# DEEPTIDE...
## Vents of Fire

# DEEPTIDE...
## Vents of Fire

a novel

by

Donald Ray Schwartz
and Steven Evans

 GoToPublish

*GoToPublish LLC*
*1-888-337-1724*
*www.gotopublish.com*
*info@gotopublish.com*

# CONTENTS

Irrationally held truths may be more harmful than reasoned errors.
—Thomas Henry Huxley,
<u>The Coming of Age of The Origin of Species</u>, 1880


Something deeply hidden had to be behind things.
—Albert Einstein,
personal note


In our description of nature the purpose is not to disclose the real essence of the phenomena but only to track down, so far as it is possible, relations between the manifold aspects of our experience.
—Niels Bohr,
<u>Atomic Theory and the Description of Nature</u>, 1934


Only by appreciating the fine nuances in their ecologies can human beings hope to understand how their actions, on the macro level, affect their micro competitors and predators.
—Laurie Garrett,
<u>The Coming Plague</u>

Without a decisive Naval force we can do nothing definitive. And with it, everything honorable and glorious.
—George Washington,
letter to Lafayette, November 15, 178

Donald R. Schwartz
2414 Sugarcone Road
Baltimore, MD 21209
*410—653—2629*
DRSRay54@cs.com
dschwartz@ccbcmd.edu

# 1

## GULFTIDE

Susan Arthknott stood at the shore of the sea. The surf, oddly rough one hundred yards out and gentle when it played the shore, caressed in foam her bare feet and ankles. She sloshed through the rough—gentle waves. She began to feel centered. She always felt centered when she saw the sea, when she was with the sea. She could be on the sea. She could be under the sea. She could be alongside the sea as she sloshed through the foam at the edge of the sea. She was part of the sea. The sea was part of her. Always had it been so. Always, for unaccountable fathoms of her life.

The water is warmer here. The surf plays out beyond the shore's edge. Then the waves roll in smooth, like soft white foam peaks atop blue crystalline hillocks. Warmer than just about any other place in the earth's ocean.

Except the one . . .

The waves of water washed in from the deep. Myriads of shells sat in the sand, some poking out as the waters receded. A few large shells, but mostly small shells, fan—shaped and curlicue—shaped, pale pink and smooth white and light gray. What happened to all the little creatures who once occupied these long lost homes? After countless centuries the sea still guarded its mysteries.

She gazed out over the waters. She thought she heard the sand give way behind her. She knew she sensed rather than heard Jennifer approaching. That too had always been the way.

"It's beautiful here."

"Yes," Susan said. White sand beaches, as they said."

"Full of these little shells though. Ouch! A person has to be careful here," Jennifer said.

"Come into the surf, silly. You're standing at the line residue of high tide."

"Yeah, you're right. Oouch. Oh. Ah. There. That's better. Wow. Water's so much warmer here."

"Hmm—mm. When you think about it, the Gulf is a huge bay. The water is deep as an ocean. See how green it is out there. But here on the coast, it's as warm as an inlet."

"It's beautiful. I think I like it as well as our ocean."

Susan gazed at her friend and colleague, Jennifer Littleton. There she stood, long blonde hair and blue eyes, a slightly large jaw that seemed to be a standard for beautiful woman and handsome men. How absurd that she should in her professional and social life link up with some perverted standard of American beauty. Why couldn't she have been a classically beautiful African—American princess, or at least short and stout? No, the woman who complimented her work and could do the work better than anyone she knew was this Scandinavian bombshell. Really, it was too ridiculous.

Now this woman, her partner really, stood on the western shore of the eastern state of Florida, at Clearwater Beach at the Sheraton Sand Key Resort. It was about two hundred yards of private beach down to the shore. This friend and colleague, the woman with a brilliant mind, whose physical appearance usurped the breath of most men and some women stood in the sand surf of the sea as the lessening waves washed over her large feet with toenails painted bright red. That was her one feature that didn't quite fit her Miss Universe face and body. Those huge feet—shovels that displaced tons of sand when walking and gallons of water when swimming.

The late afternoon gulf breeze blew the beauty's hair, soft like flax, yielding to the winds as the silk of Midwest corn fluttered wildly in Autumn reaping winds all about her head and face and shoulders. The breeze blew open her light cover dress, revealing her breasts (at least they were small, tiny almost, yet, as with everything about Jennifer, alluring) and stomach and thighs, lithe of course, in the bikini. Whilst she, the ugly duckling, stood thin, hunched, knobby—kneed, her shoulders almost fragile and birdlike, her own thighs thin, criss—crossed with veins, her light—brown hair tied back in a bun.

She pushed her glasses back up on her nose, knowing within minutes they would fall down. They stood, then, together, these two women, so different, so alike, as they stared at the sea.

Often did they gaze at the sea in this way, when working together, sometimes late at night, when out on the great swell of the sea, one could finally look up at the Milky Way of stars, away from city lights, out at the night sky and below the sea swell, as it was countless eons ago. Space and the sea and the space of the inner self. The last frontiers still to be explored. A large whitecap sneaked in, with a louder wash-gurgle than they expected. Susan looked at her friend, her brilliant beautiful assistant-colleague.

She asked what they both knew she was waiting to ask.

"Did you see him?"

"Yes," Jennifer said. "I had to turn on a little charm. He wants to hear a presenter, a particularly interesting paper on Genome mapping in the mitochondria at seven. He'll meet with us for ten minutes at ten. Ten at ten he called it."

Jennifer turned. She looked at Susan. After all these years, she did not know what to call her. Physician? Marine ethno—microbiologist? All were correct. The woman had three doctorates, and had already published several incisive articles while still in graduate school. She watched her push her glasses up the bridge of her nose. She knew in advance it was an exercise in futility.

Jennifer Littleton turned away. She resumed her watch over the sea. Gulls hovered by. They dove for their penultimate catch of the day. A large pelican followed a wave from far out to shore, then, almost lazily, banked and floated in air parallel to them. A sailboat on the horizon began to tack to make its way in to harbor for the night. Jennifer had always been able to pick on the far horizon even the feather edge of a bird's guide tail feather. Now, as she approached thirty, she noticed after considerable reading, her eyes seemed tired.

Jennifer always thought Susan was more beautiful than she thought of herself. If the woman would stop crinkling her nose all the time, trying to keep those ridiculous spectacles on which made her look bug—eyed, a not altogether easy feat considering they were half—glasses and she gave an intimidating look over them. Her hair could be let down from that tight bun, which always had wild strands finding their way this way and any which way; the frizz could be made curly. And posture. Jennifer had tried early on to get her friend to improve her posture. Finally after the woman had gotten a bit irritable, she had given up. Jennifer hated it when Susan's voice suddenly acquired the sound of fingernails scratching a chalkboard, that damn screech edge to her voice, and drew in her face taut, for the discordance and the misshapen mask transposed her almost into as ugly a harpy as she probably mistakenly envisioned within her inner sense.

What can you do with some people? Especially women. Men were easier to manage. They would do almost anything a woman wanted. She and Susan didn't always get along. Fine. Still, they worked well together. Susan had a mind that was so brilliant, it made the smart envious. She made the connections at once, miles ahead of anyone else. She, Jennifer, on the other hand, was not quite brilliant, she knew that. But if they gave her enough time, and saw past her face and body, she could almost always emerge with a creative solution. That was it, she guessed. That was how she compensated for not having a mind like Susan's. Her creativity. She had wanted to be an artist. She adored watercolors and had gotten, she thought, good at them.

She wanted more. She always had a technical bent to her nature, a scientist's manner of thinking about things. She had read an article once about some artists who could use their creative bent to fathom scientific mysteries; so she was not completely alone in the world after all. Susan, on the other hand, never had doubts. She had been a math and science honor scholar all through school, and at Harvard Medical, had been asked to stay on faculty. But there was that one thing that united them.

The lure of the waves and the foam and the great free swells. The sea.

"Satisfactory, Jennifer," Susan said.

Satisfactory. That was the highest compliment she could ever muster from her friend. Susan continued.

"Our visuals are in order? Good. Well then. In, ah, his hotel room? I see. Then let's go in, have some dinner you and I, and go over our approach again. Ten minutes. Just setting up will--well, we can only take in the hand—held. I have to change clothes and shower anyway.

The sun descended, a huge yellow—fire red dot a little to their left. The gulls and pelicans swooped out across the golden—tinged waves, flying their final fishing expedition across the surface, skimming the water as they hunted their prey. Soon they would roost for the night under bridge I—irons or on the sand of the beach itself. The two women, one broad backed and large, one thin and seemingly frail, took in the panorama one last time. They could not tell now where the clouds and sky and sea met, but the sun shot rays above the distant cloud line. Somewhere, out there in a far distant ocean, and more than a continent away, they envisioned their own prey.

At last they turned and sand—walked hack to the heated pool. A few opportunistic night—owl gulls begged or raided human caches for one last morsel of pool—side food. The cries of families and children met them as they walked the crooked sidewalk covered in durable, all—weather, water resistant carpet that led from the beach around the pool up to the side door of the hotel lobby.

They climbed the stairs to the second floor. Then they took the elevator up to their room. Jennifer had reminded Susan once that walking a flight of stairs, parking farther rather than nearer could help condition the body. Since Susan believed in compores sano, a healthy body produced a healthy mind, she had taken the advice most seriously.

In their business suits, neck wear, hose, and pumps, they clicked down the hallway of the hotel lobby. Just outside the door to the restaurant, Jennifer stopped and glanced down the hall. She peered intently. Susan, about a head shorter than her friend, looked up at her eyes, then down the hall where she gazed.

"Jennifer?"

"The convention's being held at that end of the building. I wanted to see if I could catch a glimpse of him."

"And?"

"Nothing. He must already be inside," Jennifer said.

"Well, let's get something to eat. We're going to need all our strength soon."

The smaller woman always seemed to eat more. She was almost always hungry. At times, she wondered if she ever stopped being hungry. There seemed to be some great, gnawing, insatiable hunger inside her.

Susan ordered fish, sea bass. She always ordered fish when they were getting closer to being out on the sea. Jennifer saw on the menu a sirloin steak with her name on it. Someday, she thought. Someday soon she would turn fully vegetarian, like she sometimes was and wished to be.

The food was cooked well, prepared with an aesthetic presentation, accompanied by parsley potatoes and fresh green beans. First, a tasty salad with an all right house vinaigrette dressing, and alongside hot fresh baked rolls. One thing about resorts; they had good chefs and service.

They ate in silence, each thinking at times the same and other times disparate thoughts. After the waitress and bus help cleared their table, they took out their papers from their satchels.

Susan's satchel never seemed to close properly. One of the latches hung askew. In a constant act of assured futility, on each needed occasion, the scientist tried to tape over the damaged latch. Then, inevitably, the shredded brown packing tape hung over the edge, useless. Jennifer kept half an eye on Susan's briefcase for security reasons.

"We only have ten minutes. I think in such a case less would be more," Susan said. "Jannasch's and Mottl's summary article on the geomicrobiology of deep—sea hydrothermal vents would be a good opening and an effective prequel."

"I think I can put these photographs we took into a composite that will grab his interest. Like you said, we won't have time to set up the Power Point."

They worked--the creative one, the more analytical one, hunched over their charts, pictures, designs, texts, articles, appliance internet screens, the long blonde hair and the bobbed brown hair, giving little clue to the furious and rational thoughts within their highly developed brains.

"You have the plans for the explorer." Susan looked up at Jennifer.

The woman gazed into her eyes, a look she typically reserved for men that interested her, a look she had given Cornelius Barnstone.

"Yes, blueprints, photos, and our secret weapon."

"If he has a, well, of course he'll have a dv."

"Correct. Of course. He has it. HD screen of course."

They glanced at their watches. The night wore on. Calibrated together, they agreed it was 10:00 straight up.

They collected their work into as best an organized format as they could. They paid their bill. At the door of the restaurant, leading out to the hall, however, Jennifer remembered. In her heels, as best she could, she dashed back to the table. She knew women always looked silly running in heels. Still, she ran in her heels, oddly quiet on the establishment's carpet. Now returned to their table, she deposited a 15% tip.

She looked up. She saw Susan looking at her. She scrambled through her purse and wallet again. She left an amount adding in the aggregate to 20% for the gratuity.

Suddenly she recalled the waitress had shown some interest in their work; for a moment they feared that Carstairs or another group had placed an undercover spy. Later they snickered and sniffed at their paranoia. It would be some months longer upon a strange rock island outcropping, gazing out over the living waters again, and a chill running up and down her spine, Jennifer would recall the incident and the fear. Still, at this stage, as she stood tableside now, as far as they knew, no one else had come upon the site, no one else had come as far as they, no one else had had this cockamamie idea.

At 10:05, they walked down the hall to the elevators. Jennifer glanced down at her friend. She was always amazed at the speed the woman's mind worked. At the instant they had with serendipity witnessed the phenomenon, Susan had conceived the entire plan, all the designs, even the probable time frame.

Even more amazing, Jennifer realized that she likely thought even faster than that, that Susan had conceived it all even as the phenomenon unfolded. Like some 1960's calculator which eerily bounced about on the table as it chugged out its long series of correlations of coefficient, of combinations and permutations, the woman's body quivered as her magnificent mind extrapolated the time frame intervals from the lesser eruptions to this greater one.

She recalled that almost instantly, Susan had said, "This will only last about a year and a half. We've got to start right away. Eighteen months. Two years at most."

The astonishing view before them was only still unfolding, and already she had it all calculated.

She knew her friend and colleague never slept much. Now she wondered if she slept at all. Often in the deepest part of the night, in the engulfing black shadows before dawn, in the hotel rooms they had recently been visiting, she would awake gradually aware she had been aware in her sleep. Through eyes blurred, she beheld the woman hunkered over the round table, pushing her glasses up her nose, lost under a dim desk lamp, sorting, revising, configuring. It was the only time she had observed Susan let her hair down. Really, she should do so more often, Jennifer thought; then she realized she could not keep her eyes open. She turned over, away from the single dim light. At once she found herself again lost deep in sleep and dreams. In the morning, she was uncertain which had been the dream and which the strange real vision. The dreams were nightmares, but she felt that the pre—dawn window on the world was even scarier.

At 10:08, they departed the elevator on the twenty—first floor. They sauntered down the hall, seeking suites 2104—06.

At 10:10, they looked each other over. Jennifer dug out her mirror to check her make—up. She pointed to Susan's skirt. Susan wriggled and straightened the wrinkle as best she could. For a moment, her skirt rode up. Actually, she's not a bad looking woman; she could be quite sexy, with those thin arms and legs, Jennifer thought. It was her posture. If only she would stand a certain way, a way most women instinctively understood. With one knee slightly bent, the opposite hip ever slightly pushed out. Even fourteen year old girls knew that. She had known that. Honestly. I've worked on this woman for over six years. Maybe someday.

She brushed Susan's jacket. It occurred to her that Susan appeared odd in a suit, uncomfortable, out of place. They gathered up their briefcases and portfolios. Susan knocked on the door. There was a pause. She began to knock again. The door opened.

A woman with a link—chain, silver, attached to her triangle—rimmed glasses cracked open the door. The link—chain permitted her to allow the glasses to fall upon her chest when idle.

Susan often wore a spectacles holder like that. A black cord. Her glasses, however, were half—glasses. Susan liked to look over them at the person she was speaking with. It was intimidating to some. Jennifer thought it charming.

The triangle—spectacled woman peered at them, then looked them up and down. Jennifer discerned her myopia. She noticed the woman held a clipboard, with a thick pen, attached by a cord to the clip. She took up the pen. She scribbled notes on the paper captured by the clipboard. Jennifer Littleton knew they already stood at disadvantage. A person with a clipboard and link—chain spectacles started from a position of superiority.

"Dr. Arthknott. Ms. Littleton. Please, come in. Enter. Dr. Barnstone appreciates your promptness."

Jennifer grew aware that although the secretary (Administrative Assistant?) had used courtesies, the tone of her voice had an edge to it. Was it resentment, arrogance? She knew she was the one who picked up on those types of signals. Susan was assuredly only thinking of her presentation and even the facts and plans beyond that. Her mind, she knew, was filled with mathematical formulae, the workings of Fourier transforms, and mathematical probabilities, permutation possibilities, and chaos combinations others of lesser intellect could not conceive. Later, she would come to know there was one situation even she could not possibly have envisioned. Meanwhile, her own original thought had to vie with the incidental; for example, whether she could afford Clarins new Fruit Rouge lipstick with moisturizer in the center. One could after, all, only purchase it at a classy department store, like Von Mauer or Dillard's. Often she would slip into Walgreen's for a Revlon color and some natural lip gloss.

She wasn't sure Fruit Rouge was a good color for her. The woman at the department store cosmetics counter had selected the cosmetic for her. The woman, whose name was Bambi ("Honest to God honey, ((furiously chewing her Spearmint gum))Bambi, my real name, mom had seen the movie the night just before I was born"), was buxom and had the thickest, long coal black hair Jennifer had ever seen. With her white skin the contrast was striking. Her arms just missed being hirsute; she wore a short skirt, but it was difficult to detect hair on her legs through the opaque hose. She was gorgeous. Jennifer remembered she had briefly entertained a wicked thought of cavorting naked with Bambi in a swimming pool, just to see how much hair the gorgeous cosmetics demo had upon that white skin.

Bambi sat at those counters that seduced women in to them, that always seem to recess into a bright—dim lighted place along the aisles, effused with the scents of wondrous perfume odors, a woman's haven—place in an otherwise, hectic stressful environment.

The women looked each other over, each envious of the other's particular best feature body part. Jennifer could almost hear the hum of their thoughts. "If I had hair like hers . . . eyes like hers . . .upper arms like hers, fingernails like hers . . . breasts like hers . . . legs like hers . . . this last was typically directed to her. She had been told this from an early age. And she had taken to checking it out in her several mirrors. Her mother had even said she was all legs. Lithe, she came to enjoy thinking of herself in this fashion.

She was pretty all over and she knew it, and her legs were great. Well, she could not help it nor would she have it any other way. Let most men and many women eat their hearts out. She learned early men were easy; she could always allure a man by hiking her skirt up a bit.

She took up swimming to keep them in shape. Her breasts never seemed to grow all that much more than the pathetic little teen knobs. But enough. Shapely. And she didn't mind. She penetrated the secret that men rarely told: They didn't care all that much. They simply like women, whatever their bra and cup size. Besides, she thought it helped her in her swimming career. High School good enough for a college athletic scholarship. She studied computer CAD design. She liked the artistic expression of it. But she had always been drawn to the sea somehow.

She was pleased when she landed a job for a ship engineering company, in San Diego. One day she received a telephone call from a scientist working on marine molecular biology. She had liked her work and wondered if she would work for her. It was a slight cut in pay--well, more than slight--but it meant being out to sea. That was six years ago, and she never dreamed it would come to this. Well, her legs were her best feature after all. And she was already thinking of one fantasy after another with a man she had met this afternoon. God, there she went again. Susan could care less about it all. She was sure her scientist—colleague considered only at the moment the clock—time available to them. Still, there were moments in the deep of night when the woman let her hair down and gazed dreamily aside into space . . .

"Promptness promotes excellence."

Jennifer was sure that was something the secretary with the triangle rimmed glasses and myopic eyes and clipboard muttered all the time, after hearing her boss say it once.

"Please ladies. Right this way."

Or walk this way, like the old joke. The secretary had an odd limp. She held the clipboard against her chest when she walked—limped. Her right leg flared out. Jennifer had worked with Susan long enough to know the woman had probably had a tumor and experienced successful brain surgery. There was a slight slur to her speech, after all. Suddenly she turned with a crisp air, like a soldier marching in formation, but the gimp compromised her air of authority, somewhat.

The suite was not as large as she imagined it would be. There was a kitchenette to the left and another to their right as they entered. Then the room opened to about the size of three hotel rooms. He stood to the left. He held some papers in his hand. Another woman sat in a corner chair, but not far. She held a drink. She looked buff, Jennifer thought. Wiry. A woman of action.

Jennifer liked trying to read people up front. Arthur Conan Doyle was one of her favorite authors. She always tried to intuit people by appearance as Holmes had done. Holmes was based on a true person, a Doctor Bell. Bell was Conan Doyle's professor at medical college. Prior to any examination, Dr. Bell would diagnose a patient's physical or mental incapacity merely by those clues in appearance alone presented to his keen observant eye. Conan Doyle became an ophthalmologist. In those days an ophthalmologist was referred to as an oculist. Conan Doyle hung a shingle outside his office, painted with a huge eye. But his true diagnostic vision was his great detective creation, who gazed at clues with his eye through an enlarging glass, Sherlock Holmes, Dr. Bell's fictional alter ego.

"Dr. Arthknott. So pleased to meet you. I've been looking over some of your articles. The literature is fascinating. After Ms. Littleton spoke to me this afternoon, I investigated your work. Quite impressive. Ms. Littleton. Good to see you again. Please, ladies, would you like a drink? Good. Daiquiri. Scotch on the rocks. Why, Ms. Littleton, I am even more convinced now you are a woman after my own heart."

Jennifer felt a familiar weakness in her knees, and a warm flush in places she knew she should not at this interview be sensing.

He fixed the drinks himself. He was surprisingly in good shape, rather fit, Jennifer thought. She remembered thinking that this afternoon. He had to be in his late 50's, yet his body seemed well formed and firm. He either had a full shock of hair or the best toupee money could buy. But it was his eyes--deep blue and piercing. Jennifer suddenly felt warm and not only under her armpits, suddenly realizing she could comprehend how younger women could fall for older men. She noticed for the most part he addressed Susan. But he couldn't keep himself from looking at her. She was suddenly conscious of her feet. They were so huge. It was the body part she hated the most. She thought they must look like shovels to everyone else, huge scoops. But she knew that they had helped her in her swimming meets. Now, she couldn't get them to cease quivering.

"The overall theme of your work appears to be 'Life Origins at the Molecular Level in Deep Sea Vents.' Clearly you've made or confirmed some interesting discoveries. These tube worms, for example. But I don't see yet any empirical evidence to support your theses."

"You've read Gold, Van Dover, Lupton's report to the Pacific Marine Environmental Laboratory?"

"I've read your references to them. I intend to pull them later."

Susan cleared her throat. She rubbed her hands together. She rubbed slowly. She rubbed fast. Then slow again. Jennifer knew this meant she was getting down to brass tacks. Usually she took longer but they only had seven minutes left. Jennifer had looked at her watch. She knew Susan had a punctual internal clock.

"Dr. Barnstone, with all due respect, when you first uncovered the findings that nitrous oxide could relax the cavernous areas of the penis, did you think at once you could develop a compound to retard impotence in men so quickly?"

"Actually almost at once. But now we're working on retarding the aging process."

Dr. Susan Arthknott perceived her opening at once. "Aging process at the molecular level. And we can find the very origins of life, which could provide for you the biology of DNA genesis, the secret to longevity. The Holy Grail, the compound, the pill that would enable a healthy fulfilling life to 120 years before the aging process starts in. Who can say, perhaps 140, 150 years might not be unheard of. More perhaps. The extraordinary wealth that would be generated . . ."

Jennifer was a bit taken aback. She had never heard Susan speak of wealth before. Still, she had their budgets worked out. She had known for some time Susan was complex; Now she thought even more so. One thing was clear. The woman suddenly held this man's interest.

"Go on."

"It's not just worms or whatever they are in these vents. Life forms erupts at any new vent that opens, and dies when they shut down. These are fantastical creatures of every description, clam—like, crab—like; here are some pictures we took over the last four years."

"You have three minutes, Dr. Arthknott."

"I know, Dr. Barnstone."

"And I have seen most of these before."

Susan looked at Jennifer. Jennifer nodded.

"Three months ago, we went out beyond the Gorda Ridge. There was something about the color of the water, the green—percolating—whiteness of it perhaps, that got my attention. Well,in truth, Jennif--ah, Ms. Littleton's attention, actually."

Cornelius Barnstone and Jennifer Littleton looked at one another.

"It was improbable, quite unlikely. Who could imagine it, such a phenomenon? We were over 100 miles beyond where any of the vents had been seen. The volcano birth places, the tectonic plates were far behind us. But then we saw a bubbling on the surface. As you know, it was our last grant money that we had use of the Alvin sub from the Institute. We submerged. If we may show this video . . ."

Jennifer inserted the video. She adjusted the set so all could see. At first the images appeared hazy, blurry, murky. Then, as a camera lens comes into focus, or a person realizes she is awake just before she awakens, as if from the thickening fog itself like an amorphous blob suddenly taking defined shape, out of the mist emerged a huge fissure, with hot steam escaping at every crevice. Sticky and worm—like tube creatures floated in and out of the fissure and up the steam bubble wall for awhile. Jennifer noticed Barnstone was now leaning in to the picture.

"It opened even wider just as we arrived. Watch."

"Is it as huge as it looks?"

"Wait. Let me fast forward. We sent out a buoy for size comparison. Wait now, should be just about here, no, back just a bit, I think--there!"

"Ah, most satisfactory."

Amazing. In many ways his mind was like Susan's. He saw the whole thing at once,in advance. He used the same vocabulary. Then, for a long while, no one said anything. All eyes peered at the screen.

"Dr. Barnstone."

"Yes, I know. I see. Everything. How much will such a design cost? Have you run a projected cost analysis? Ah, good. Let me see your spread sheets."

"Cornelius?"

The woman in the corner chair spoke for the first time.

"Hmm?" He kept his hand in the center of the spread sheet packet. He looked over at the woman. "Delores. Don't you see?

They're going to chase these creatures all the way in. They've found a portal to the other side, the possible spawning ground for life itself!"

Susan and Jennifer looked at one another. Jennifer retrieved the plans and her rendition of the OVIDSIFOE.

"We call it the Gee—Ex—Gee. The Genesis Explorer, Gee Whiz. Ex—Gee for short. Its actual designation is OVIDSIFOE, Oceanic Vehicle Deep Sea Intra—Fissure Origins Explorer. Its quarters are, well, at this stage of conceptualization, ten feet by six feet, about the same as Alvin. Its bulkhead is squatter however, to withstand the tremendous pressure."

"How do you propose to withstand the heat?"

"Notice that the outer shell extends another foot. We propose a heat shield design, roughly similar to the space capsule and shuttle tiles for re—entry, and here, this-- "

Jennifer put her hand on her friend's shoulder. Barnstone looked over at Delores. The two women were so different. The little mousy brilliant scientist, this gorgeous blonde with great legs and big feet who made these renderings; yet somehow they were the same; or, at least, somehow they understood one another. In an instant, he had an idea of what the marine biologist was going to say. Some sort of spent uranium shield. Well, he had always had the sense of things before anyone else. That's what kept him well above the underachievers. He had the feeling of something of biblical proportions was coming. He half expected the scientist to exclaim, "Behold."

"See. Here is a three inch space. Note it adds volume but no weight. And here, on this space, with three inches on the other side to the bulkhead of the ship, is a spent uranium full closure shield around the entire ship. It would take a temperature beyond anything we've recorded on earth save for an atomic bomb blast, to get past this last line of defense, for a while, anyway.

"I know our time is up. But we have an animated video of how the ship would look--"

"Define 'a while, anyway.'"

"Yes, a while. Hmmm, forty-five minutes, maybe. With luck, an hour, and, twenty-forty minutes. Then conduction would generate too much heat for the crew, even if integrity held. After all, we are dealing with unknown factors; that is, no one has ever--"

"Go on."

"Well, as I was saying, uh . . .

"The video," Jennifer whispered.

"Yes. The video. If we may. Our computer generated projection. Jennifer is a CAD expert, and with some CG animation we did at a California studio, that is, how it might appear going through the fissure. However, there is one other thing I haven't told you."

This last bit of suspense had been Jennifer's idea, hopefully to pique his interest. A ploy, she knew, but she wasn't sure they could close the sale without it. She wasn't sure now, even with their, well, their perfume spray, so to speak.

A pervasive silence clutched the room. Suddenly Jennifer coughed. It was awful. It was one of those sudden violent coughs, unexpected even to the cougher, as in a springtime allergic morning. The sneak attack, with neither warning nor forecast, like the horrid moment with no foreboding when one feels stabbed in the eye with darts, clearly indicating a sinus infection or, at least, a headache was about to rain torment. She found she could not stop. The more she tried to stop, the worse it got. Susan patted her back. It helped a bit, but not much.

The secretary, Mrs. Perkins, arose from her chair behind Barnstone. She limped over to the kitchenette counter. She picked up the water pitcher. She brought it over to Jennifer. She bent down. She filled a glass of water for her. In the tension, the water pouring made an oddly comforting gurgling sound, like a minute vent or vortex bubbling.

"Thank you," she gasped, between coughing and breathing with hoarseness.

"You are quite welcome. I'm sure it will help," she stated with an austere, superior air, not a compassionate one.

Mrs. Perkins retraced her steps. Before she returned to her seat, she replaced the water pitcher in the exact same spot from which she had lifted it. The water ring on the counter had not been wiped. The return of the pitcher, condensing droplets and fog on its glass walls, produced a squishy click—thud. Mrs. Perkins picked up the water pitcher. She held it in her hand. She limped behind the counter. She picked up a roll of paper towels. She attempted to tear a towel with one hand. Unable to acquire a secure purchase, with neither design nor intent she tore more than one towel at a ragged angle, beyond the scored line. She replaced the paper towel roll in exactly the spot she had retrieved it. She wiped the counter from the other side. She replaced the pitcher. The little squishy part of the click—thud was now missing. Mrs. Perkins limped around the counter. She returned to her seat.

Jennifer drank the glass of water. She coughed again. However, already it was better. The tickle felt not as inevitable. She sipped more water. She cleared her throat. But for occasional minor lapses, at last she ceased coughing. She cleared her throat. Then her right foot, the one even larger than the other, began to quiver. It shook, up and down, down and up.

Damn! She could not get control of the palsy. Surely everyone was watching her now. She was letting Susan down. She hated herself. He probably hates my hair too; and my small knobby breasts. Even Susan and this crippled Perkins woman have larger breasts. As for Delores, it's difficult to tell if she's a manly woman or a womanly man.

Susan rubbed her hands the way she did, left over right. Then she adjusted her glasses. They fell down her nose. She removed them from the bridge of her nose. She allowed them to dangle upon her chest. She put them on the bridge of her nose. They slipped down. She adjusted them. They slipped. Delores sat ramrod straight, peering at them seemingly with disdain. Mrs. Perkins tapped her pen on the clipboard, a steady rapping and tapping, as if some visitor were coming to the suite door.

Barnstone held his first two fingers of his right hand over his mouth. His right thumb played the outline of his jaw. Jennifer had the idea for a moment that they were all sitting at the defendant's and prosecutor's tables at a murder trial. The defense had just given an objection. The decision hinged on whether an important piece of evidence could be presented or not; or an answer by a witness that could give confirming proof one way or another.

Barnstone sat as the judge. He opened his mouth. He closed his mouth. Jennifer become aware of a clock ticking somewhere. Odd she hadn't heard it before. A cloud passed overhead. The room darkened. Soon the cloud began to pass, restoring most of the light to the room. Barnstone's hands came down. He folded them over his chest, just above his diaphragm.

"Let's see the video."

They were never more as one, the two, when they silently felt their collective sigh of relief. Jennifer found the video in her hands. She didn't remember pulling it out. She started to put it in the machine. Why wouldn't the damn thing go in all of a sudden? It worked fine before, in all the other machines.

"Pardon me, Ms. Littleton," Mrs. Perkins said. "But of course you must remove the previous one before inserting the new one." Obvious. Officious. Disdainful. Damn that woman. Still, she had given me the glass of water when I needed it.

If only I could act professional and not high—schoolish; And my flipper—feet. They're always swinging in the way, tripping me up.

"Oh. Yes, of course." And she gave that nervous girlish laugh and giggle that she hated women giving, in serious business moments, but they always seemed to give it and she hated it most in herself.

Damn, it was hot all of a sudden. She hadn't noticed it before. When the cloud swirled past on its merry way did the temperature rise at once in some bizarre meteorological phenomenon?

She removed the previous dv. She placed her disc at the flap of the slot. She began to push it into the slot. Her fingers fumbled. It dropped to the floor. It made a soft cracking sound, twice, as it careered upon its edge, then onto its side. She cursed, softly under her breath. Still, she knew all had heard her. She knew all eyes were upon her in the room, suddenly grown very small, tight, crowded, cramped. She knelt down. She knew her skirt rode up high on her thighs. She hoped that wasn't the first hint of a thirty year old's cellulite she had seen earlier this morning when she put on her bathing suit. She giggled, that damn stupid silly high school girl giggle. Once more she felt small, like an unpopular kid at high school, a gangly tall girl who had to endure the jibes about big webbed feet. "Duck—feet," "goose-stepper," and whose only friends were on the swim team. Good friends though. She had kept in touch with them for a good while.

Well, it couldn't hurt that much, in fact let him knock himself out looking at her. If only it wasn't so damn hot. Ordinarily she disdained deodorant and make—up. Now, she could smell the sweat in her armpits and wished this morning at least she had used that roll—on she had for emergencies and tense situations. Why had she forgotten it when they changed clothes for the evening's wear? If only the disc's integrity didn't shatter when she dropped it on the floor. She tried again.

Finally she got the damn thing in. In an instant she realized the "Play" button had disappeared; or it was a manufacturer's defect. They had neglected to put on a play button. What was it with these manufacturers? How was such a thing possible? God. Breathe, Jennifer. She felt Susan's hand touch her arm. She knew she was fine. The button came in to view.

She pushed the button.

A slight momentary hum whirred. The word "play" appeared on the blue field of the screen. Thank God. Then the image suddenly appeared.

It was one of those computer generated animations. Jennifer was indeed a craftswoman. The film unfolded better than most, richer, more three dimensional even than a Japanese mangra anime. It seemed to the viewers they were in the fathoms of the deep, approaching a huge vacuum fissure with steam, fish, eels, bulrushes, reeds incredibly rising in the percolating water. One almost had the impression of the sudden creation of a world. Bizarre creatures--huge red shimmering worm—like tubules, ameba—like moving forms from a pilot's viewpoint. Then the objective view of the ship: A squat, oblong, gray—white entity, almost like a sculpted whale. The tiles were visible. In the rear a small propeller spun. Two holes to either side rested above the spinning propeller.

"Rocket engines?"

"A small nuclear propulsion system on board to generate ion emission. Fully generated and controlled by a Cray processor."

"Ion propulsion," Delores said. "Because you won't know if the propeller will work on the other side, deep within."

"Exactly."

"Visual?"

"Three panel Plexiglas, matching the 3 X 3 inches bevel of the tiles and spent uranium. An ergonomic mechanism closes the windows in one level with titanium shielding if necessary. Of course two cameras forward, two aft, one starboard and one port side. The bow and stern zoom from five inches to infinity. Wide lenses static on the sides. As long as they last.

"Sound system has directional density microphones all around, again, as long as they last. There are backups in the design stage. Six torpedoes firing capacity forward. Three aft. Laser beam forward. All sonar all four sides. Navigation by chip memory to back out as we entered; we call that the Minotaur Naviguide. Vernier propulsion rockets, two lateral with 180° mobility for multi—directional movement. There's much more of course, but that's the gist of it. The computer will figure the angle for entry. Ah, here you can see our conception of the initial encounter."

It seemed the ship hovered above a stream bubble column, then defined a double helix curve, like a slow solid whirlpool twisting within a vortex to squeeze through an opening.

"Tight fit."

"The ship should be thinner but it would then be unprotected. If we can get there in time we should find a crevasse on the western edge. That's where the largest one was. They're probably all connected somehow. Of course, we can only hope--"

"Yes. That is, at least as large as the one you enter."

Susan rubbed her hands, left over right. She adjusted her glasses, then took them off, to leave them dangling. Jennifer tried to get her foot to stop shaking, then returned to thinking about it shaking.

"Yes," Susan said. "That is correct." She rubbed her hands, right over left. After a moment she began again.

"The cabin has minimal living conditions; or, rather, travel conditions. We estimate we can only be down a few hours at most.

"There's a considerable amount of control equipment, of course. Internal weaponry, harpoons, firearms, flares, and so on. There's also . . ."

"Continue."

"We're designing an electrical charge to the entire body of the ship. In case anything should be large enough in there to want to consider us on the menu."

"Nemo's giant squid."

"Exactly."

"Please continue Dr. Arthknott."

Jennifer was breathing easier now. She noticed it wasn't quite so hot any more. She thought she might be able almost to gain control of her foot. She looked over at Susan. She knew the woman was warming to her subject.

"These creatures don't use oxygen nor do they give off carbon dioxide. They are chemolithotrophic. They, well, they give off of, from, to themselves, simply put, in a feed—back loop we don't fully comprehend as yet. Or, don't comprehend very well at all, to be more accurate.

"That is, to summarize and reiterate. There are large colonies of chemolithotrophic bacteria in some sort of symbiotic relationship. That will be one of the key questions we'll want to investigate. Quite frankly, we'll be in a brave new world, so to speak. More accurately, perhaps, a very old one."

"Or, a foolish old one. Never mind." He placed his hand along his lips and jaw line again, playing his thumb, back and forth, forth and back, almost in a rhythmic pattern that could bring on a hypnotic trance. He lowered his arms. He folded his fingers across his belt buckle. "How long. How much?"

There! Just like that he had said it. There it was. They were well over their time. Jennifer looked at their work. Hot magma conduits, bizarre creatures floating and, yes, swimming, locomoting by. The disc ran its course. She retrieved it. She placed it in its plastic container. She had to force it a little. Finally it gave that satisfying tiny pop. Her colleague and mentor continued.

"We have a budget. The main thing is we think we have only a window of about two years at the outside. More likely eighteen months. Based on projections of when the more well known fissures opened and closed."

"Crew?"

"Crew of five. That's all that can fit somewhat comfortably. Enough food, water, oxygen for thirty—six hours. If anything should be needed. One never knows what one will find. After that, well, there's only time for one, and we can't afford the luxury of designing inter—ship passages. What I mean is--"

"Yes, I understand fully. There won't be any rescue ship coming in."

God, keeping up with either of them. Jennifer was no longer sure who was the quickest. Susan apparently already understood she had met her match or nearly so. She did not acknowledge his attentive interruption. She merely continued.

"A mother ship above. Jennifer will be in charge of communications there. A lesser submarine ship below, just off the edge. We'll try the Navy's low—frequency underwater telecommunications band, but we won't know for sure if it will continue to the other side, although--

"Indeed. In theory, it should."

"Six months to manufacture. Six months to trial, re-design, re-calibrate, and retrofit. Three to six months to proceed. I know. A very tight fit. There's no question it's a gamble, all the way around."

Jennifer waited. Susan waited. Then they received the answer they had only dreamed of.

"Delores Hundley is an ex—Coast Guard Cutter captain. She used to ply the waters off the Alaska coast. She'll be your captain. Her men are still loyal to her. Practically her entire old crew has agreed to sign on. One of these, Delores tells me, is the best pilot in the business. She'll hand—pick others for back—up. I want one of my own microbiologists along, probably in the secondary sub. With some later adjustments that should make out your crew. Well, that's it then, ladies. Mrs. Perkins will show you out. She will be in touch. To the other side."

"To the other side." They drank their drinks.

Mrs. Perkins showed them out. Again Jennifer thought of the stupid old joke: Walk this way . . .

In the hallway, they embraced. They punched the air. They gave high fives. They held hands and did a little dance.

Sooner than it might seem possible, they were about to be the first people to go inside the deep mysterious interior of the earth.

# 2

## COASTTIDE

They waited six months for their vessel. Barnstone had been true to his word. He had pulled out all resources. He found an engineering firm to drop everything, to go on twenty—four hour shift to retool, and to give this project clear and uncontested priority. By now Susan and Jennifer had Dolores's men and Barnstone's scientist. The crew was motley, as the saying goes, Jennifer thought. But, in spite of herself, she couldn't help looking at the pilot, Josh Margule, in a certain way. Allen Johnstone, an African—American was also quite attractive to her. She thought of doing both of them, first the joy of some Norwegian or Swedish hot blood, then the contrast of her light—toned skin against the other man's brown flesh. It amazed her that she could work and contribute at this level, and still thought of men as some high school or college conquest. Well, she was who she was and it was all a heady atmosphere and thrilling. Hodges, a large hulking man, perhaps an ex-football player, seemed curiously interesting as well.

Honestly, how did she get any work done at all? The microbiologist, with an odd name of Samson Magruder, filled out the crew of the compact explorer.

Names came into focus. There would be many others in the surface crew she would have to learn besides the Ex—Gee and the secondary sub. It was starting to emerge as a significant project indeed.

It turned out to be Allen who first girded up the courage to ask her out for dinner. She was beginning to wonder about Josh. She had given him enough to look at, but he seemed more interested in one of the surface crewmen. Once she turned a corner and thought she saw them holding hands. Well, she probably had caught the better man after all.

Susan was preoccupied with the design and building process. She wanted Jennifer to spend more time at the CAD to design the adjustments and re—designs; daily they increased. They worked fourteen hours a day; soon, she knew, the woman scientist would forget to eat and barely sleep altogether, if she didn't look out for her.

Allen emerged easy to talk to. He liked to walk along the beach with her at sunset. He laughed at her jokes. She expected he would eventually tell her about emerging from a poor background. But it hadn't been so. When she found out, she cursed herself for holding onto the stereotype.

One night, during a delicious fresh fish dinner, he told her his father had been a doctor. They had always done well, and he, a young man, wanted to be a doctor too. But he had met Delores at the Coast Guard Academy. There was something about her; she had a commanding presence. He put his career on hold to follow her on this adventure. Then of all things he met this astonishingly beautiful and intelligent woman.

Jennifer blushed. He was charming. She looked at him. She smiled. She knew this was the night he would get lucky. Yet, there was something he said that wasn't quite right, something nagged at her mind . . . her perfume and the scent of the ocean, the washing of the waves, the man—scent from his desire for her, the foods and the breezes, it was too much, she couldn't think straight.

It was the night they agreed the explorer sub would be dubbed, "Stanley." They had considered, "Nautiless," or the "Pequot"; but, after <u>Alvin</u>, the African explorer seemed a more viable choice. Ships received feminine names, usually, or triumphant ones, but it seemed deep sea explorer subs were dubbed according to male nomenclature.

They sat at a poolside table not far from the beach and the ship works. Barnstone had built a facility up the northeast coast, off the Maine shore at a secret location. The ancient wild woods rose in mystery behind them. Perhaps Massasoit of the Wampanoags or the woman chief of the Pequot and their warriors had roamed these woods.

Barnstone had explained how he came by this retreat. He had built it as a power training facility for his executives.

During their intense time here, the resort served as sleeping rooms for the crews of boat builders, dock workers, spent uranium experts, and legions of other experts, welders, computer experts, and service and support staff. She tried to calculate the investment, but wearied at the impossible changing and challenging figures. She wondered why they hadn't built their facility on the west coast. Susan had explained that the skilled help and this facility were on this coast. Later they would fly the prototype to an undeveloped sound at the western edge of Oregon. From there, after some fine tuning, the final stages would be accommodated from the modules, they could set out, the Ex—Gee on board the <u>Parsonage</u>, the old freighter Barnstone was having retrofitted on the opposite coast.

So the plan went. Later, even as the project unfolded, events led to a different ship awaiting their arrival at Pacific port.

Something nagged at her. It seemed when they arrived the facility was already laid out, or nearly so. That would have had to have been done very fast, indeed. Then, she had turned a corner once, and saw a strange yet familiar marking on the side of one of the buildings. She had seen it before, but couldn't quite place it.

They heard a shout. They glanced out toward the ocean. The crews were running some practice programs down by the beach. No doubt they had just been dismissed for the day.

"I hope that means things are going well," Jennifer said.

"There have been glitches. But by and large . . ."

For a few moments they were silent. He poured her some more wine. She drank half the glass. They looked at each other.

"I don't think we have much time left. We'll be leaving for the coast soon. Would you like to come up to my room tonight?"

"I've been hoping you would ask," Jennifer said. Stupid schoolgirl heart racing, she thought.

They kissed for a long time, Jennifer adoring being submissive and seduced, at least for the moment, feeling his rough—gentle hands over her. Women never quite got it right. They were always so gentle, so considerate. Men were gentle then rough as well. At just the right moments, if they sensed their woman. She felt his desire rise up against her, a wonderful feeling.

She could never help herself. In an instant her whole flesh seemed alive, pulsating, and full of desire. When they found themselves in bed, she acted as she always did, suddenly turning with a near growl into the aggressor, more like a man than a woman, compelling him over on his back and mounting him almost violently. Allen took it like a submissive woman. She liked that, watching them submit beneath her. He almost moaned and begged and cried out like a woman. And she, finishing as she did ahead of the man, more like a man really. Whatever could she do, such a hopeless case?

They lay entangled in each other's arms, as usual finding it nearly impossible to get all four arms and legs in a position that inflicted no nerve damage. The cuddling was the one feminine moment she held onto. She knew men only cuddled for the benefit of their women. Alas, poor men: They always had to do things they would rather not do, go places they would rather not go to, simply to make us, their women happy. They always seemed to want to do anything to make us happy. And we are never quite satisfied. What a strange coupling our species is.

It was nice, laying here like this against him, feeling his smooth flesh, the sound of the ocean not so far off. She became aware she was no longer certain she was awake or asleep.

She had an odd thought, one of those halfway to sleep, when the dream—mind attempts to make illogical sense from logic, or logical sense from illogic; they lay there, the two of them, spent, but not gone, like used—up uranium. She saw herself and Allen as spent uranium, their light and dark naked bodies glowing, in the sea—dark, extruded and stretched over a ship's bulkhead. Something was wrong. Something was tearing at the fabric of their being. They were being torn apart. If she could find him, if they could find one another . . . a warning bell sounded. She saw it as well as heard it, a huge fire alarm bell. Down theyt plummeted through a vortex into the deepest oceanic void, the whirlpool's depth defined by a giant maw of some horrible enormous creature, their extended naked bodies spinning like a fantasia . . . the bell rang again and again . . . above her, way above her, she saw or thought she saw another Allen, a whole man, flesh and blood, holding something, a large black dumbbell shaped club, or, wait, was it blue? Had he turned? That bell! No, the bell stopped ringing. As at a distance she heard him.

"Yes. Who? Susan. Yes, she's here. Hold on. Jennifer. Jennifer!"

"Whe--what?"

"Jennifer. Come on"

"I, we're falling, torn, Oh God, a nightmare."

"Come on. It's Susan. Here. Are you ready?"

"Yeah, yeah. Hello? What? Susan? What? Slo--What's wro--slow down."

She motioned for Allen to gather her, their clothes together. He knew they would not be returning together tonight.

"All right. All right. I'll be right over." She realized she had just popped up fully awake. "Yes, right away." She hung up. "What, damn, what time is it?" Well, maybe not fully awake. "Co--hmmf, coffee."

"I'll get it."

"God, my head. How much wine did we drink?"

"Jennifer?"

"They ran a full computer simulation. Some of the tiles flew off into the ether. Temperature inside the cabin rose to 122°"

"Jesus. What, how--?!

"I don't know. We thought, I don't know what we thought. Could I just have some coffee please."

That damn annoying female edge of irritation to the voice she hated in other women. We are so bitchy and we always take it out on our men who are perfectly innocent. Women are just crazy people who are hard to live with, she thought. Why do men put up with us at all? Well, we are pretty damn good looking; Perhaps that's the reason, she supposed.

"It'll just be a moment." He shouted from the other room. "I know you like it hot and, let's see, cream, no sugar?"

A good boyfriend. He stayed in shape. She liked his body. For a sweet moment she pondered it. The coffee would be hot, steaming even with cream in it. She laughed to herself, not knowing if the giggle was heard in the other room or not; hot tiles, hot coffee. One flies off, one goes in. It was stupid funny. She knew that. But she laughed in spite of herself, sitting dissolute in a rumpled bed, awaiting coffee from her lover, needing to get up, get dressed, and get on with her mission.

It was the air space. It created a bubble from the inside that flared out with overwhelming heat overwhelming the tiles. The pressure built up. Then exploded off. The heat transferred to the spent uranium bulkhead. She knew it all even before getting to her design protocols. Maybe Susan was rubbing off on her after all. Or, maybe she had known all along. Damn! What possible solution could they come up with? Then she had another thought. How did Susan know where to find her?

She padded to the bathroom. When she came out her coffee was ready. He took his turn in the bathroom. She sipped the coffee gingerly. It wasn't McDonald's hot. It would do. Hot enough. She would get another one at the design facility. Or maybe a diet coke would be better. She thought one of the machines had a diet Dr. Pepper. That would hit the spot. A half a cup of hot coffee and a cold diet Dr. Pepper and she could face the enemy.

God, how to keep the pressure heat from building to keep the tiles on?

He came out. They got dressed. From the time Susan called, it took less than twenty minutes for Jennifer and Allen to arrive at computer — command central.

Two main consoles sat, one in the middle of the room, one angled to the side, about ten feet away at a 45° angle. Two old school — wall light green smooth metal sentries with push — button red and white lights. The facade of the consoles was beige. The lights, the push — button indicators, aligned in neat rows upon the face of the facade, with one or two alone or isolated from its fellows. The button — lights were large, about a half inch square. Large enough to allow a man's or woman's finger or thumb to press clearly what needed to be pressed. Jennifer liked the push — button indicators. They didn't give too easily, but they made a satisfying clicking sound and the light came on or went off when pushed. Of course that meant a desired function was activated or turned off. There was a side panel on both. These buttons were not buttons but had the sense where simply touching them on a flat surface activated the function. However, most of these were for calculations and not for commands.

Some of the lights held steady. Some blinked. Some were dull, off, but occasionally blinked on, then shut down again. They all had bold black block lettering names underneath their positions on their panels. Susan sat at the console in the center of the room. Jennifer noticed that Delores sat at the second console, surrounded, as it seemed she always was, by her coterie of men. Delores barked orders and they hove — to.

Jennifer thought of Catherine the Great. The innocent German girl — Tsarina had usurped the crown from her husband by winning the army to her side. An army that would assassinate for her, slay for her, follow her anywhere. Every night Catherine visited a different barracks. In the morning she returned to the palace, another platoon fiercely loyal to her crown and monarchy. What army wouldn't follow such a woman? Is that how Delores . . .? But she looked so strong, almost manly herself. Still there were men who . . .

"Jennifer! Come on. Get to the CAD. I've run the damn thing three times. We'll solve it eventually of course, but we don't have the usual luxury of time. Damn! What did I overlook?

"Jarrod," Delores said.

"Yes, ma'am," Jarrod said. Like most of her men he was burly, a wrestler or a football player. He sported the standard military haircut. Come to think of it, they all . . .

"Check all CB's, fuses, light bulbs. Run a systems diagnostic on C—1 and C—2. It's going to be a long night."

"Yes, ma'am. Jarrod crossed to the shelves of computer drawers about five feet in front of the main console. There was a Circuit Breaker panel between Computer Command 1 and 2 shelf drawers. Little light bulbs illuminated, seven rows of little lights, ten little lights in a row on each C—shelf drawer. The shelves had security handles which had to be released to pull out the drawers. Once pulled out, a chip or a circuit board could be extracted and replaced. Jennifer had heard also that a man or woman with the skill level could solder around circuits on the boards. Supposedly, this would occur only in emergency situations. This was significant, because the drawers with their logic designs and commands would store in memory what they did here, be pulled out, and installed on their vessel.

Now, each of the 140 little lights blinked or ceased blinking, as they monitored a logic sequence or absence of one, a seemingly random sequence display. One session, they had received training on the logic sequence. They had followed the schematics through every combination and permutation of the And, Or, and Not logic gates. She was sure she had forgotten half of it or more than half of it already. Each of Delores's people, on the other hand, seemed to be quite proficient in this skill area.

Jarrod pressed a button at the bottom of each shelf. All the bulbs but for one lit up at once. He released the button. The lights extinguished, but for the continual monitoring sequences. He went across the room to a storage cabinet. He took out a small bulb. He came back. He pushed the same button. He replaced the burnt out bulb. Now all the lights lit when he pressed the bottom button. A small fuse box sat above the cabinet. Jarrod had a key for the latch. He flipped the latch. He opened the small metal door. With a pen flashlight he examined the fuses. He closed the door. Jennifer heard the latch yield a satisfying snap as he locked it.

Three other men surrounded Delores, looking on. She looked up. She now saw the couple who had come in. Jennifer realized that all eyes were upon them. For an instant the men and women in the room were more concerned with gossip, than with scientific curiosity and engineering practicality.

"Allen."

"Yes, ma'am."

"Come here. I'll bring you up to speed."

"Yes, ma'am."

He crossed to her console. So, even her man was really Delores's man, Jennifer thought.

"All CB's lights, fuses check. They're a go, Comman--ma'm."

"Roger that, Jarrod. Stay your position to monitor sequence."

"Aye--Yes ma'm"

Suddenly Jennifer realized another of her sudden insights. Admittedly, it now was not difficult, and required little psychic energy. Still, it made connection to that empty, disconcerting, disturbing, nagging, itch—void that had been crawling up to her thinking brain from her primitive brain, from cerebellum sparking out to the higher cortex regions, never quite getting there, until now, with the crew's obvious slips of tongue, their own cortex circuitry betraying them, Broca's area relaying signals before Wiernecke's area interfered with interpretation.

Barnstone wasn't merely conducting scientific research, imagining scientific scenarios to be played out for the development of cures and treatments. The money wasn't only coming from his pharmaceutical firm's deep pockets and stock options. This mysterious facility was a secret base for submarines, perhaps even enemy submarines captured during the cold war or even today.

"Jennifer, don't stand there staring. You're needed in the center of things. Come on. You know the clock is our enemy."

Jennifer hated that shrill brittle tone to the woman's and scientist's voice. Her eyes never looked so myopic, peering over those damn glasses, rubbing her left hand over and over her right, then reversing the process. She stood by the chair.

Behind Susan's console, Jennifer's CAD computer sat. Jennifer sat in her chair. She looked out at a huge glass enclosure. Through the looking glass, at an odd angle, like some exposed ant colony of which half the side visible to the world, workmen at all hours tended a bulky gray—white object, seemingly suspended in space, a ten foot by five foot teardrop or whale outlined blobby mass. It was taking shape, Jennifer thought. Just like her drawings. But now something was wrong.

She began to enter index codes, matrices, nexus—limits. Soon she saw the problem. Her insight had been right. And, almost at once, she thought she knew what needed to be done.

"It's the tiles--"

"We know that, Jennifer," Susan said.

Delores picked up the criticism. "We've run that sequence three times, Jennifer. If you and some other party which I won't mention his name had been here like the rest of us you would have known that also."

So the woman was not just a man with a hole in the middle after all, just another bitchy woman. She knew what they really meant, the bitch—scientist, and bitch—engineer. Jealous they were, jealous of another woman—competitor because they hadn't had a hunk in their bed tonight. She was the artsy—fartsy—craftsy—touchy—feely one. What did she know of thermodynamics, and geomicrobiological statuses and sequences? Six years she worked with that woman, her friend, and she still would turn to show her the scientist's arrogant know—it—all ass face and shrill voice. Well, if they knew so much, why were they watching her as she worked the three dimensional design in front of her breaking it into fractoids, redefining our own plane of reality?

Her graduate instructor had once told her she reminded him more of a geneticist, a genome worker splicing recombinant deoxyribonucleic acid than a commercial design specialist. Marcus was his name. He was great. They had spent long languid dissolute afternoons on another beach, with Brie and Chardonnay There was something about him, and he was the one man she had been fully submissive with, for some reason. A warmer beach, a longer time, a time far away yet captured in dream moments of our memories . . .

"You remind me of a protease inhibitor, a phantom scissor cutting parts and re—analog—categorizing them."

"I remind you of . . .?"

"You remind me of a magnificent as yet unknown creature evolving moment by moment, beauty and intelligence formulating geometrically into greater intelligence and beauty." Gaw——who would not give herself to such a man?

"When the shuttles re—enter, there is a finite time, usually not much more than twenty minutes until the known time ends. The specs call for more than that, of course, but even at a stretch, they wouldn't experience the practically constant thermo—pressure that our ship must endure. Therefore the failure of the tiles is inevitable." Jennifer cleared her throat. She downed a sip of the diet Dr. Pepper she had been nursing since she purchased it topside and came down to enter the room. She waited.

Grim silence stalked the room. Someone coughed. Someone shuffled papers. Susan looked up. She and Jennifer caught each other's eyes as they always did when they had the same idea.

"We need to cool them," Susan said. Jennifer nodded.

"Cool them?" Delores said. Her men shuffled uncomfortably. Jennifer noted that when she was unhappy they were unhappy.

"Or, more accurately, displace the heat. Air condition-- no, more like . . . "

". . . a refrigerator," Jennifer said.

"A small compressor."

"That's nonsense. It will add too much weight," Delores said.

"Not necessarily. We could get a small one. It doesn't matter if it burns out in six hours or so. Heck, two or one, even."

"And, as you see here," Jennifer was working furiously at her keyboard. Tiles were flying off the unit and returning at different patterns. The model in the large glass enclosure changed angles. "We could cross—patch the design. Remember now, the one advantage we do have in our equations, our heat is constant, in fact a constant for a formula we could employ in our work could probably be derived; we could call it Hc."

Jennifer was enjoying herself now. They could all see at last she wasn't just an artsy—fartsy good looking broad. Uh—huh. She could spin out a scientific query or hypothesis as well, well, almost as well as they could. She continued. She observed they were all listening to her, intently.

"Anyway, the heat in and around, and probably within the vents will not change very much, will not increase. (At least we hope not, she thought.) That means less tiles are necessary, compensating for the compressor unit addition. And we already have--"

"--We already have coils in the design for the electric charge. We just piggy—back through a generator switch—gear. A small one, of course."

Jennifer said nothing about the interruption. Susan had always interrupted her, often finishing her sentences for her. It was a damn irritating habit. She had it right, though. That was what she was going to say. She simply wasn't that convinced it would work. She looked around her. Oddly, for the first time, for the second time tonight, something that had been nagging at her connected and was revealed.

It had struck Jennifer as odd before, but now in her mind it coalesced, the eclectic manner the equipment was laid out, computer control drawers from the 60's and 70's console and chip equipment from the 80's and 90's and some of the panels looked colorful and flat of a contemporary design; somehow it all worked. It was as though this facility had been here for a long time and upgraded, refined, remodeled in stages. Susan continued.

"It should add little, if any significant weight. We can run the transform projections and polar coordinates later. For now, Jennifer, design . . . Jennifer! Design the model and run it through the scenario. We'll try three different sequences. Even three hours will do if it must."

Jennifer noticed Susan was starting to bark orders like Delores. She felt like saying, "Aye, running sequences, Aye, ma'am." She looked over to catch Allen's eye, but Delores had him occupied with a chart. She turned and began to design and run programs.

She ran nine sequences and it was only then they realized it was morning, that there might be light in the sky. They knew at once, like a boulder suddenly falls from the face of the mountain, after being perched in one position for so long, they were exhausted. It hit them like that. It slammed into them. Bit by bit, product moment by product moment, they found the weight and distribution of the new equipment and design down to less than one per cent differential.

Again and again the three women and the three consoles tried varying tangents of degrees less than .02%. The men watched the sequences on the control computers or read ocean charts to determine that the thing could move through tight squeezes. The model beyond turned this way and that sometimes propelling through a red laser lit faux — opening slit the smallest size which Susan had proposed the vent might be when they realized that they had reached a realistic probability and could possibly crystallize it later. They decided to get some breakfast and rest until the afternoon.

Then a blare of blares blared forth!

The klaxon blasted their ears! Lights flashed all over Delores's screen. Jennifer covered her ears. She couldn't think the horn was so loud. Susan looked like a deer caught in headlights. She didn't know what was occurring.

"Intruder. Perimeter A—1. No, wait. A—2. Damn, they're fast. A—4. Heading out to sea. Jennifer barely heard the women's voice.

"Turn the damn thing off!" Jennifer said.

Allen went to a near wall and interrupted a circuit by tripping a Circuit Breaker. To the great relief of all the horn, a great fog horn but at a higher decibel, went silent. Susan looked around for instructions. Jennifer went to her and held her. It never ceased to amaze her how fragile the woman's bones seemed to be. Jennifer noticed the platoon running to a wall cabinet behind Delores's console. Suddenly AR15's, M-16's, and clips emerged from the cabinet expertly locked and loaded by the troop. A gun belt and Glock 9mm for the commander. She snapped the clip, pulled the bolt, knocked off the safety, brought the first of 15 into the chamber, expertly slid her finger out of the trigger casing and rested it along the barrel. It seemed it was all done in a blur, 8 seconds or less. They were already headed past the large blast door and up the steel frame stairs, their boots metal upon metal.

"Jennifer, what's happening?"

"Let's go up. It will all be clearer up there." It occurred to Jennifer as they followed the unit up the stairs that their roles were reversed. She was the one who was leading and taking care of the needy one. Halfway up, she stopped and faced her friend.

"Susan. I want you to know something. Barnstone, he, things are not what they seem."

"How long have you known?"

"Only earlier tonight. I suspected--only earlier tonight."

"Then we had best see what's happening. Hadn't we?"

The edge to the damn bitch—voice returning. She was starting to gain control.

They looked at each other. Jennifer saw she was disappointed with her. Like any academician a scientist's life is full of political intrigue, careerism, innuendo, back-stabbing. Jennifer suddenly knew Susan felt she had betrayed her somehow. It wasn't true. Damn! She should have been working with her all night instead of . . . She nodded. They went upstairs. They opened the door that led to the outside world.

Delores's merry band was using its flashlights even though grey light broke through black in the sky. Then almost at another glance, Homer's rosy—fingered dawn stretched toward the trees at their backs as they traipsed the beach and glanced out to sea. Then, Jarrod, or was it one of the others, Jennifer could not be certain, shouted.

They ran to the spot. It was the one known as Hodges. He was the biggest and most intimidating of all. Apparently he also had the sharpest eyes. "Out there."

He gave the binoculars to Delores. She peered out at the sea's horizon.

"Dingy. Three men, persons, possible two men and a woman. Heading out to their mother ship. Came in from the sea. They knew how to avoid the infrared trip sensors. Probably had a vis-detector to see the sequence patterns. Messed up on one when they hauled out at pre—dawn."

"Yep. Sums it up all right. Sure was a hole in our defensive scheme, all right." Jennifer saw silhouettes. She could not be sure who said it. One of the guards topside, who, obviously, had been in another sector location for a while.

"Shall we go after them?"

"Negative," Delores said, in command voice again. "They're too far gone. May be a sub. Or a freighter along shore lanes. We'll double permutations. Let's buy some mechanical devices. They may not he ready for the simple items. It's possible they don't know we detected them and they might return."

"Jennifer."

"Susan, Barnstone wasn't fully honest with you. He's made some kind of pact with the pentagon. Delores and her cadets here never left the military. They just haven't been wearing their uniforms is all."

"Why would the military be interested in this work?"

"Why don't you tell her, Delores?"

"That's classified, ladies. I suggest you stay out of my business."

"Why? You're in ours. Is it biological or biothermal weapons. thermo—devices of some sort, or, oh my God."

"Jennifer?"

"Don't listen to her doctor. She doesn't know--"

"You want to find subterranean passages for, for, what? Her mind raced now. Is this how Susan often felt?

"Espionage, sabotage, troop transport?"

"That's quite enough."

They stood facing each other. "What are you going to do, Delores? Tell me then kill me?"

"I said I've had enough! I'm responsible for this mission and you'll fall into line."

"Come on. You're a big woman. You've got all the moves, I'm sure. Foot, hand, finger. Do me in. One less mouth to worry about."

"Commander!"

"Commander, now. Even the pretense is gone. Isn't it, Commander?"

"Coming."

"Jennifer, am I to understand that the army is behind all of this?"

"Some of it. Probably most of it. Barnstone Pharmaceuticals will still get first benevolence crack. If that means anything."

"Then we'll pull out."

"What. This is your life's work."

"I won't be party to some new ghastly weapon design."

"Weapon! That's it! They want to harness the vent's sources. Control their eruptions, somehow. And I slept with one of them."

"Dr. Arthknott. Could you come over here? We found something."

They waddled—ran the beach to a high point looking over the sand. Someone had dropped a strap of some sort. One of those extra camera straps that no one seemed to use. Susan took it from Jarrod's hand. An etching into the strap had an unmistakable symbol of a Model—T automobile and a curving stairwell.

"My God! "Carstairs," Susan said.

They returned to the control center. Susan sat at her console. Delores stood over her. The platoon stood around the console. Jennifer stood by her colleague—friend, her hand on her shoulder.

"Tell me about Carstairs. Is he working for the Russians? Chinese? ISIS? Iranians? Serbs? Don't act like you know nothing. This is my mission now. I won't--"

"The hell it is!" Jennifer looked down. She was once again proud of Susan. The scientist had looked up at the military officer with a deep—set glare she had not seen before, or had not seen for quite a while. She knew it because her colleague had turned to look at her immediately after, breathing hard, a muscle on her cheek twitching. Susan went on.

"How dare you. Now you listen to me. I am certain that the reason we are able to live and work with the relative freedom we have--"

"Relative? You don't--"

Susan raised her voice. Jennifer had heard the screech before. She hadn't wanted to hear it again. Now here it was, almost a harpy—skree. It resounded in the water—chambers of her ear. Anything withered in its path when this seemingly frail scientist rose to her full height and expanded the depth of her intensity and desire.

"I say relative. From the standards of your watch and the men and women who guard our shores and stand at the ready so we need not fear the knock at the door at midnight and for it we are all grateful."

Jennifer noticed the group stood a bit taller, their shoulders a bit more braced.

"But make no mistake. This is my idea. This is my project. This is my design. This is my say—so. It is for science and, ultimately, good therapy for now incurable diseases. It is not for any destructive element that could impact the world. Thus spake I!"

"You know nothing of the workings of the world." The military officer and the scientist stood face to face now.

"I know about its sea—bottom. I'm the one who knows the most about it. In fact, we can settle it now. I don't go, you can't go. You won't know the first thing of the geo-biological entities or movements or tracking of the vents. I don't go, you don't go. And I only go when I'm in charge, as from the beginning."

"I could command you. See about this grant money."

"Go to hell." For a moment there was silence. Susan sat down. Then, looking up, she spoke. "Or rather, go ahead. Inquire. I'm sure Dr. Barnstone would like to hear about it. In fact, we'll call him right now. Jennifer."

Jennifer removed her smart phone. She touched the speed dial. Delores nodded to Hodges. A big man, still she was amazed the speed of his approach. He propelled her phone out of her hand.

Delores sighed. A crack in the armor. The first. Small. But a crack, like a fissure at a vent letting off the first steam ball.

"All right. For now."

Susan had called her bluff. Jennifer felt a little elation. Delores repeated herself, with a different tone. Her authoritative hum had at once returned. "For now."

"All right then."

Hodges returned Jennifer's phone into her hand. Had he kept his hand on hers a little too long? Looked into her eyes a little too deeply? It didn't matter. Not any more. Once she might have worked her way through the group. After all, they seemed attractive, fit, excellent specimens. Her right big toe was larger than the left, a huge toe on huge feet. Men she was with often commented on it, embarrassing her; a few great guys placated her tenderly, then turned to it with high eroticism.

It always twitched when she had one of her insights. She realized it was twitching now; for she suddenly recognized the reason behind her promiscuity, her dissolution (albeit she was always very careful), her problem. She liked men. And more than this: She regarded them as specimens to study, to see how each new body reacted as she took it beneath her. Each new body smelling of maleness undulating and moaning beneath her, like some great mysterious tubule creature, her bedrooms and motel rooms laboratories. It was only when her experiments in her lab were complete, when her dissections and catalytic conversions could show results, when she conquered them fully, only then wouldst she explode in her own exquisite pleasure shower of release. So powerful sometimes blazes of light cascaded in the back of her brain, and, for a short moment, she lost consciousness.

She had dallied with a few women as well. She allowed they weren't too bad. She liked their perfume. She liked their soft red—painted lips which left rouge hues on her body. She liked the different anatomical protuberances and digressions of their bodies that went in and went out, where softness turned to firmness and firmness to softness. Oddly she found men to be better kissers for the most part. There were some women, she knew, who didn't like kissing men because their whiskers raked their fair skin. She considered these women fools. A little pain was part of pleasure, and men's facial hair was part of what defined them as men.

But she now knew her true problem with women was she often found herself submitting, lying beneath them, or at least alongside. One, with an odd name, Zelda, liked to spank her with a large black belt. She let her, lying as submissive as a slave, for it gave Zelda great pleasure and at that moment that was all she wanted to do. Almost to the point of welts and they were somehow thrilling when she finally was allowed to run her fingers along the pink—white flesh incarnadine of her person.

How strange she was, to want to be bound to women but to dominate men. Even her relationship with Susan might be defined that way. She had tied herself to the scientist, for she admired intelligence and hypothetical inquiry. Susan had entered her life, rescued her from the mundane of mere drawings to the adventure of discovery. She knew she would do anything for her.

That was it. With women, she suddenly knew, she was searching deep inside them, for that long ago locked away clue to our origins, hidden in the unyielding depths of the ocean and mirrored somewhere deep inside the astonishing feminine body. Really, women were treasures to be adored. If only more men realized it. Well, they certainly better realize it where she was concerned, when she was with them. Now she knew that was part of the equation as well. She felt her nipples expand. She felt her breasts yearn. She felt wet in her womanhood. She felt at once one with earth and sky and sea.

But her toe twitched even mightier than before. Her right foot quivered. Surely everyone would see it. Why did she wear these damn sandals? She would change to full covered shoes in the future. But they always looked so huge, like giant yellow earth — moving shovels and back — hoes. As she always did, she tried to find a way to hide her feet. She moved a bit more behind Susan, trying to slide her feet under her friend's chair.

Well, now it was hopeless for these men. She, they, Susan and she had been deceived by this butch — bitch woman and all the queen's men. She didn't like it. None of them would get lucky again on this watch. None would know, well, none else would discover what she knew of the beautiful male body and what she could do, if they would only submit to her will and her wiles.

"But I need to know about this Carstairs." Quieter. Almost submissive. She equested.

Jennifer knew the commander was entitled to know. If she didn't the unit could not protect them from a harm perhaps as dangerous as the way deep they were headed. Susan didn't like to talk about it, she knew. Jennifer looked down. Her scientist friend took a deep breath. She gazed into space. She peered into the not so distant past. Jennifer had always wondered if . . .

"He was a professor of mine at Pacific University and later at Wood Hole. A brilliant mind. He had a theory that the vents intertwined in passages on the other side, were all inter — connected somehow. It was one of those old resurrected flawed scientific theorems that began with the discovery of Mammoth Cave in the nineteenth century, reared its fallacious head in the 1920's, when for some reason, a number of spelunkers in caves around the country were lost and never found. Some of our caves today still bear the names of these lost troglodyte explorers. Basically, it went something like this: All caves and underground channels in the world interconnect; the proof would be if you could locate two underground rivers hundreds or thousands of miles apart, and throw into the one a colored dye, the color would at some later point in time appear in the other.

It's been on occasion attempted, but the hypothesis is never supported by evidence. Adherents claim that the experimenters didn't wait long enough, or that the underground rock filters out the coloring. Once a theory develops, and no evidence can be found, still some adherents will hold on to their ideals. There's a name for that postulate: The infinite displaced theorem or something like that.

"Carstairs's analogy of the inter—connecting cave—channels in the earth: Therefore, all these vents were somehow connected deep within as well, and, more than this: The theorem expanded, a super—connection in all caves and fissures of the earth no matter how deep or shallow,like cracks in an egg. The grand— under— the—earth Northwest passage, he called it. I tried to remind him about the moment of Meriwether Lewis's antithetical moment of truth, his anti—Epiphany, when he stood at the source of the Missouri River, observed boundless mountains and valleys before him and knew at that instant there never would be found a Northwest passage. He smirked. 'Lewis, as you know, simply sniffed out the wrong track, ' he said. 'And he hunted his prey in the days before nuclear powered submarines. Today the technology exists to prove my theory.' My protest was waved off.

"I begged him not to publish this hypothesis, not till we could test it somehow. After all, the cave conceptualization had decades earlier been regarded as crackpot. I knew this line of reasoning could lead only to disaster, academic suicide. I persisted. But Will had a maniacal vein and he could be--"

She paused. Silence reigned in the compound. Delores fingered her weapon. One of the men looked about, as if someone were invading past the blast door. A compressor revved. Soon dripping as through from a conduit pipe was heard. Jennifer noticed it at once. She was certain Delores noticed it. Susan gently rubbed her left cheek with her right hand, as though she had been slapped there. The compressor hummed. The water dripped. Drip. Drip. Drip . . .

"I'm sorry. He could be most persuasive and imperious. Cruel. So cruel, right even when he was wrong.

"The article generated some controversy and he lost his post. He lectured for awhile, then took me and other followers . . ."

Jennifer had heard the story before. Susan wasn't telling all of it. The scientist (selectively?) deleted details, most unimportant, one or two significant. Jennifer had met Carstairs once. It was an academic party soon after his controversial article was published. Clearly he was trying to woo the Dean and Trustees to his side. But it hadn't worked. The six men and two women, dressed in tuxedos and gowns, had left early. The ax had fallen a week later.

Jennifer allowed that he had piercing light blue eyes, almost translucent. He was captivating, compelling somehow. His company to salvage had made some money; but Susan knew what he was really after. She left when she began to entertain her own, seemingly more realistic premise, although she still maintained a loose connection with the university. More than once he had followed her. She had solved or thought she solved the thermo—pressure problem. She waited for the right vent to blow its top to steam. She was beginning to believe she would never discover it until it was too late for her, when Jennifer's sharp eyes had caught the strange long green ripple in the ocean surface. Susan told her for some time she thanked her lucky stars for the day she found her. She suddenly recognized Susan hadn't told her that for some time.

Susan knew Carstairs wasn't far behind. Now he closed in, circling like a shark terrorizing its prey before striking with its razor shearing teeth. She knew these were his subtle touches of espionage. He was too assiduous to leave something by accident. She knew Susan knew it was his signature, his calling card left in her mailbox.

"If I were you, I'd track that strap. It may have a listening device in it."

"We buzzed it already. It had a bug. We're going to send out false messages," Delores said. She breathed. She continued.

"There's more, isn't there? Something you're not telling me."

Susan slumped in her chair. For the first time since she knew her, Jennifer noticed a tear in the eye of her friend. She had been right. Carstairs had taken advantage of her in more than one way.

There was another silence. The compressor stopped. The drips continued. Louder.

Jennifer put her arm on Susan's shoulders. The woman's range of emotions, hidden and now, not so hidden, were becoming complex and somewhat predictable.

She had never seen her so vulnerable and compliant, and just moments ago--she suddenly hated this man. She vowed he had best not get in her way.

"Susan." She bent down. She put her lips close to the scientist's right ear, nearly touching the flesh. Susan had strange ears that ventured back at an angle, and pointed a bit. Her helix curiosity almost caused her to look like Mr. Spock, the Vulcan, a character drawn so well, that, like Sherlock Holmes, he almost seemed to enter our dimension of reality. In fact, there were significant congruities between the two rich characterizations. Well, and besides, who was she, with her foundation feet, to dwell on someone else's anatomical peculiarity? She had known several men whose--God, she had to stop it. Things were becoming much too important. "Susan." Not louder. More intent.

"I don't know what uncomfortable feeling grew on me. But I began to come home early. I noticed men leaving the house as I entered my own driveway."

Coming home early. Leaving the house. Her own driveway. So the story was complete. She had lived with him. I always thought so, Jennifer thought.

"One night I came home early and entered through the back. They saw me. They left. But not before I heard some things."

"Go on. You're doing fine now, Dr. Arthknott. Good, Ms. Littleton. I think she can use some water. There. Good. Now. Please. Continue."

Well, that's it, after all. Except. Except I believe I now know who those men were."

"Yes. It's all right. You can say it now."

"I now believe, I didn't want to, that they were Russian, Syrian, and Iranian agencts.."

"And why would they--"

"Stop. You know why better than I."

"Say it Doctor."

"It's obvious now, isn't it? It's all too obvious. Oil for weapons. Technical know—how to send to the Chinese, the Columbian cartel, the Russian mafia, the Iranian qud. They're all interconnected like some giant octopus or squid sending out its tentacles everywhere. Anything to circumvent the United States, the western alliance, Israel, friendly Arab nations. Big money. Big guns. Big technology. Isn't that what you wanted to hear? I thought it was X—files paranoia, until that day. And science goes wanting."

The compressor waited for that moment to return on. It sounded as though it was sucking in air, perhaps their air. It certainly seemed to be hotter and colder in the room at the same time.

Jennifer suddenly felt as though this machine, wherever it was in this facility, somewhere in the basement, was the spy or worse, a malevolent entity which was slowly but inevitably draining out their oxygen, as though they were deep and the channel to climb to surface vented a tiny shunt of air. Unconsciously, she held her breath. Susan ran her right hand over her left cheek. She ran it slowly back and forth, forth and back.

Jennifer shivered. Allen came over to her to put his arm around her. She pulled away, hard, perhaps too hard. She stared at him, a woman's wilting gaze. He saw the truth. He stepped back a half step. She spun away, with a look in her eye only women were capable of, one they reserved for men who had betrayed them, or thought they had.

The group finally allowed that exhaustion reigned. They agreed to get some rest. They would return in six hours. Delores had wanted three. Susan, the scientist whose idea had generated all this, and who was in charge, produced a plethora of biological and circadian rhythm rationale and published articles and insisted on six. Delores, realizing that Allen had gotten some sleep, put him on a four hour watch, with orders to wake her for relief. She lay down on a cot in an upper level of the command—control center. The others headed back to their assigned rooms.

Susan and Jennifer walked side by side. Jennifer matched the fast pace of her colleague, step for step, but at a slower pace, for she was taller with longer strides. She sensed the tension between them. Indeed, when they arrived at the entrance to the converted hotel, Susan walked to the roundabout.

Jennifer knew now this was no hotel but something military designed to appear and act like one. She suddenly realized one reason was probably to fool satellite photographs. She stopped. She turned. She looked. After a while, she realized that this had probably been some 1920's or 30's seaside resort that played out for some reason during the Roosevelt era. She had read there were a string of these seaside remote resorts in those days, most of them defunct in a decade or two. The military had no doubt commandeered this one during World War II using the excuse of national emergency. After the war, intelligence had recognized its remote potential, with a decent infrastructure in place.

She didn't want to start and go through this with Susan. She felt drained, exhausted, bone—weary. Jennifer thought of her uncle then, a man she thought of from time to time, as she did all her deceased relatives. He was a sweet man, God rest his soul. He never married. He lived with his sister, Jennifer's aunt, the aunt's husband and two children, Jennifer's cousins. The man, Ben, held a steady job. He contributed to the economy and affairs of the household. He could pack luggage like no one else on earth could pack luggage. He had a strange ocular disorder in which he could see oddly in front of him only if he cocked his head about thirty degrees to the right oblique. He uttered various original bon mots, neither vulgar nor sophisticated epithets of pith that were earthy but astute. One was, for example, when it was time for dinner, and the people yet milled about in their conversations, he drew all to table at once, by announcing clearly, "Food's ready; park your carcass."

I just want to haul my poor tired ass to bed and park my carcass, Jennifer thought. I don't give a damn about men or ships or undersea monsters or women scientists and their goofy ideas. I just want to--

"Susan, I'm tired. I'm only thirty—one years old and I'm so tired."

"We can't talk in our room. It's probably bugged."

Jennifer sighed. She dragged herself to the drive circle island. Let's get this torment over with.

"There's something terribly wrong with this whole thing. Forgive a scientist's poor pun, but something smells fishy."

The woman actually snickered at her pathetic joke, a nerd joke. Jennifer suddenly recalled her high school days: To everyone else it seemed she was the top of the line high school girl. Cheerleader, date of the football quarterback, all of it; yet even her high grades and honors ironically indicated her conflict with how she was secretly jealous of the so—called nerdish group, their always having first crack at the computer systems and discussing mathematical and scientific indications. She wanted to join those conversations, those clubs, those groups. Yet she was somehow herded into discussions of hair, boys, nail polish, nail polish remover, boys, lipstick, other girls not being discussed, and boys. She yearned for the others to call her in to their groups, and worried that they would.

"I've always been conflicted," Jennifer said, only then realizing she had said it out loud, instead of inwardly, which she had meant to do.

"What? What does that have . . . Never mind. There's something fish--wrong. Yes, I know. I think we both know.

"No. No. I know you know that. I mean--" Here Susan drew even closer to Jennifer, as one of Brutus's conspirators might have drawn closer to whisper in his ear just prior to Caesar entering the room. Jennifer's heart skipped a beat. It always did that when something significant was about to occur. At first she had hated it and hated herself for it. Later, she came to rely upon it as an aura of some sort. Susan whispered in her ear, but it was quite loud resounding against her eardrum. "I think Carstairs has a spy in our group."

"My God, Susan. Why? How?"

"After I realized what kind of alarm system they had, I knew it. The codes are random and complex. The layout of the patterns could not have been discerned or even guessed at."

"Allen said they probably used night vision goggles."

"That could be it. That could accomplish what they needed to do. However, these patterns change at randomly selected time intervals. Even invaders with night vision goggles would get caught in a fuzzy logic driven vector at some point, unless--"

"Unless the timing sequence codes for that night had been given to them, so they could download and match, match the pattern precisely."

"Even--"

"Even predict it within what, what tolerance, seconds?"

"Tenths of seconds, probably."

They sat. They stood up. They kept silent for a long while. In near—despair, Jennifer realized she wasn't sleepy any more. On top of everything else she'd have trouble falling asleep. And I am so tired, she thought to herself, careful this time not to give her complaint voice. Instead, she gave Susan the only logical counter—argument.

"But they did get caught. That's how we found out."

"A mistake. Human error. The chaos factor. It's inevitable. But they were out there a long time before it happened. And they did not get caught. Indeed, they were long gone."

"OK. OK, you've stimulated me back awake." Susan deserved it and she was going to get it in. "But who?"

There it was. The question which sent even greater chills up and down their spines. They spent the next few moments going over the personnel. Susan was a bit bitchy when she came to Allen, but Jennifer shrugged it off. Hodges, the big man. Jarrod Wells, the thin guy, the Norwegian—looking one. Jones, they called him, of course, "Jonsey," a technician of some sort, peeking and probing here and there into their consoles and mainframe stations, like a praying mantis reckoning its prey, and Magrugder, that strange short man bulging with muscles who obeyed his orders but made it seem like they were his idea. Almost an aloof, autonomous individual, who seemed to know what was expected of him before it occurred. Jones had not procured a weapon. He was probably a techie only and would stay behind. But the others . . .

"Don't forget Delores," Jennifer said.

"I haven't forgotten her," Susan said.

At last, almost in her state of desperation, Jennifer said, "We won't figure it out here tonight. Let us get our nap. Sleep on it. It'll be clearer that way."

"Very well. Perhaps we can resolve the matter while we sleep. It happens that way sometimes."

Jennifer caught herself from letting out a great sigh of relief. She appeared analytical. The scientist was correct on two counts, of course. Our problems can sometimes be helped or resolved in our sleep and dream states; and rest would surely bring more clarity than she could fathom now. Her head burst, full of problems, concerns, CAD designs, men, the sickly-sweet charged odor of electronics and plastics, women, and weariness. She was condescending. Even with these new challenges, she began to feel sleepy again. Anything to get them to their bed. It was always a problem. Susan needed so little sleep, working all hours of the night. She almost always felt tired, and needed to rest. "Yes, Susan. Of course you're right."

They began to walk to the door. In the distance they heard buoy bells, odd with the sun up. Jennifer had one of those strange insight thoughts spark in her brain only when she was too exhausted to make a further connection. For a moment, she stopped.

"Susan, what did you mean, when you said, 'Only I know what's out there?'"

The scientist, her friend, her colleague, her supervisor, did not stop nor miss a step. Even over her shoulder, she spoke, walking away, difficult for Jennifer to barely make her out.

"Come on now. We both need to sleep.'"

Allen blinked his eyes. Immediately, he jerked awake. At least for a moment. It was a court—martial offense to fall asleep on watch detail. He knew it. But the sleep he had had before had been fitful. The woman kept moaning in her dreams. She kept thrashing about. She kept kicking him.

The sex had been great, sure. There was something about white women. Some special allure. They smelled different, reacted different, somehow.  Not better; women of his own race smelled and reacted better; but different somehow. Sooner, faster, maybe. Almost as much as men, some of them, like, like they were always just about ready for sex. Their skin folded in creases in erotic places, and when those beautiful pink—hued white bodies fell back or rolled over on top of him he felt his member would pulsate through his skin.

But it had been draining. He was exhausted. And the commander put him on watch. Two and a half hours to go. Man! And then only two hours. He'd try to talk the commander into another two. He was sure she'd give them to him. They could cover him for that period of time. Otherwise he was going to collapse. Bivouac was never this tough to stay awake.

Two hours twenty—five minutes. Water. He needed water. That might help. It was as though he were asleep with his eyes open, that's how he felt. The console lights and security video screens of topside jumped and fuzzed, bluing this way and that. He thought maybe he had seen or sensed a shadow behind him. It seemed everything was OK. He could almost hear the commander snoring in the room above. Two hours twenty minutes. He had to keep awake. But was he now awake or asleep? Something had moved! He went to the stairs. A shadow crossed at the bottom. Radio. Where was his radio? The commander was upstairs. He needed to call. He hardly noticed the little dart pricking him in the thigh, through his pants. As he blacked out, all he could think of was who should be his counsel in his court— martial. A strange figure with no face floated up toward him. Then there was no doubt as to whether he slept or not.

Susan watched Jennifer thrash about in her bed. Later, Jennifer would tell her of the dream. She was naked. A man held her by the ankles, a woman by her hands. They were laying her out on one of those medieval torture machines which stretched a body and broke her bones one by one. She was lashed to the machine now, screaming in agony as the malevolent couple turned the screws of the machine with greater increasing torque. It began to smoke. Straps and gears snapped, broke. The evil couple looked chagrined, concerned. The whole thing collapsed. She was suddenly free and free of pain. Clothing floated down from somewhere and instantly she was dressed with modesty, refreshed with make—up and hair—do. She sat up. She stood away. In a darkened room the bad couple had fallen under the collapsed gears, belts, levers, straps. They lay mangled and bleeding. Then, suddenly, cool water came down, a cascade, a falls. She felt refreshed, relieved. Then a giant worm or squid chased her. Its great maw was about to consume her. She bolted awake, drenched in cold sweat. Susan was close looking at her.

"Susan."

The seemingly frail, but in truth tough scientist, cast off her veneer, and held her friend, like a mother consoles a child.

"It's all right, Jennifer. It will all be all right. You'll see. Nothing bad will happen."

"I. I think for the first time, I'm scared."

"I know. But it will be OK."

And she sang her a song. She held her in her arms and crooned a lullaby. An old Irish lullaby in a soft voice. All of a sudden, Jennifer was transported back, being held in strong but loving feminine arms, a woman's voice sending her serenity in song. She remembered: A memory so old and deep and buried, as though before time and oceans and air separated, a memory that few in their lifetime are fortunate to remember, something from a time that was timeless, and that, always, throughout our lives, though we are not aware of it, we wish we could return to it.

They sat like that, the two women, in an ancient Jungian icon of relief and comfort, for the remaining twenty minutes of their respite. The singing ceased. They broke apart.

"You do know something, don't you?"

"No, Jennifer. But I have some suspicions, suppositions."

"Why?"

"They're speculation for the most part. And antithetical. I, I can't, well, I've gone over and over the readings we took when we were out there."

"I know."

"The vent describes an opening of an astounding 37 to 50 yards at least, perhaps even nearly 90. That's huge. An amazing phenomenon. Allrocker's Ridge vent lines were thought to be the largest, and they're measured in feet. Anyway, the smoke and fumes on our ridges make it difficult to tell for certain, from our photographs."

"We knew it was the largest. That's why--"

"No, no that's not what I mean. Look here. Where is it? Yes, here it is. No, that's not it, where did I put, oh, for crying out loud, I had it earlier--here! Wait. Let me turn this, now. Look at the spectrograph. The thermographs and the visual. Here, in the area . . ."

"It, but that's impossible. The spectrometer shows these red and yellow—red ranges all through until, but here it's reverse from--

"Yes. Perfect description. Reverse from. Here in this, say 20 or 30 yards, if these are accurate--"

"The cold water is being sucked into the event."

"Yes."

There was a long pause. Jennifer envisioned herself working at her CAD, drafting cool spectrometer scale water into the vent. She looked again at the thermographs. She was sure she would see a denial. After all, she had looked at them a hundred times.

Now she saw the truth of the matter. In that part of the range, no steam rose. There was no smoke. There were no bubbles. There were no weird creatures. She fairly ran across the room. She grabbed her briefcase. She pulled out the video she had shown Barnstone that day, not so long ago but which seemed like an eternity now. She snapped it in the machine, expertly this time. She hit "Play." Soon the murky images became clear as the fantastic creatures appeared in as much focus as possible. One thing was certain now. In that place, or close to it, no steam arose, no strange vent—creatures floated by or undulated in relief. How had she missed that before?

On either side, bubbling, frightening steam and red creatures which should not live there belched forth and twitched after.

"My God. You think that--"

The phone rang! Susan picked it up. Jennifer heard the conversation as at a distance, as though in a haze of steam of strangeness, until Susan mentioned Allen's name.

". . . been hurt. Right. No. We're up. We'll be right down."

Susan had never seen Jennifer dress quite so hurriedly.

By the time they ran in, the entire group surrounded him. They knew how to treat for shock. They had already administered their xylocaine injectors into his chest. He gazed at them. He blinked, as though seeing and not seeing. Jennifer had the idea her lover seemed a rag doll, like the old Raggedy Andy consort of Raggedy Ann, flailing this way and that. It was an odd contrast to the stalwart and strong man who had been so firm just hours ago.

Susan, the competent health practitioner, arrived at her patient's side in an instant, already into her patterned physical exam.

"We've got him awake at least, but his pulse is so slow. I've never--"

"Move over, let me see, Dr. Arthknott ordered."

The doctor—scientist felt his pulse. With a small pen-light she always had with her, she peered first in one eye, then another. She tried to look close into his eyes. Soon, she stood up.

She announced her diagnosis; or lack of one. In an instant, she remembered. She knew what to do.

"He's been drugged with, I don't know, nothing psychotropic, nothing hallucinatory. Something exotic. Damn! I can't, I don't know wh--wait a minute. Let me look at his eyes again. Here. Hold his head here. This way. That's it. If his eyes turn--so. I saw this once in, damn, where was it, where, come on, come on. Yes! Haiti, on a small island off the main one, the loa ritual, lwa, actually. I recall .. . All right everyone. We have to get his clothes off."

"What?"

"Don't waste time. Hurry. Pants. Shirt. It could be anywhere. Look carefully along. Here let me do it. I'll start at his feet, ankles."

You had to go slow and careful and even then backtrack. Even then, you could miss it. And it was more difficult besides on dark skin.

Indeed, she almost missed it but decided to go back up from the left ankle a third time. She saw it. A tiny red circle. There was no dart however. It was probably in his pants leg. She would look later.

As she suspected, she had seen it once, on her Caribbean investigation of jellyfish.

"Tetrodotoxin. From the, wait a minute, extracted from the, what, what, yes, the puffer fish. It's used in the petro black magic rituals, part of the zombie trance death—look drug. The evil side of Voodoo. If treated properly, the patient can make a full recovery, sometimes quite soon. I think the dart failed to deliver the full amount. He would appear dead and who knows what we might have done. You've all done splendidly. Not only saved his life, but we'll be able to bring him out of his coma with little or no damage.

"The terrible thing is, he sleeps a deep sleep, yet, somewhere above him, he is suddenly aware he knows everything that's going on. Don't worry, Allen. You'll be fine. Jennifer. Hold his head. Talk to him. Right now he's terribly frightened. I have to return to my room. I have some contraindication medications.

They will significantly reduce his time in limbo. Jennifer. Tell him that he'll be perfectly all right. He has to tough out about four to six hours is all. That's if I can find , . . . it would be best if he could simply go to sleep but he may be too full of anxiety."

"Hodges. Go with the doctor."

"You know something Delores? I think I won't turn away a bodyguard. How the hell did someone get a dart in him down here?"

She zipped out the door. Hodges trailed after her trying to keep up, clutching his holstered Glock in tight against his hip as he ran. Jennifer comforted the dazed patient. Delores started barking orders to the rest to check all around for clues. After a while, the two women found themselves at their patient's side.

"How is he doing?"

"A little better, I think. It's difficult to tell. I've just been reassuring him. I think I saw a glimmer for a second in his eyes. Delores."

"I know what you're gong to ask, Doctor. I don't know. I was upstairs in the cot for my sack time. I violated a cardinal rule. Always post two men, never one alone. But we're a small unit and we'd all been up all night, except for, well, I'm sorry. I didn't mean . . . "

"No, it's OK."

"I'm calling for reinforcements. At least until we haul out of this station. We'd better check all our equipment. Wells. Run a simulation check on all major sequences. Check all switchgears. Battery back—ups, fuses, light bulbs, the whole lot."

"Aye—aye, Commander."

"Damn. This operation's turning into a Custer fuck. And it's my ass strapped in."

"Where did you find him?"

"Here. Over here, at the head of the stairs."

"what's downstairs?"

"The switchgear. Backup generator. And--Jesus! The download back—up. Every entry into the analog buffer system. A bit of the dinosaur era but accurate as hell. If the tape's been moved--watch him."

She bounded down the steps three at a time. A big woman, solid, muscular, Jennifer was always amazed at how gracefully and lithe she moved. Like a wolf in the wild.

Jennifer watched the commotion swirl around her. She moved occasionally to get comfortable. Fortunately she had worn pants this time, so she didn't have to worry about the guys sneaking looks at her exposed parts much. She talked to her patient lying in her lap, as Susan had comforted her only an hour or so ago. She sang soft songs, trying to recall the one Susan had sung to her. Finally she heard Delores and Jones coming up the stairs.

"The tape was off seat an eighth of an inch. It could be a normal drift. But I'm afraid someone got a heck of a lot of our data. But how did he get in in the first place?"

"It was Carstairs," Susan said, holding three syringes. "He's a ghost. Besides surely you all realize by now, someone in our group is feeding him the scanning codes to get in and out."

"What?

"Who?"

"It could be anyone. Even Allen. The dosage should have been higher but for the dart falling out. Delores was here, asleep. No one knows. We were all asleep, weren't we?"

Everyone looked at everyone else. Clouds of suspicion hovered as loud as the silence. Susan bent to her patient. She injected the syringes. Allen emitted a faint moan.

"Well, a good sign. A very good sign."

Jennifer sighed. She relaxed. She lifted up her eyes. She suddenly realized the men in the room gazed at her, then at Susan, then back to her.

"I think it's time you told us just what we are to expect out there. Reinforcements are setting up now. They've expanded our perimeter, including three miles out to sea. I've ordered double watch, double detail. We won't have any more security breaches. Clearly something of great significance and moment lies under the ocean currents in some place only you know about. My men and I need to know what to expect down there. Obviously a lot of people know more than we."

"Well, not a lot, really. A few."

"Nonetheless, Dr. Arthknott."

Jennifer peered at Susan. She glanced at Delores. Moment, the woman had said, in the correct usage. Who were these people? She had heard that Special Operations specialists had high intelligence, facility with languages and systems, as well as their formidable physical prowess and highly advanced training. What really was going on?

Jennifer sighed. She put her fingers to her upper sinuses, the ones underneath the brow ridge but next to the top of the nose. They hurt. So always would they hurt when she was under stress or was tired. Now, here, a double whammy—benefit for the sinus demon. She pushed in, harder, almost breaking her nose cartilage. Sometimes her self—inflicted pressure—pain helped.

She had gone with a man once who she would have married simply because he had a magic touch in gently massaging her sinuses, making the pain go away, opening her breathing passages. She would lay her head in his lap, like an older dog who knows precisely what familiar ritual position will elicit the desired affection. His long tapered fingers, sculpted almost like a woman's, relieved her agony. His fingers canon: Nose sprays, antihistamines, decongestants, ointments, steam treatments, these were mere pea shot by comparison.

Afterwards, they shared some wine, domestic, and . . . In the morning, she would awaken always to find him gone. The sinus pressure and pain and clogged passages returned later in the day. One night he simply stopped coming. Later, she heard he had taken up with men. Men! Ah well, if only he were here now.

She felt cramped. She shifted her position. Several hours had passed. They checked their work. They double—checked their equipment. Nothing had been interfered with. But it was clear they had been compromised. It probably wasn't too bad. Delores felt she had awakened soon after the attack on her guard and had scared the guy off. Unless he was still there; but they had scurried about and poked into every nook, every cranny of the oddly designed place. In fact the new men and women, apparently some ranger or other special ops group, investigated still.

Allen started to come around. Every so often, Susan checked his vitals. Occasionally she examined his eyes. It became clear she grew increasingly satisfied with his progression. He peered in a strange fashion, as if seeing a time afar off. His spoke still slurring, in a mumble. Jennifer remembered a time she was very depressed, enshrouded in dark fog. She recalled she could barely generate the energy or link thought together to stimulate her lips and tongue to move in a manner that would produce intelligent and articulated speech.

"It was weird. I could see you, hear you. But it was like through the small end glass of a telescope and I, I couldn't, I couldn't . . . I kept waking and sleeping and, and . . ."

"Shh. Rest, Allen. Just relax and rest. Your recovery will go faster, that way," Susan said. Jennifer covered him with a blanket after Susan completed yet another exam.

"Dr. Arthknott."

"Yes, Delores. Yes, quite right. It is indeed time to try to understand what all of you have signed up for. I presume this is a volunteer mission, as they say. Good. Well then."

Jennifer was reminded of her old campfire girls group. Like her campfire—mates, this group gathered in positions as comfortable as they could arrange in some sort of pattern pre-ordained by the commonality of the gene pool. They settled in for the story. Jennifer immediately recognized Susan returned to her familiar persona of classroom lecturer. She struck her professorial poses. She engaged her teacher's tics. She paced. She projected her lecture—voice.

"As early as the 1800's divers in pressure suits with air hoses attached to their helmets, limited to an extent only by the length of their precious air umbilical cords, began to report the existence of strange creatures never before seen. Since underwater photography was not yet a particularly good technology, marine biologists, zoologists, and taxonomists could only rely on their reported observations and, in some cases, their renderings based on memory of what the divers saw or thought they saw.

"Many scientists, knowing well the inadequacy of those early suits which subjected the divers to bends and oxygen deprivations, thought they might simply be experiencing a common form of temporary hallucination. As the decades proceeded and the equipment and training improved, the reports persisted, often quite consistent in descriptive detail: Elongated, eel—like creatures which glowed in red or golden auras, as a future fictional spaceship's electro—harmonic shields; semi—circular creatures with huge pale blue eyes, a sort of folded about manta ray with spikes raised all about its partial shell—like, partial soft skin; these and more, crab or lobster like creatures that had fins or something like them and swam with agility.

"By the 1970's the reports were accompanied by decent photographic images or film. Whatever remnants of skepticism somehow remained were finally put to rest. Well, for the most part, anyway. In fact deep sea divers plunged ever deeper now, into abysses of ocean valleys, crags, caves, and beneath overhangs of mountains.

"Soon, reports of thermal expulsions from vents began to surface, if you'll pardon a bad pun. Both situations stimulated submersible explorations. Conventional wisdom dictated that no creature could exist therein. The question was how could they live at such depths without sunlight? There was always the question of the holy grail of marine biology. Archetuthis, the giant squid, a creature never seen nor discovered, but whose existence is all but known. It must exist at some incredible depth. Only recently has it been exposed, a picture of it.

"That satisfied some scientists. For the rest of us, soon scientific shock. There were creatures there, in and around these thermal vents! But extraordinary, even weird. Nothing like we'd ever experienced and suspected. Still, these were creatures much like others. They, for want of a better word, inhaled oxygen. They expelled carbon dioxide, or, if plants, as we understand the natural order, the reverse. The universal premises of the living kingdoms stood upheld even with little or no sunlight. We've since come to learn there are chemical reactions which emit temporary bursts of high intensity electromagnetic wave radiation. Some of these random events emit sufficient light and heat for the processes we consider normal to occur. Of course the creatures' evolutionary adaptations in metabolic homeostasis allows them to consume, to expel, to locomote, to reproduce, or, again, if somehow meeting the definition of plants, to engage in some sort of synthesis that expels heavy or light oxygen molecules.

"As for this direction in investigation and inquiry, well, it's an entire other area of interest, as it turns out. As we speak, some of these forms have been brought to the light of day, after assiduous assessment of how to reduce any trauma or harm. Currently these specimens are being studied intently, then exhibited in various aquariums about the country. But the creatures at the vents and fissures, which we discovered later, well, these were something else again.

"It happens that the bedrock that forms the basis upon which the biomass builds life is not so stable as we might think. The rock is in plate form, as we call it. If you think of a cafeteria with trays touching each other on the cradle—bars, and one of them turns at an angle, a hole develops. If the cooking serving—holders of food lay directly underneath, the steam would expel upwards. So it is with these plates of rock. They shift. Holes develop. Steam or great heat emerges. Remember we're talking about enormous depth--7, 8, 9 miles down."

"Twenty thousand leagues under the sea," Hodges said. Jennifer looked at the hulking football player or heavyweight wrestler. She continued to develop new found respect for the troops' intellectual capabilities.

"Not far off, Mr. Hodges. Now at this depth the force pressure is so huge however, bursting bubbles at times emerge all the way to the surface and it changes color."

"That's how you found this one"

"Yes. We call it <u>Fissure</u> <u>Gargantuans</u>. None other has been discovered this enormous. It was further out in the great swell of the sea than most. It took some experience in knowing what to look for, a keen eye, and fortuitous serendipity.

"Extrapolating the time the smaller ones are open, I calculate that, as we speak, we have remaining about a nine months window of opportunity."

Jennifer felt a twinge of something she did not like in herself, when she realized Susan failed, whether by memory slip or by design, to indicate her as the experienced, keen eyed, and serendipitous discoverer.

The men peppered Susan and Jennifer with questions. To Susan they were directed formally, as students at seating to the classroom instructor; to Jennifer, someone would lean over or cozy up to her and whisper a question while the formal addresses were being made. Like a co—conspirator, Jennifer leaned to her questioners' ear and whispered her best quick summary response. Eventually, Susan directed her sternest schoolmarm's gaze, the all-foreboding raise of the one eyebrow, the right, at Jennifer and her personal questioners to bring order to the room so that all could hear and engage every question and answer.

The two explorers, scientists, researchers, and teachers continued to alter their view of this brute force. Impressed, they began to admire their intelligent nature and informed curiosity.

"So they all close. Eventually."

"Yes, that's right."

"And we want to get this ship in and out before it closes."

"Correct."

What do you hope to find?"

Susan stopped pacing. She usually paced when she lectured, Jennifer knew.

"Strange animals. Perhaps even their birthing grounds. And-- but allow me to continue in a logical progression and organized methodology. I assure you, all will be revealed; and with a clearer understanding for the foundation developed.

"In 2011 an advanced sub-capsule out of Woods Hole by chance submerged deep just as one of these, for want of a better word, erupted. Within hours, hours, mind you, there were myriads of creatures. As I said, it had first located them in the late 1970's. But no one was aware how this life, how soon it formed, so to speak.

"What kind of creatures?"

"More like those begun to be found in the 1880's?"

"No. Not like those. Not like anything seen, known, or even suspected before. They seemed alien. They do not need oxygen for example. They do not need to have an ecosystem of plants supplying oxygen for animals, animals pollinating plants and providing carbon dioxide. All rules of basic zoology do not apply. They are chemotropic."

"They rely on chemicals they themselves produce?"

"It's somewhat of a simplification of the process; but in a very real sense, yes, that's right."

The silence seemed heavy. Now, even more than on the previous occasion. Susan didn't have her overheads nor projected screen Power point. But she retrieved the hand—out photographs in her briefcase. She indicated the pictures as she continued.

Jennifer gazed about. Although the secret was now out between the two groups, she noticed Delores and her men still wore civilian clothes. The new troops, the additional security detail, wore camouflage battle gear. They were no—nonsense military. They had secured the perimeter in short and efficient fashion. Jennifer imagined these men and women, well, woman, could also be no—nonsense when the time came. Now, however it was clear their scientific curiosity had been piqued.

Jennifer knew them better now. She went about the room as she had before. This time at a more comfortable level. Strangely, for a moment she felt like she had a camera and was performing one of those panoramas of the characters, stopping at each one to expand, to discern, to--then she realized what she was doing. Any one of these could be a domestic or foreign espionage agent. She looked for a tell—tale sign, perhaps, in a thematic twist of the classic Poe story, the beating of his, or her, nefarious heart.

It was hopeless, of course. He wouldn't give it away. Still, she continued her observations, hoping for some sort of psychic intervention.

Jarrod Wells. He had blond—reddish hair, the color she thought, of the last gasp light reflecting off the sea at dusk, a sailor's delight crimson light prism. He was Norwegian or Swedish background, probably a Minnesota farm boy. Once in a while she caught his blue eyes and she almost felt that old familiar feeling come over her, even some wetness in her womanhood. Sometimes she hated herself for liking men so much. She wasn't sure about Wells though. But he had one wining smile that caused a little tendon in the back of her knees to quiver.

Allen Johnstone. She knew him very well indeed, at least in the carnal sense. He had a mole on his left thigh, just above the knee. She suddenly couldn't get his sexual anatomy out of her mind, how it bent or tilted slightly to the left and up toward his stomach. He had begged her to be gentle when she took him into her. Maybe she had been too rough on him. Perhaps he deserved a second chance. He was charming and gentle in his way. And she loved the feel of the skin of African heritage men. It was so smooth, almost like that of a woman of her own race, like silk.

At that moment, Delores said something to him. He nodded. He went over to the small table at the entrance blast door. He poured a cup of coffee. Black. He brought it back to his commander. Jennifer felt a twinge of envy. Her man, that bitch. It's my feet, she thought. He hates my feet. And my hair. I've just got to do something with my hair. Already the bun unravels in strands.

The short stout swarthy man with the unlikely name of Samson Magruder. He was the most difficult to read. He looked like an Afghani. Only with a mustache. Did Afghanis have mustaches? Those horrible misogynists seemed always to sprout scruffy beards; but mustaches? She couldn't remember. She decided not to decide. He did speak with an odd accent. Perhaps he was one of those foreign microbiologists, if he was a microbiologist at all. He seemed to always be fooling with a gray box and gazing furtively about. It suddenly occurred to her that microbiologist might be a cover; he probably was the munitions or bomb expert. In an instant she realized that thought made her particularly nervous. Every time she looked at him he was looking away from her. She had the impression he averted his eyes just in time, that he really had an instant earlier stolen a wayward glance at her, the way some men become expert turning their lecherous looks aside at the right moment. He coughed. He spit into a handkerchief. He pulled up the lid of his gray box. He worked with something inside it. Occasionally Delores and Allen came over to peer in. Delores would then say, "Hmm mm." They walked away, leaving him to his work.

She examined herself and Susan. They had decided to return to their field wear. Loose khaki pants, bush jacket shirts and boots. It was functional. They now, that is, she now, like Susan, pulled her hair back tight into a bun. As she did when they were at sea, she wore little make—up: Some base and special lip—gloss to protect against wind and weather. She sat like a man, legs splayed a bit, when she wore clothes in this fashion. The only reason she could divine the men glancing at her now was to continue their amazement at her huge feet. She tried to pull them under her chair. She knew it was futile.

She gazed about the room again. From the command console in the center, she could gaze more than 180°. Four drawer units stood in front with space to walk between in a semicircular array. Lights blinked on the faces of these units, in a pattern both planned and random, but understood by everyone on the team. A second console stood off left of the main one, at a 45° angle.

Jennifer wasn't fully sure of its function. Usually Delores sat at it. It had something to do with communications and, she thought, a double—check monitoring system.

A circuit—breaker panel and military cabinet stood on the far curving wall beyond this unit. It was from this cabinet the men had quickly retrieved their weapons and armed themselves. Jennifer's CAD console stood against the stairwell and faced the glass window beyond, where, within the small wind—tunnel room, the real—size model of the ship maneuvered through its hydraulics as design indications and flaw corrections were calculated and entered.

Susan now paced between her and Jennifer's console. Delores and her troop sat all about on steps and stairs. They appeared enthralled. It was a good lecture. Susan was warming to her topic even more, for she had begun at a high level as it was.

"Let us begin with life as we know it, or, rather, have known it up to now. The premise we operate from is that life is life; this a truism recounted in a fictional piece, oddly enough, not so long ago, is that DNA, deoxyribonucleic acid, that double helix shaped protein strand, or, more accurately, series of strands, discovered by Watson and Crick, is the most powerful force in the universe.

"Indeed. It is. Given any degree of possible habitat environment within a much broader spectrum of parameter than we at one time thought, DNA will emerge, survive, procreate, and exist longer than any non—living matter, even the very place of its origins. Nothing of that magnitude exists in any known dimension.

"There is a species of spider that lives only at the highest elevations of the world. Now nothing else lives there. Nothing as yet discovered. Still, this creature has found its niche and has evolved to exist in what to any other creature or plant or fungus on earth is descriptively inhospitable, in fact, fully hostile.

"The question arises as to its food consumption. After all, arachnids are carnivorous. Well, like certain species of scorpion, its metabolic rate is so low it does not require much; still, it is alive, it must metabolize energy somehow.

"Although never observed or proven, the only current assumption can be either of prey--a second species at that altitude as yet undiscovered, or, some form of cannibalism, but, obviously, not so intense as to deter the species from ascending into succeeding generations.

"We know other creatures, some of them arachnids,that in fact engage in cannibalism. Some female spiders and insects will attack their mates with viciousness once his fertilization contribution act nears its end. However, upon most occasions, she is not as consistently successful as popular thought would indicate. Still, once in a while, she oft presents an alternative meaning to the concept of honeymoon consummation."

A joke, Jennifer thought. A palpable quip. A scientist's lame moment of pith. Jennifer had observed Susan once or twice engaging such a joke, followed by the instructor's own sniggling high—pitched girlie giggle. Her class emitted almost a nervous laugh, as though snickering at their instructor's strange humorous self—indulgence than at the punch line itself. Jennifer looked about. These were serious people.

"There is a species of snail that lives at deep sea levels. Few other creatures can survive at its depth of habitat. Yet it survives quite well. Its locomotion quality appears to us agonizingly slow; perhaps to the snail it moves at a rather good clip. Still, as it imperceptibly yet inevitably progresses along the sea bottom, it constantly ingests sea bottom creatures as its ongoing food requirements.

"Viruses are still a mystery to us, seemingly no more than random strands of DNA or RNA, they exhibit faculties that clearly define them as separate living cogent entities. I say cogent; at admittedly a metaphysical and not empirical level, beyond our conceptualization of the bio—physical—natural world, they almost seem to possess some kind of intelligence or will we cannot begin to comprehend.

"A highly metaphysical proposition is that they are all strands of one huge unseen entity, guided by this 'golem's beyond being's being.' This out of body body, if you will, progresses toward what ever motivates its desires and so compels the facets with which we must contend.

"I have entitled this non—scientific proposition the 'Star Trek Episode Syndrome.'"

To the side of Jennifer's CAD, stood white plastic boards, with magic markers, the antithetical chalkboard. Susan had written, "DNA," "Adaptation to habitat," "Viruses" upon it in black marker. Under "Viruses," she now wrote in blue marker, "Metaphysical"; below this, in red marker, indented a bit, she wrote, "Beyond Being's Being," and "Out of Body Body." She capped the black, blue, red markers. They snapped, each in turn, a satisfying click. Click. Click.

The aroma of the pungent ink permeated the room. The unique odor combined with the peculiar scents of plastic and silicon, of floor cleanser that clung to mops, no matter how mighty one washed and squeegeed, of anxious men and nervous women, and a certain indeterminate sweet quality.

Again Jennifer gazed about the room. She caught Allen's eyes. Perhaps playing too much the coquette, she turned her glance away. Hodges and Magruder, and one of the new guys, Smith, Smithson (?) caught her gaze. They turned their glances away. She wore khakis and field shoes. What were they looking at? Probably her feet. Her hair. Next time she would comb it out straight like she liked it, like everyone else seemed to like it. Or maybe they liked it this way and that was why they stared. Was she really so beautiful as everyone said? She never believed it, not fully. Somehow she had fooled everyone. Not she with the extraordinary feet and ordinary hair. Maybe they stared because...

With the experienced and confident lecturer's flourish and flair, Susan removed the cap from the green marker. This action produced a slight squeaking—click sound. Her presence and the squeak—click brought silence to the several hushed conversations about the room. All eyes returned to her.

Magruder walked over to the table by the entrance. He poured another cup of coffee. Susan waited. The liquid slowly filled his cup. Steam welled up. He poured sugar into his cup. He stirred the beverage. The spoon occasionally clinked the inside of the cup. He put down the spoon. He placed the coffee pot on its heating beveled pad.

Hodges walked to the refrigerator located by the table. He pulled out a diet Coke. He closed the refrigerator door.

"Bring me one too, would you?" Jennifer said.

"This is the last. There's, wait a minute, let me see here. There's some, I don't know, this off-brand here."

"That will be fine."

"I'll have one also, if you don't mind," Susan said, still standing at the marker—board, the green felt tip piece in her hand. Her hands and arms already appeared as an impressionist's canvas, streaked with red, blue, green colors from marker ink.

"Are you sure? I can go topside, see if I can track down another carton."

"That's sweet. No. Really. That will be fine. I just need something to drink and a little caffeine. It is diet, right?

"Yeah, it's diet."

"That will be fine," Jennifer said.

"Doctor?"

"Yes. It's all right. Thank you," Susan said.

Hodges opened the refrigerator door. He pulled out two red and blue striped cans of an off—brand diet Coke. Hodges brought the cans to the women. Jennifer looked at the can in her hand. Her long fingers caressed almost fully about the can. Sometimes she played her own game. She tried to stretch out and bring her fingers all around the can to touch the edge of her palm. She could always get her nails to scratch the area. She smiled, not sure exactly why it made her feel good.

She always took care of her nails. She didn't like the different colors and designs however. She preferred red. She stayed with it. Occasionally they chipped and she was so busy she could not find time to deal with it properly. It made her feel bad. She looked at them now. They were doing OK. The left pinkie had started to peel. That was the one that always gave her a fit.

Jennifer the commercial artist held and shifted the can in her hands. She gazed at it through different angles. She turned it over and around in and out in different space dimensions. She examined it. It began to condense. Her hands and fingers felt the familiar, always refreshing droplets of water upon them. She put down the can on a small table next to her. She rubbed her hands with the condensed water upon them. She peered at it on the table. At once, as it always did, all came into focus for her. She thought of three designs more conducive to the product.

The brand probably came from a local distributor. Perhaps she could find out and contact the distributor, the executives later.

She was certain she could increase their sales figures fifteen per cent right off the bat.

She glanced up at the refrigerator. There was no Coke machine on the immediate site. The men and women had to keep the stock up. But there were machines and a restaurant back at what everyone called the hotel, the old resort. Did all the service personnel have top clearance? What about the company men and women who had to refill the machines? Was that a weak area, a possible security breach? She was amazed. She had been around military people for a short time and already she was beginning to think like them. She decided to open her can, to drink the murky clear refreshing elixir. Still, she could not help examining the design further.

Occasionally, others of the troop, mostly men, maybe three women if you counted those who would come and go from topside, the new troops, got up to get coffee. Doughnuts were passed around. They were the kind boxed for long term keeping. They were a bit stale, but not bad. The satisfying snaps and subsequent whooshes of the cans being opened caught a bit of silence hanging in the room. Even the compressors stood off—line at that moment. The team drank. A few ate the near delicious snack. Susan drew a line in green, giving it an arrow point. The arrow pointed to the side of the board at which she had begun. She capped the pen. Another satisfying snap. Somewhere below the compressor whirred online. She continued her lecture, projecting a bit more.

"Let us return to science as we know it. To continue with viruses: They are our predators. We have taken dominion, or so we like to think, over practically every place on earth. Yet the smallest of creatures, invisible to our eyes, visible only with the strongest of instruments of our own design and invention, thwarts us, stalks us, intends us (or, in true science, by random or chaotic acts) inflicts upon us great and irrevocable harm. Most of them we survive, but only because they "allow" it (you perceive how difficult it is to discuss these beings in purely scientific manner). They are the ultimate genomic engineers, reducing our puny attempts at recombinant reconfiguration as pathetic. For every action we take, they counter with three or four, and are always, or nearly always, well ahead of us and prepared for anything we might do. Against them we must be ever vigilant.

"They mutate. If they are so virulent as to destroy us, their hosts, that is suicidal; when we die they die. That is, at least some do. Since this is absurd and futile, they mutate again to emerge less harmful and thus to survive longer within their hosts. This fortuitous accomplishment of generation assurance (remember, generations, with these creatures, are not measured in years or decades, but in hours, minutes, seconds) allows them to multiply astronomically, not merely geometrically. Many of these move on in some fashion to other hosts. Others "sacrifice" themselves simply so their fellows may proceed on to other hosts. They mutate. They survive.

"Most of them we survive as well. Then our antibodies manufactured can defeat the next attack, and the next, and so on. This is immunity. Vaccines can be developed against many viruses. The more virulent mutate constantly and it becomes like hitting an object traveling nearly the speed of light with a projectile traveling near the same speed. It would depend on considerable random chance. But we'll progress to normal metabolism now. I shall discuss immunity's significance later.

"All animal life, so it was thought, metabolizes its food, by taking in oxygen, processing, and expelling carbon dioxide and other waste by—products. All plant life, it was thought, metabolizes through photosynthesis, takes in carbon dioxide and expels oxygen. Thus a perfect eco—balance on planet earth.

"Like a yin and a yang, plants and animal species need each other to survive. The basis of life is carbon; the fundamental need for animal life is oxygen. Animals are living beings which ingest oxygen, expel carbon dioxide, locomote, reproduce. From bacteria to ape along the scale of evolution. We knew this defined animal life. We knew what defined plant life.

"Until now!"

People in the group shifted positions again. They'd been sitting awhile. Jennifer stood up to stretch. Two of the others did as well. Hodges, who had been standing since he served the beverages, found an old secretary's chair behind the kitchenette corner. He wheeled it over. It had a crack in its green plastic cover. He found some duct tape. He stretched out the tape. He tore the strip. He taped over the crack. He replaced the tape in the supply cabinet by the refrigerator. He sat down. The chair creaked. It expelled air from its cushion. Wells stood up. In his lanky stride he went over and stood by the stairwell. Susan continued.

"These vent creatures do not take in oxygen. They do not consume food from without their bodies."

An undercurrent of murmur passed among a few of the men. They looked at Delores. She said something to Magruder. She looked out at Jennifer. Jennifer looked away. She returned her gaze to Susan. The others took up her lead.

"Your question obviously is how do they survive? Everything has to take in energy converting substances. Well, as far as we can determine, they don't survive for very long, and they are born or generated very quickly. In—between, we now have some knowledge.

"Look at your pictures. Witness their tubule—bodies. These--just a moment, let me come around and point them out. Here. No, here, right within them, and then down here on the floor."

Susan meandered about the room, pointing out certain images in the photographs. She had a silver—plated pen that telescoped into an elongated pointer. Often, at the lectern, she drew it out for dramatic effect, then pointed at her visual aid.

So she did now, leaning over her participants. Jennifer noted she leaned quite close to Hodges, seeming to ensure her breasts fairly brushed against his shoulder. He looked up at her, close enough, it appeared to her, that he might be breathing on his instructor's neck. He had been looking at her, after all. Could he, she . . .

At first the images were difficult to see by the untrained eye. Most of the troop caught it soon enough. Susan went around again to the rest, explaining with the patience of an excellent teacher.

"These are scores, hosts of scores of colonies of bacteria, so astonishingly numerous the full colony can be seen with the naked eye, as snowflakes gather into a snowfall. Through some symbiotic process as yet little understood, there is an exchange between the bacteria colonies and the tubule—creatures. Look closely; the bacteria colony can still be perceived even within the confines of the opaque membrane walls of the tubule creatures. Remember this is not oxygen—carbon dioxide metabolism. In fact, it turns out the chemical basis for these beings is mostly sulfur and its compounds, such as sulfuric acid. There is some silicon and manganese influence as well."

"You're suggesting these are sulfur, manganese, silicon creatures." It was the first time Jennifer heard Magruder ask a question. She knew it was him without looking. She had not yet become accustomed to being surprised his voice was high pitched, like a woman's. Even so, she had that funny feeling at the nape of her neck. He seemed to know more, have some insight. Or was it just that strange high voice from a man well manufactured in muscles?

"Yes. In a fashion," Susan said.

"It sounds like a Star Trek or--" Jennifer had known that Hodges was smarter than he looked and tracked the lecture with comprehension.

"Yes. In a way it does." Susan said.

"But this is here. On earth."

"Precisely. And it is not at all fiction. It is proven zoological fact. We are now questioning the fundamental principle of the definition of life itself. At least the survivability of life. If life species as we know them can exist at elevations beyond conventionally thought life support, and at depths few other forms can fathom, if you will (again Susan giggled, covering her mouth with her pointer and hands at her pun; soon enough she continued and if life as we don't know it, or, rather, don't as yet understand it, can exist at places above 100° centigrade, then who knows what exists anywhere on any planet or moon in the universe?"

The compressor turned off—line. The command center cast into silence. Jennifer swigged her Coke, killing the can. She could hear the liquid compound with precious water necessary for life gurgle down her throat, felt the coolness in her esophagus, drip into her stomach, where it would began its metabolic passage to give bathing catalytic life to her cells.

"We believe, that somewhere, inside these vents, may lie the answer to the mystery of life itself. That life may have begun not by carbon combinations, but by sulfur, or manganese or something else, deep in the interior of the planet. Perhaps this may happen anywhere in the universe. On our planet, sometime in the distant past this life exploded through steam released vents. As the organisms floated, bubbled, twirled up to the surface, there were occasional mutations; remember what I said about viruses, mutations, antibodies, immunities. They found they could survive in the sea and ultimately above it, on an alien environment to them, land. This is our supposition. This is, in whole or in part, what we hope to discover over there, or, rather, under there."

Delores stood up. She had it, Jennifer saw. She had been listening intently and now she had the whole thing.

"We're going to be looking for the birthplace of life itself."

Susan paused. She smiled, a slight, knowing Cheshire grin. She often did this for effect, before answering a question, the pause, the wily smile. Then she spoke only one word.

"Yes."

The commander sat down. The compressor revved. It seemed louder this time. Jennifer wondered if she was always the only one who heard it hum up to specs, or felt the silence when the thermostat opened it went offline.

Susan confirmed Delores's conclusion.

"Do you understand the implications? Life forms, life on earth before it mutated and evolved. DNA as it was originally designed, without error, without the misspellings and corruptions of the code that have come down through uncountable generations and genetic challenge."

She was an experienced classroom lecturer. Now, for the first time, she observed some eyes start to spin. They were getting away from her. She had to simplify. She needed an analogy to bring them back.

"All right. Let's go at it this way. We have no more than 20, maybe 25 times the number of genes that does E. Coli And we already know there is a vast amount of homology, of metabolic commonality, even between E. Coli and us. For that matter, let us examine Drosophila, the simple fruit fly. It has about 10 to the 8$^{th}$ base pairs in its DNA. We have only a little over 10 to the 9$^{th}$. Consider it: Only one dimensional number away, meeting then a similarity, a vast, huge similarity between us, a higher life form, and them, a supposedly lower life form completely similar in metabolic pathways, in genetic function, in enzyme control, in homeostatic and other physiological maintenance."

Her next preliminary phrase would be the clue, she knew, where students registered for credit would scurry to scratch in their notebooks, if any still did, or on their ipad or other sophisticated devices, knowing the material would be featured on the exam.

"I emphasize this: Extraordinarily similar; fully overlapping."

They were coming back. Soon, she knew, for she had the entire methodology mapped out, as if she had spent weeks in preparation for this moment; in a real sense, she had spent years; soon they would be in her palms, and, as any competent lecturer knows, the old high feeling of wrapping her fingers about them. What a glorious thing to be a teacher, when all flowed so well.

Susan Arthknott warmed to her material. Her excitement grew, a felt pulse of energy about the room. All felt it. She pushed her glasses up once nearly every sentence as she grew clearly agitated. All faces were on her. Jennifer could see a transformation in her that was rare, a passion that rose up, like bubbles bursting upon the surface of green—blue deep water, something she had never seen in her friend before.

Suddenly a red flush painted her flesh, near her ears; it reminded Jennifer the blush she had witnessed upon her lovers as she teased them to submission, and spread in streaks upon her own skin, she knew, since she could often feel the same heat generated from deep within her body, welling up to her skin, like life from below edging to the surface.

She wondered if she were exhibiting the same ruddy hue now, any change in coloring that would give her away to the group. But like the others, she could not take her eyes off Susan. It seemed like Susan's voice, like that of an opera diva capable of eight high C's a night, emerged not from her oral cavity, but from a vortex area defined within her forehead.

"Now imagine, just imagine a creature a little more complex than the fruit fly, probably at least 90% a direct homologue to our DNA. Or what would have been our DNA if we had not been challenged by viruses, bacteria, evolutionary insult, and more.

"Our DNA is like a computer operating system that has been corrupted and patched and patched and fixed for millennia! Now we could obtain the master configuration. The cellular level control, the singular presentation of intra—cell transport, the primeval metabolic pathways and precisely what depended upon what! Here we would have the original design, the original message as God or chance had first intended. Compared against the current form, every error, every mishap could be literally calculated, every mystery of life's and disease's code: Uncovered! Revealed! At last, known, all known! All mystery of life known!

Susan breathed heavily, rapidly now. Her nostrils flared. Curiously, she stopped pushing her glasses up. They hung precariously low on her nose, and there they stayed. It was obvious at least to Jennifer that Susan wasn't looking at the group any more. Indeed, she might of a sudden not be aware of their presence. She spoke to some other entity. She reached deeply in to some pure part of her mind that raced ahead, dashed to a finish line climax that would be as explosive as any Jennifer thought she could remember.

"Every gene in that creature, governing every pathway would be pure and primitive. Deleting that gene would tell us precisely what process went awry. Each gene would be the target for some drug as a remedy. Where we now have predominantly several dozen classes of fundamentally different kinds of drugs, we could imagine developing several thousand! We could map the DNA variations that characterized the "cause" of virtually all the disease of aging: Cancer! Heart Disease! Arthritis! Osteoporosis! Diabetes! Myasthenic Syndromes! Wrinkles!"

Susan was in control. Nonetheless, this last choice drew more laughter than she expected. But it had the effect of starting to return her to the level of the group. She let the pause continue, for effect, as she had before. She worked the crowd now, and she knew it. At last she pushed her glasses back, to focus her mind, to glance over the rims in her intimidating fashion upon the faces that did not leave hers. They were riveted. She was riveting.

"All curses of ills and ailments could be genetically determined. Once determined, the efforts of medical research could be surgically focused on a cure, on a repair, no longer wasted on why or how.

"And the reverse would be equally true. This, I make a presumption, is what your superiors may want; this is what I most fear; this is why science should remain in charge, for the good and not for the evil in our souls."

She needed not to glance at Delores. The military officer knew to whom that last sentence was directed. There was one flaw in Doctor Arthknott's reasoning that Delores and all good military commanders knew, know. It was a distinct false assumption to believe that wondrous scientific discoveries and technologic inventions would be used only for beneficence; their use eventually would be bent toward some weapon of horrific destruction as well. This had become the hallmark of American military strategy in the aftermath of Pearl Harbor: To divine the technique first, to be prepared to counter, to be prepared. Therefore, as Susan continued, Delores had already intuited most of what was coming in the lecturer's denouement.

"By knowing exactly what our most basic cellular processes were strictly dependent upon, we could devise chemicals which in effect could be deadly disruptive with no longer a concern that the organism had evolved a defense. Even HIV: we know patients, or, rather, subjects, with HIV who can not progress to AIDS because of a "genetic mutation." Our DNA mutates and maneuvers like a virus, adapting, building in redundancy, alternatives, defenses to challenges. Some persons evolved defenses against smallpox, a disease once so virulent it wiped out towns and villages. But with an understanding of the pure and fundamental processes the target creature or creatures could provide us, we could disrupt homo sapiens's metabolic processes with synthetically constructed chemicals for which only the chemist creating the agent would have the antidote. A Satanic Arm of the Agents of Death: Angels of Death, with no recourse."

Susan's tone had shifted gradually over the few moments when she offered the cornucopia of a disease-free world to one with perhaps tens of thousands of molecular poisons for which cure would be impossible, perhaps immediately lethal, except to the agent creating the DNA plague whose arm she imagined outstretched just as she stood with her own arms stretched out. She dropped one slowly, not so much for the impression it made but for the fact that it was simply too hard for her to hold it up any longer. She dropped her other arm, again, slowly, feeling the ether, flowing this way and that, almost as if it appeared a billowing jellyfish in the order of the deep sea.

She pushed her glasses up again, for now she stared at the commander. Everyone could feel her look heavy upon her. The commander did not flinch. She was tougher than that. She stared down any challenger if it meant going to her grave with both eyes open, unblinking. Susan's intimidating gaze then toured the room.

"Don't you see," Susan said. "This will make possible a unified field theory of the most powerful of all forces known to sentient existence. For good . . . and, alas, but hopefully not soon, for evil. And we don't have to go out there to find it: Not to Mars nor to Venus nor to Titan nor to Io. It is here, burning deep in the soul of our planet earth. It waits for us to come to it. It calls us to come to it, calls over the eons of time. At last we are ready."

Susan hurled the last marker over her shoulder while looking triumphantly at her students. As if with unerring precision and not random chance, the cylindrical object click-rattled-landed in the board tray. Jennifer wondered how many hours alone she had practiced to perfect that impressive skill.

Susan's eyes glistened. She experienced a slight tremble or spasm. Jennifer had been noting it for a while. It was growing worse. It grew worse when she was excited. Then, suddenly, in one of her mind's saber flashes, she knew the entire story. She said nothing now, however. It was Delores who first spoke.

"It is a doorway."

"Yes," Susan said. "If we find the birthing place, we'll have the basic pattern that started it all."

There was a pause. No one moved.

"We can save the world. Don't you see it? We can save the world." Jennifer looked at Susan. The scientist looked like never she had looked before. Her arms spread upward again. A grin, more of a grimace than a smile, shadowed her lips. Shadows seemed to cross her face. Her eyes waxed wide and wild. Her voice reverberated.

Most of all, the frail, thin boned woman seemed larger, huge, puffed up was all Jennifer could think of. She seemed almost mad with ambition and delirious with the potential of her discovery. She repeated her penultimate statement, her voice a voice echoing itself as if generated from a deep hollow vent. All stared at her, as disciples must stare at their cult's leader.

"We can save the world."

Considerable murmuring and talking broke out about the confines of the place. Everyone seemed to jump up and about and talk in little groups all at once. Jennifer went to Susan to congratulate her. It had been a brilliant lecture after all, one in which complex terms were handled in reducing language and understanding to lay terms and facility. Still, Jennifer knew that

Susan had purposely omitted or briefly covered the more complex terms, as well as some significant items of information.

The two friends and colleagues hugged. Delores spoke to Wells. Jennifer still tried to get a read on him. He acted even more mysterious than the small group which had preceded him. Hodges, Magruder, and Allen formed a group. Susan stood just outside this latter circle.

Jennifer realized Susan wasn't finished yet. Still, the scientist tried to compel errant strands of hair back into her bun. For the twentieth time, or fortieth time, Jennifer long ago lost count, in her presentation the scientist pushed her glasses up her nose. They soon fell down. Unable to get her class's attention, she took the green marker and struck the board. She needed to strike three times before the excited murmuring died down, then ceased.

"Now, Delores. I don't suppose you'd care to inform us of the military's interest in this."

"You know I can't do that, Doctor."

"No, I suppose not. Still, I've been developing some suppositions. Care to hear them? Well, one of them, I suppose, I have already--"

Delores's troops protested. The commander raised her hand. They quieted down. Jennifer stood by her friend-colleague's side, realizing Wells stood at Delores's right hand seemingly ready to pounce at a moment's notice. She noticed that the military group and the science group were divided. They faced each other over a gulf, not merely a geographical lacuna.

"Go on, Doctor."

"At first I worked two premises, both of which seemed a bit far-fetched, but these days one doesn't know."

"Please. Continue."

"I thought the pressure and temperature seemed inviting, perhaps the development of some sort of fantastic Flash Gordon type Heat Ray; then the theory of the infinite intertwining labyrinth, inter-connecting caverns: that disreputable theorem that all caves and fissures in the earth are somehow connected. Well then, a troop ship could enter off the coast of Hawaii and emerge in the middle of the Black Sea somehow, or a cave in Iran or Iraq. It might need a little help of an earth digging device or laser ray, but the element of surprise would be maintained.

"Then I realized my best supposition yet, which I should have at once. You're after some horrible biological weapon. With the potential knowledge gained within the site, as I have indicated, there'd be no antidote. But there might be a vaccine. Your soldiers--"

"Our soldiers, doctor. Yours as well as mine."

"-- could destroy the health of an enemy force while remaining free of symptoms themselves. The perfect battlefield weapon. In fact, the perfect weapon that military minds have been seeking since Alexander. Do you know what Aristotle answered him when he asked his teacher for such a weapon to conquer the world?"

"My God," Jennifer said.

All were silent now. The silence was deafening.

"This is nonsense," Delores said. She turned away, as if to go somewhere, though it was clear there was nowhere to go. The soldiers began to murmur in agreement. They died down when they noticed Susan was going to speak again. She still looked taller, Jennifer thought.

"The answer lies within you, my son."

"How does any of this make me any different from you, Doctor? Your desire to see how we got here, how it all began, the secrets to the universe. How am I any different from you?"

"You want to destroy the world. I want to save it."

"No. You're wrong," Delores said. "You see Doctor, we're the same you and I. That's the key. That's what you can never understand. With all your brains and knowledge, you still don't get it. If we don't now, some evil ones will. We have to be the first and the best. We both want to save the world. We just want to do it in different ways. And who is to say that whatever lurks down there, once unleashed, whether from science's viewpoint or the geo-political viewpoint, that anyone will ever be able to put that genie back in the bottle?"

They were quite close. They stared at each other. Jennifer felt a chill carry up and down her spine. She started to take Susan's hand. She noticed it once more experienced a tremor. Susan broke off. She retreated to behind a column. Jennifer followed, though at a distance. Susan reached in her pocket for one of her pills. The capsules fell over one another in the yellow-opaque bottle, rattling. She twisted the cap. She lifted a capsule out. It was yellow, with tiny black lettered writing on it. She replaced the round white top of the bottle. She downed the capsule with the last dregs of her soft drink, tipping the can high and her head back to catch it all.

The compressor was off-line. Susan returned to Jennifer's side. Coming to her, she looked in her eyes, then looked away. She said nothing. The two groups stood gazing at each other for a long time, in silence, before they returned to work.

The remainder of their time passed quickly. With the new security personnel and measures, no further security breaches occurred. The codes were changed. No one worked alone in the command center. "Task on target, deadline on target," Jennifer heard Susan tell Barnstone, whenever he called her or she called him on his personal secure line to report.

Jennifer deduced the reasons. Since the security breach and the night of enlightenment (as she secretly called it) there had been little or no social life. All had bent to the tasks before them with new found industry, fervor, purpose. Jennifer attributed it to any number of things--a clarity of purpose, greater understanding of what lay before them and its significance, the odd sort of paradox,a renewed camaraderie albeit infiltrated with an inherent dislike of their seemingly polarized mission.

They worked together. Left to their own devices, without security distractions or lusts after the flesh, they soon caught up. In fact, if anything, they emerged a few days ahead of schedule. For Susan, Jennifer now knew, an additional, more personal incentive floated under the waters far off any chartered coast.

One fine autumn day, a day of clouds and blue sky, a last gasp day of incredible beauty before winter's onslaught, the thing, the first module, this ship which had been designed and constructed for an environment never before seen, was ready. It had been nine months. Nothing like it had ever been made nor seen.

They went down to the docks and launched it. Seagulls and cormorants flew overhead, occasionally diving into the water. The waves were becalmed and, in this inlet bay, lapped the shore. The East coast ocean always seemed calmer to Jennifer than the West coast. The Atlantic could be terrible and violent and cold, she knew, but the Pacific always seemed wilder, more untamed. Jennifer knew she was just a west coast type of gal. Well, they'd soon be returning to their part of the world. She had, for some time, been looking forward to it.

The maiden voyage proceeded with little difficulty. A few warning lights appeared. Pressure and depth indicators. They realized they were attempting too much too fast. After troubleshooting, with some adjustments in mechanics, hardware, software, they tried again. There were clearly further adjustments needed; all in all, things proceeded well enough.

There was a cove with some rocks and caves located about twenty miles south and a few miles out. The depth was nowhere near what they required but they would test it at those depths on their way west from their secret Washington state station. For now, a detail on a scouting mission found this aperture was about the right size.

They needed to see how the verniers would maneuver the craft in tight spaces, spaces as closely aligned as possible to their mission. The tension mounted, conjoining in an amorphous unseen entity; each person knew it, this cloud, dank, grey, heavy, the fog of mutual trust and distrust, that the group had been working under since that eventful week. It was a tight space they found themselves in. Somehow, they had to wiggle a way out ensuring they all survived.

Stem to stern, she was forty feet. She looked like she had a semi-circular outrigger, that being the first line of defense against the gargantuan heat and pressure. The engines appeared oddly insufficient as those of commercial jet airliners sometimes seemed to its boarding passengers. But, once in, it was felt, they did not need to generate much more than a few hundred pounds of thrust. The shields covered over the windows smoothly, within second.

Inside, deep in the bow, Susan and Magruder sat side by side at a console. Delores sat beneath them at another control panel. To their right Hodges sat low with about two feet before him; to her left, Susan sat monitoring a control panel. The panels all looked different. When Jennifer saw them before returning to the control boat, she was struck again with the odd combination of twenty-first century technology and 1960's and 70's technology. The upper panels had a triangular, flat surface, sensitive to touch and roll-ball control. Susan's panel, completely push button laden, had little window clasps over a few of her buttons. It was, she knew, the control of their weapons array, and no mistake of firing could be made. A key sat in a lock above the panel. Clearly the weapons systems could only be activated upon a direct command. Magruder and Susan could peer out the upper window, as well as regard the four television monitors in front of them. Delores and Hodges could peer out the lower window; they also had redundant monitors in an array between their own. Susan could gaze at a panel above her, at an angle. Here she relied on thermographic and telemetry readings from an array of encased electronics in the titanium needle poking out from the front of the ship. From her perch on the bridge of the support vessel, Jennifer thought it looked like a thin dugong, with a bat-wing front, accented narwhal. For a moment, she had a thought of Noah's ark, so vibrant to her of a sudden was the animal imagery. Allen sat with his back to the others, a little below Susan and behind her, but not as low as Delores and her group. He had a little window as well, but his monitors had a more panoramic view of the rear. Allen's panel had many redundancies so he could match telemetry and operate weapons from his position.

"It's time," Delores said.

"Remember," Susan said, "We don't enter the hole until I say it's OK."

"Of course, Doctor. It's your project. You're in control."

Jennifer didn't like the sound of the woman's voice. She was sure she detected, what was it, deception? There's an amazing thought for you, Jennifer pondered, a deceptive woman. I remember people saying men should step down and let women rule the world. God, you think we have politics now.

Jennifer assumed her place in front of the communications panel. Wells sat to her left. To her right the support ship looked like a fishing vessel or small freight-trawler. Inside it too was brimming with communications panels, radar, sonar, and weaponry. A small helicopter stood in a space covered by a green awning, like a car port.

"They're beginning their descent," Wells said. After a moment, with some urgency in his voice, he continued, pointing to the screen. "What's that?" Jennifer gazed at the sonar screen. A white outline seemed to swim toward the ship.

"Porpoise, I think. Curious. Investigating this new creature." In the next instant, Jennifer noticed for the first time Wells rarely spoke in sentences longer than a few words.

"We warn them?"

"I think she sees it. Look, there's more from the pod. They'll go away soon enough. Once they determine it's of human origin, they'll go to a safe distance, probably hang around just enough away to keep half an eye on things, so to spea--there, see? The scout's returning to the entire group. Besides, they probably don't care for the shallow depths near the cove. OK. Here we go. Descent OK. NA-1, NA-1, you're looking good."

"Roger that. NA-2. We are approaching target area. Releasing robots."

From an attachment along the belly of the vessel, the navy tethered robot submersibles appeared as though shot from submarine torpedo tubes. A small submarine with flood lights, still camera and enough software to configure directional diversions, the submersible played out its tether from the "mother" robot and entered the dark opening under the sea. Soon, its flood lamps clicked on. Some fish swam by some algae covered rocks. The human observers watching their television monitors noted that past the entrance the space opened out in a few hundred feet into a fairly good sized cave.

On board the Ex-Gee, Delores made a request. "Doctor?"

"Yes."

"Let's see what she can do."

"Proceed."

"Mr. Hodges. All ahead. Into,into the breach."

"All ahead, aye." Hodges had a stick and rudder, similar to combat pilots in high performance aircraft. Now he pulled this way and that, looking askew at the window, a small eyepiece out from his right eye. He maneuvered the intrepid vessel through the veil.

On the support ship, Jennifer's visual signature was lost.

"Telemetry excellent. Reflection buoy activated. They're doing great. Tight squeeze but they're in and maneuvering within parameters."

"Who's giving the orders?"

"You mean who's in command? Well, I think that's a problem for all of us. You see, there can only be one queen bee in the hive. And man, we got us two queens down there."

"Two queens," Wells said. "Only one stays in the hive."

Jennifer suddenly felt sick. She sometimes felt seasickness and nausea wave through her, but this was worse. She watched the screen. After a while, the large grey-white shape returned.

"Well, looks like she did all right. Reckon we're in business."

Jennifer felt cold. She shivered. She couldn't stop shivering. No one noticed. No one came to put a blanket on her. No one draped a coat over her. So often the center of most men's and many women's attention, she now knew the heartache of those who move through life as if invisible. She knew she should feel ecstatic. She felt sad, angry, confused.

She felt something else, some uneasiness she could not identify, a growing, palpable sense of something akin to the monster that chased her in her dream. She suddenly realized she remembered it, this memory so long ago lost.

She remembered that as a little girl, there was a monster in her hall. Her parents kept the bedroom doors open. Each night, before she fell asleep, a great large hairy monster would start to enter her room to do her great ill. The only thing she could do to make it go away was to close her eyes and stay awake. When she opened her eyes, the monster had returned to the hall. He entered her room again. She closed her eyes again to protect herself. Again he retreated. This approach for attack, and stratagem for defense, proceeded for some time. At last, during one of the times she closed her eyes she fell asleep.

She heard her parents talking in their room. She wondered why they did not come to her assistance. Every night the monster began its attack. Every night, through her specially designed defense, she thwarted him and sent him in retreat. After some years, it didn't come every night. She slept better. In time, it stopped coming altogether. She forgot it. Until this moment.

She shivered, as though someone had stepped on her grave. A huge wave rose their boat high to draft. The bow came down and she tried to find her sea legs.

Some gulls drifted by, unusually high in the firmament of the heavens. They played in and out of clouds and blue sky. Then they swooped to the surface of the sea and skimmed over the waters. The sea now calm. The boat floated gently. One of the gulls turned and flew directly in front of her, his wing tip not five feet away. She gazed into his deep dark eye.

She wished she could identify the feeling. She could not. The engines revved to life, jerking the boat. The boat began to return to dock.

Jennifer turned to face the prow. She wanted the wind to play her hair. The gulls headed back out to sea, seemingly to the far horizon; then, all of a sudden, they turned. Together in formation and synchronized in wing stroke, they followed Jennifer and her crew in to shore.

# 3

---

## DEEPTIDE

Slowly she stirred, propelled by heat waves from one fiery chamber into another. Then, almost guiding herself with nearly a voluntary movement, she entered the cool chamber, the wet one. It was a new sensation. As much as she was able to, she basked in its novelty. Had she been more able to comprehend its matter, she could have reveled in its degrees of suspension of weight, its allowances of freedom of movement; but then, most of these she had already experienced for a time beyond record or any being's comprehension. She survived the coolness of the waters as she survived the heat of the fires. Always she survived.

In a time almost to the horizon of infinity had she drifted in this fashion; she could not fathom it, nor comprehend lesser concepts. Eon past era, worlds and stars created and destroyed, all so far in the distant past that what semblance of awareness she might have had was lost in stardust of fire-rock and water courses, and something else which the sentient ones had never been able to define. For them, it remained a factor undetected, unsuspected, as yet unknowable.

In the near semblance of a particle of a micron of memory, she almost knew there had once been a time of near nothingness and then she was. The cosmos transcended time. Time transcended her. She transcended time. A moment could be an era. Eras drifted by her, drifted as flame borne bubbles and fire smoke mists gurgled and wafted by her always as always she floated, propelled by the fire, and now the water, currents.

As the eons and eras passed, somehow she grew almost aware others existed and that they had emerged from her. Some floated by her on their way to disappear from her chambers. Some re-entered her to be absorbed internally for what she could not comprehend was to her benefit. Others would become and remain and flow with the fiery flow as she had always flowed. She never wondered. She never questioned. She could not.

Yet, as a degree of awareness unfolded, dimly, she nearly became aware that she was almost aware. She almost knew she could only float within the channels and caverns, not out to where the bubbles escaped. Something different lay out there, though this complete thought she could not have generated; nor, once nearly generated by random chance, certainly she could not have entertained or maintained it. Once, her semblance of thought produced, in what had become, in a most primitive sense, her nerve spot, a hint of memory that she had been able to float through all the channels, not just the large ones. Had she the power of reasoned thought she might have intuited she grew in size. She, however, was not so blessed nor so cursed. She was only dimly aware she was aware and that the fire bubbles and steam hisses compelled her undulating definition of form to flow as streams extruded through filters, whisked about.

Over the eons she became nearly aware there was fire and light and eruption of fire, that she was impervious, that others seemed to emerge out of her, that they were impervious. Even this vestige of awareness could not comprehend that in a different place, fire was harmful to life. In her world, all was simply as it was, as it had always been. So long past, even a semblance of a memory could not grasp the distance in time, some of the others that had come from her had been drawn into the places wherein the fire bubbles and steam hissed and escaped. This was of no concern nor consequence to her; indeed, it could not be construed that it ever should be. Still she was almost aware that it had started and had gone on over the eons. It never occurred nor could it occur that something existed beyond the fiery and fire cloud realm, that great transformations seemed to be happening there.

Great white sheets of individuals so numerous like a snow blanket against the red-fire caverns floated in the bubbles of flame and air. These, too, she almost became aware, emerged from within her somehow. They also re-absorbed into her and gave her something and then left her again. Some of these blankets also vanished in the escaping channels.

Currents of cool and heat expelled her again into the channels of fire. She was almost aware that this new blue green elemental had only recently invaded the fire and steam channels. She could not consider this to be for ill nor for good.

She was.

It was.

Is.

Be.

Only the near-memories in the vague near-quality of stirring thought almost let her know it was something different, unique. There were floating, shimmering things in its quality also, but different somehow. Propelled down through a huge channel by a great fire-cloud hiss, she nearly could imagine these were from her also and had also returned. But they were different from that which she had known somehow. They re-entered and gave her something. But they did not go out from her again.

Somewhere, in the deepest darkest recesses of what almost begins as consciousness, there was a dim, vague near-sense that more and even stranger ones would soon be coming. The cosmos spun. Time and timelessness passed with no commencement other than what was and what will be. Only now, she almost felt an indefinable sense that her existence was not eternal, that she sensed the unfamiliar sense of fear. Or so she might have, had she been able to. As always, she floated and stirred wherever the fire currents took her. Now, however, she almost sensed a different concept. Had it been possible to sense it, she'd have known it as this:

She waited for them.

# 4

## COASTTIDE

Off to the port side of the ship a pod of whales surfaced. Almost at once, they dove in a rolling pattern more like porpoises or dolphins. Their flukes, out of the water low, waved calm, relaxed against the sky and the sea. He heard the basso Tibetan monk-like chanting of their songs. Hodges always listened for the songs of the sea. At times, he hearkened, to believe he discerned meaning. Over time on the waters, he came to comprehend they used tones and length of tones in an auditory glyph-system not unlike rudimentary symbolic vocabulary. He squinted. He peered through his binoculars. Grays, heading back to the Baja bays, probably. Found some squid out here perhaps.

Hodges never felt more at home, one with the world than when he was at sea. He liked taking watch. He could stand and walk around all areas of the ship topside. He liked this ship, the Starr, an old Navy destroyer retro-fitted to carry on its once-modified deck for helicopters the Ex-Gee submersible explorer. He looked back at it now. It was small for five people, a mini-sub basically. But that strange bat-wing or whatever it resembled gave it a larger appearance, gazing up at it this way.

He walked back toward the stern. He sauntered around the entire once of a kind technology that earth and sea and sky had never seen until now. He walked fully aft, then about the starboard side, as an experienced art appreciation student revered a sculpture and other three dimensional objects d'art.

On his government's service, a secret mission. He'd been on many. They all had. The Persian Gulf mines. Forward air, a quick in and out vector directive for the Chinese embassy in Belgrade. He liked that one. He had rarely gone that far inland. But they had tracked the spy with his disks and dots for days. That bomb design would never reach Beijing. Not all of it anyway.

Once they almost had Bin Lauden. The damn slippery eel had zoomed through the seaside Pakistan village. He had been scheduled to stop. That was why the guy always seemed to elude them, he supposed. He regretted that moment. Now another team had been successful. He knew it was due to that Holmesian crafted woman. Beautiful and brilliant, a deadly combination, deadly at last for that bastard of bastards.

He wished now he could be in that endless caldron, the Syrian desert area, to bring those barbarian ISIS bastards a good blow. He read the reports. Our bomb raids have killed at least 15,000, while 16,000 new recruits show up. Still, one call-in . . .

Now this. He had never regretted putting his life on the line for his country and his mission. But this seemed like a suicide mission and for no real military benefit he could discern. After all, if there were caverns yawning to other oceans of the world of seas, how could a troop possibly get through, how could they withstand the environment for that length of time? Besides the earth under that heat and pressure was sure to shift. Channels perceived by their sensors might close up in minutes or seconds; and what sensor could hold up in such a hostile environment?

Even this thing was only going to be in and out in forty-five minutes at most, perhaps only half that to have a chance of surviving the awesome forces down there according to the description. Maybe there were scientists who knew more than he. Still . . .

And the biologics? Hodges knew from military seminars and scientists and his own strategic training and wealth of experience that they were the worst tactical weapons of all. Eventually they would flow back upon the perpetrators in one fashion or another. To accomplish the mission was to destroy the enemy's ability to wage war, to demoralize the civilian population, and to occupy the soil that the enemy formerly occupied. Biologics and nukes could certainly accomplish the first two. But all three could only be said to be accomplished when the foot soldier stood without contest on that ground. And he, or she, could not do so if it was horribly polluted.

Hundreds of Saddam's own troops and so-called scientists had been affected in their genocide attacks upon the Kurds and other ethnic villages. Parts of Khurdistan were an ecological disaster, another storied Russian area isolated from human contact because of a test gone wrong. What leaked to the world by the wretched monstrosities in surrounding areas, the Russians called it a chemical spill and radiation from nuclear testing. But it was a genetic altered bacteria with neither vaccine nor effective anti-bacterial developed. So far they had contained it to the large area within their own borders. No travel was permitted in or out. If someone should sneak out, or if it mutated and became air transmitted, the entire world could suffer, probably most horribly. It was all kept top secret, by the Russians and the US, and any other intelligence that discovered the truth of the matter.

The public should be trusted more. Citizens in a republican democracy needed to know how to act in times of high stress. Information and awareness were key. That was, after all, why he served, why he had taken his oath: To uphold and defend the Constitution of the United States against all enemies, foreign and domestic. I might disagree with what people say or think, but I shall always defend their right to speak it or think it. And the more they knew . . . there must be another reason for the secrecy. But his was to honor the secret, at least for now.

The Israelis were reported to know about it, as well as the toxic junk from the other mid-east nations. At their own top secret medical labs, they were reported to be developing antibodies peculiar to recognizing effects only in the bloodstream of their own citizens, but that was far too complex a dimension for him to consider. Perhaps he would ask Dr. Arthknott about that at some point. She had, after all, alluded to such a genomic possibility during that amazing lecture she gave months ago now (had it been that long?). He found he had not been able to take his eyes off her. Then, was he imagining it, she had come especially close to him, to point out her visual aids.

Increasingly, he found himself thinking of her. Well, what would she, a sophisticated scientist and doctor, that is, what chance could he have?

He returned to his consideration of the problem he could manage with his own unique background and experience. Guns, bullets, bombs, robots, explosives, artillery, air power, sea power: These could be controlled, armed, tactical strategy determined, designed, and, with the political will of the mission, the commanders, and the populace, be carried out to full effect.

That had been the policy that had guided US military might since its inception, and especially from the middle to the end of the twentieth century. Somehow, commanders of the Vietnam War had let that get away from them; and, at the end, the Persian Gulf Wars as well.

He turned. He looked over the starboard bulwarks. The ocean breeze always made him feel at one with the sea, the land though it be far away, and the heavens. He looked up at the clear blue sky. An intuition, developed over many years of standing at ship's railings stirred. The light was odd at an angle severe in a shaft to his right, to the east. Over there, a few days now, was California, Oregon, Washington. But the sun only came so far. He felt the ship pick up. He looked down. The waves grew to whitecaps. The wind shifted just at the moment he knew it would. Before he turned to gaze behind him, he knew what he would see. Already the gulls, too far out here, a bad omen, were turning and heading up north to the Alaskan shore and island estuaries. Other sea birds, more common out here, even they soon followed. None glided nor drafted. They were flying hard, with intent. The wind hit him, full. It would get to us, he estimated, in about four hours. He had nearly reached the forecastle at the bow. He looked up. Already in mid-afternoon he could see the lights in the bridge.

He pulled out his LF radio. He adjusted the gain. He noticed the whales began to sound. Their flukes went high in the air. They took deep dives. They would be under a good long while.

"Bridge. Watch 1. Over." It was a long way away but he thought he could already make out lightening and the grey surge wall. The wind picked up. Static interrupted his band. He adjusted his gain. "Bridge. Watch 1. Do you copy. Over."

Delores's voice came through. W1. Bridge. You are 4 X 5. We copy. Can you see it? Radar shows it's huge. Over."

"That's affirmative. Grey wall cloud south-south east. 50-60 miles, maybe. Estimate 15 mph. ETA our position--whoa Nelly--lightening out there. I say again, ETA our position 3 hours. She's picking up. Does radar confirm? Over."

"Stand by 1. Radar shows large wall cloud, wave pattern estimate at current levels 20 to 60 feet elevation 32 knots on increase. ETA 3 hours 20 minutes." She paused. "Give or take. Any ideas? Over."

"Head to starboard. We might make Akku. Alpha base zero." Static. No cetaceans nor fish stirring in the sea's waves. They were full whitecaps now. Damn, that sucker's gathering fast. Sea birds flapped furiously now to reach any landfall.

"W1, you are 3 X 5." Static. "--ti r-dge."

"Roger that. I'm on my way. Out." Hodges lurched on around to port. He gazed out. The wind hit him square. He looked to his left. There was no shaft of sun, for it disappeared in the grey throbbing cyclone of wind and whitecap and ocean surf. He heard a strange bellow he recognized, usually hearing only in the south sea. He looked up. A huge albatross flapped his wings, flying north. A long way from home and heading north. Another bad sign for a sailor. Well, any port in a storm. He reckoned it in an instant. He was a huge strong bird. He would make it. He was even less certain than before about their mission, however. The wind already started to swirl. Damn. Less than three hours. It had come up sudden. More like a storm in the Atlantic.

Already the ship cut through eight foot waves. He felt the old sea-sickness come upon him as the ship rode swell and crest. As always he took a moment and willed it away. Fresh water from the sky came down upon his face, mixed with the salt-droplets of wave crests washing over stem, bulwarks, stern.

For a moment he stopped on the companionway, attempting to gather his sea legs and get to the bridge as ordered. There he thought he saw another large shape loom before the cloud. One of the whales get lost and confused? Were those lights or--the Starr heaved. She descended unwillingly into the valley of a huge wave, for an instant the wave curling above her, her crew perceiving, not the blue-grey heavens of sky, but the temporary vault of the waters of the ocean. She struggled to return above her water line. She rose again. Clearly, helm faced a terrible struggle. It took a strong, skilled man in such weather, he knew. He peered out again, attempting to penetrate the grey-dark clouds. Already he could not discern where sea and sky met. Whatever it was, it was gone now, lost in the gathering storm.

He turned. He found the steps to the bridge. It occurred to him someone should tell the scientists to stay below.

In the large sophisticated pilot house of the bridge, it was dry and calm. Hodges realized he was quite wet. He hadn't thought about his rain gear. Uncharacteristically, Delores acted like a concerned mother, sister, wife.

"Take off those wet things, the shirt at least. Go below and change." Her military bearing returned. "Wait. Come over here. Look at this."

All about the room, men and women peered into scopes, making adjustments. The green hues reflected back in faces grim, and not merely from military bearing, training, professionalism. Delores and Hodges peered into the largest scope. The tall, lanky, light-haired man seated in front of it had been in their group on the east coast.

"Wells?"

"Aye Commander. She's a brute. Picking up a head of steam. I think we're down to less than three hours at this heading."

"Hodges."

"That's affirm, Commander. We need to get this bucket into port. The Starr will be all right, but I don't know about her baby back there."

"It'll set us back days, maybe a week."

"We may have nothing left if we don't. That's some very delicate instrumentation back there."

"I've been with her since the mere idea of her. She's built to withstand tremendous pressure."

"But not wind like that or lightening."

Delores turned to Allen. It seemed odd he was the only one she called by his first name. Hodges wondered if he was military or . . .

She asked the closet port or station.

"Aye Commander. Akku Island. Alpha 1 Bay Station Zero. Stand by one. Two hundred twenty kilometers."

They all did the math in their heads.

"It's too close in time. We'll never make it. I'm open to suggestions."

There was silence. Finally, Hodges said what he had not wanted to say.

"Standhope."

For a moment, no one said anything. Then the expected retorts followed.

"Are you crazy? It's a rock, an outcropping. It's off limits, out of shipping lanes. It's not on any charts or in data base profiles. We could run right into it in this storm. No one's been there for decades."

"I've been there. Commander's been there. I suspect Mr. Johnstone has been there. Haven't you Allen? Not all that long ago, I should think. We can find it. It's about seventy-five kilometers North-Northwest. It will take us out of sea lanes, sure; but we can protect our mission. Our return will be shorter besides. We can put in under three hours at flank speed. Shorter in, shorter out: We won't lose as much time overall."

All eyes went from Delores to Hodges to Allen. Hodges looked at Allen. Allen gazed back at his scope. Hodges knew he knew. They turned again to look at Delores.

"Navigator, set course. Hodges will assist, Wells. All ahead, ahead full."

"Course set, aye. All ahead full, aye."

Except for occasional professional radio chatter the crew bent to their tasks in silence. After a while, something blipped or may have blipped on a screen.

"Commander," Allen said.

"What is it?"

"I thought I saw something. It's gone now. Wells?"

"What?"

"Did you . . ."

"No. Nothing. Nothing at all. Lightening will do that sometimes."

"Right. Lightening sometimes."

"Hodges," Delores said.

"There is a pod of grays sounding. Probably heading south to skirt under the storm. I thought once though, maybe--."

Commander," Wells said.

"Go."

"Command on the satellite. Say they're having trouble reading our signal. They want to warn us of an approaching wall cloud."

Delores sighed. "See if you can let them know our position and heading. Tell them to keep trying with SGP. We'll try to boost our signal. I don't want to tell them about SH until we're almost there, but I don't want to be out here all alone either."

"Aye, skipper."

"Damn, that sucker's picking up. I don't know if we can even reach Standhope," Wells said.

Silence. Hodges felt something he usually didn't feel in tight situations. Slight perspiration on his upper lip.

"Destination targeted. Sixty-three kilometers. ETA 2 hours 55 minutes."

"Continue flank speed."

"Flank speed, aye Captain."

Hodges gazed out the port side of the pilot house. He wondered if he might detect the lone large lost whale or whatever it was. His military background gave him that old shiver in the back of his neck. It occurred to him that perhaps it would not be a bad idea at this time to secure weapons.

The ship heaved in the waves and crests. Hodges estimated they were already seven feet high. Some eighteen or more. The old destroyer showed her seaworthiness. But it was a ways to go yet in trying to outrun a bad storm that had gathered upon them unexpected and clearly gathered much momentum.

During World War II, a navy submarine received its orders for a top secret mission. It was to enter beneath Tokyo Bay and take measure of the ships that anchored there--battleships, cruisers, destroyers, frigates, armament crew numbers. Over three days it was to determine the entrances and exits into and out of the harbor. There was a military concept that from Midway an aircraft carrier would steam within 100 miles, and the time of most ships in anchorage being known, a sort of demolition payback for Pearl would demolish a significant part of the Japanese fleet.

As it happened the sub's mission was quite successful. Numerous records and night surveillance photographs were taken, at substantial risk, before the sub retreated safely from its espionage mission. Prior to the second phase of the mission being carried out, however, the tide turning Battle of Midway ensued, Japanese carriers were sunk in valor nonpareil by American naval and naval air forces. Following this turning point battle of the war, the photographs of the sub's mission were forgotten, and deposited in a dusty corner file cabinet, with their secret classification intact. Attention turned to the Coral Sea and Guadalcanal.

Meanwhile, on its return, the Standhope, the fleet's submarine on the secret mission, returned on the major sea-war lanes, engaging enemy ships when she espied them. She sunk 10,000 tons on that voyage, a quite respectable job for any warship, until a sharp eyed Japanese crow's nest lookout on board a destroyer with full compliment of torpedoes and depth charges caught sight of her periscope cutting the surface of the water in relatively calm seas. Nearly destroyed herself by the vicious attack, and only through the cunning of her captain and crew, persuading the destroyer's captain she had sunk her while gasping their last gasp of air and passing dangerously close to no ballast pressure until the enemy ship departed, they surfaced by night and limped-returned to Midway Island.

The voyage outbound had been nearly as eventful, though not quite as dangerous. Avoiding major shipping lanes, passing about 800 km south of the Aleutians, they were fortunate to be riding by surface by day to conserve fuel. But for a sharp eye in the coning tower, they might have crashed into it, as the Titanic hit the iceberg.

It was an old volcano, inactive, that had been a full island once, eons ago, in all probability. It looked like some outcropping that belonged about 500 yards or a half mile off a shore line. But there it was, in the middle of nowhere, a basalt rock nearly red from the sea, wind, and sun erosion. From a distance, it appeared like Chimney Rock in western Nebraska, that strange columnar island of a demarcation that conveyed to nineteenth century pilgrims on wagon trains or on horse or foot that this was the point of no return. Upon closer examination, for the Standhope took a few hours to explore the curiosity that day, it was revealed to be not as tall as its cognate landlocked geological formation, and set within on the northwest side, two water caves, large enough to accommodate Standhope class (later Dallas class and larger) submarines.

A few years after the war, while cleaning and re-organizing classified files, an imaginative vice-admiral came across the old Standhope report. The navigator had carefully reported the position -- x° longitude, x° latitude. These quickly were classified Top Secret. The outcropping was soon investigated.

During the term of the Cold War, 1950's, 60's, 70's, and 80's, the Soviets could never intuit how American subs were able to respond so quickly to events and crises in the Pacific and Arctic Oceans. Undersea LF and satellite positioning communications had not been perfected. They suspected a secret base. They never found it. Recently declassified KGB files reflect the brilliance of the logical assumption and the growing frustration at lack of discovery.

Later, although the outcropping could be detected by satellite cameras, it would not appear as a structure worthy of investigation. Seabee engineers prepared an undersea entrance into the base port. Only two subs were permitted at any time. Traffic was kept to a minimum.

It remains today one of America's best kept military secrets, revealed here, but not its geographical locus, for the first time.

The odd formation was named for the submarine that had discovered it. Most thought it only a rumor. This was the port in the storm the Starr desperately raced toward at flank speed.

Hodges looked back out the pilot house of the bridge. He needed no radar scope. He knew at once the situation. He knew the problem. He knew there was only one answer. He also knew he might be compromising one of the nation's best held secrets.

It occurred to him that the scientific leaders of the expedition were nowhere to be seen.

They stood, facing each other. They had not gone this far before. They gazed into each other's eyes, in their strange love-hate relationship fully generating the sparks of energy they felt. Ironic at that, for it was for a beneficent reason on the part of one of the partners that brought on this impasse.

It started well enough. The two consulted. Their magnificent minds worked together on final preparations. They poured over their work with industry in their pressurized cabin whilst their 747 flew at over 35,000 feet. Occasionally they glanced out the window. They both knew it was near seventy degrees below zero outside. They said something together. They realized they both realized they were cutting across a space of extraordinary cold to a space of extraordinary heat.

They journeyed across the continent, with the Ex-Gee specially mounted on a 747 like the space shuttle. They had access to military secret air lanes so that as few as possible would catch a glimpse of them from land or air. Jennifer had always liked flying. This trip was wondrous, clear practically across the country. The green and brown cross-patch pattern of the Midwest yielded to the large expanses of farms and ranches. The Rockies seemed to reach toward the cabin of the plane, as if aching to scrape the bottom of the fuselage. She thought she saw condors floating on updrafts from the cliffs and gorges. Occasionally she caught sight of an eagle far below, once, she was almost sure, for she always had exceeding range vision, with little ones perched atop her pinions. This day, it seemed all flew across the great North American continent on eagles' wings.

In a sound of the Washington coast they landed at a strip unknown to the flying public. It took a full day to transport the vessel to the old destroyer. The scientists understood it had been specially modified, in many ways to their specifications.

At last, on Susan's heading, they were off. The women knew they were steaming between known lanes. But it was the fact they had originally swerved off course which had allowed them to locate the anomaly.

They settled in to their quarters. They explored the ship. They were familiar with the sea. On any vessel, within a short time, they felt quite at home. Then, again, they dove into work, more than once missing full meals in the galley.

Gradually, however, Jennifer began to get the sense of unease she had recognized in herself off the main base. She couldn't quite place it. She simply sensed the tension, the danger, that something was amiss, not quite right, nay, not right at all. When Susan dropped her coffee cup, she knew what it was.

"Well, that's it, isn't it?"

"What are you muttering? Hand me that towel, will you? I've got to wipe this up."

"Here. Look at you. It's getting worse."

"What are you talking about, Jennifer?"

"Oh, you know."

"No, I don't," Susan said. She attempted to wipe the spill. She concentrated. She did well for a moment, visualizing the round strokes. Then, just beyond her control . . .

"Look at you. It's worse."

"You said that."

"Your hand, Susan."

Susan pulled her hand into her side. Jennifer continued. "It's shaking so hard, it's all you can do to wipe back and forth."

"I can control it. It's nothing. It will be all right."

"You're going to be operating that ship, for God's sake. How will you . . ."

"I said it's nothing."

This was the moment they stared at each other, ice looks. This was the moment the ship began to tilt harder in the water. They didn't notice at first. They resumed their disputation, a bit calmer and quieter now. Jennifer noticed Susan's hair was not staying well in the tight bun. Loose strands jumbled, frizzed, wandered all around. Jennifer presented her diagnosis.

"It's Parkinson's, isn't it?"

"I don't know. One of the autoim--I don't know."

"You haven't been tested."

"No."

"Physicians are the worst patients."

"Don't placate me. I know all those bon mots, clichés, common sayings."

"I'm sure you do. Placate. I'm not placating. Fine."

"What? Well. Go on. We've come this far."

We are all dependent on you," Jennifer said.

"I have it under control. I've been on Neurontin and Tenormin. It's gotten worse lately. Nerves. That's all it is. Nerves. Nothing more. I'll increase the dosages. Add Prozac or another cholinesterase inhibitor; They are all safe drugs. It will be all right, Jennifer."

"It's the real reason you want to go down there, isn't it? To find a cure."

"For me. And the world."

Jennifer thought she had it figured out. Now she realized she only had half of it and made the connection.

"Oh my God, Sus--"

At that moment the ship leveled and plunged about. The women did all they could to find a way to stay on their feet.

"What the hell?"

Jennifer looked out the porthole. "Oh my God. Susan, it's a squall line. And it's coming right for us."

"Damn."

"We aren't going to make it, Captain," Hodges said. He stopped. Men and women glanced up at him from their scopes and stations.

Years ago, when a lad, on more than one occasion, Hodges's father took him to hunt deer. Now, a hardened combat soldier on his government's business and arm of political will, yet, man or boy, he could never fire the shot at the peaceful, graceful defenseless creature. But he always remembered the eyes of the hind or hart, the doe or stag, the terror and the fear and the knowing. He was at sea, a seaman in a tense situation, and he was but a lad, plowing through the underbrush, trying in vain to satisfy his father. For that look of fear was the look the women and men in the pilot house looked upon him now. He had their attention. He continued. He knew they wouldn't like it.

"She's a good vessel for all that, for riding out the storm. But she can't plow through wind and wave crest at flank speed. You'll not only tear her engines out. You'll destroy the Ex-Gee."

They looked out to port. They looked behind them. In awe they realized the truth of the great sheet of gray-black smooth entity: She lived. A predator, she hurled toward her prey, lightening spark-lashes its crooked fangs and dragon-fire ready to crush and burn bone. Splats and pings upon their Plexiglas windows, sheets of rain, at once individual drops and a complete curtain fall hurled almost at sixty degrees angles upon the glass; whitecaps stretched over the bow and bulwarks to spray the top deck.

"We've no alternative," Delores said, for the first time in a voice that didn't instill confidence in her charges.

"We have one."

They turned. Against the wind, howling in a skirr, screeching like a banshee now, they had not heard the door to the bridge open from the starboard side. Two women stood there, one thin-boned, slightly hunched over, the other taller, standing on the balls of her large feet, as if taking a strong stance.

"Dr. Arthknott." Welcome to the brid--"

"We have to take the Ex-Gee below surface."

"Excuse me, Doctor, but with all due respect, you being the scientist and all, but are you mad? Have you lost all sense of reason while below in this storm? It took a loading crane to get her chained in. There's no device capable. Certainly not in all this."

"Especially in all this. If we don't, she'll be destroyed, or damaged beyond any non-port repair. All those months for nothing. We have only this one window of opportunity. None other. Forever."

"There is a way," Jennifer said. Her voice was much less impassioned than Susan's, quieter, so quiet they almost didn't hear her. But it was just as intense. It brought silence in the room. God, I hate that screechy witch's voice when she gets upset, Jennifer thought.

The silence continued for what seemed a long time. Beyond anyone's belief the wind picked up. Rain lashed the windows. A forty foot crest picked up the vessel, hurled her into a valley so deep it appeared the ship was in a canyon, then another huge crest lifted her again. Scientists and military personnel nearly fell over each other in a successful enough attempt to maintain their sea legs.

Delores gazed out the windows. Spider web crackling lightening within the grayness of the cloud sent yellow flame reflecting in her eyes. She turned toward Jennifer. "You've got my attention, Ms. Littleton," Delores said.

"We tied down the chain locks with pyrotechnic explosive bolts. The devices are generated from within the controls on board. All restraints will explode off her. If the Starr's bow is rising and her stern is down at that moment, or not much later--"

"She'll slide down the rails where she sits, like she's being launched from a dock," Hodges said.

"It's risky as hell," Delores said.

"It's our only chance," Susan said.

"Wells."

"Aye, Commander. ETA 1 hour 10 minutes."

"Damn. Slower approach. Reduce speed one-third. All right. Get the crew ready."

"There's one other thing."

"The umbilical?" Delores said. She had guessed what was coming. Susan continued.

"We can't. Not in this. We'll be out of communications for a while."

Damn. Yes, all right. Hodges."

"Aye, Commander."

"You go with them. I'll continue on. In this weather, I'll be in the cave before any satellite can see anything. I'll go in the ad cave. It'll be a tight fit but it'll work. You bring in the Ex-Gee to the deuce cave. We'll link up, wait this out."

"Aye, Commander."

"Let's do it!"

Jennifer and Susan ran out the door. Slowly against the storm, they made their way to the module at the stern of the ship. They looked back. Hodges followed. He was a big man. Yet he ran with grace and ease, like a gazelle skipping o'er water-wave mountains. Jennifer knew men. She knew this one had been around the block a few times, a good man to have in their situation. It seemed Susan had looked at him in, no, surely she was imagining it.

In spite of it all, Jennifer smiled. Susan could not see it. She was going underwater with her design after all. Susan tripped. She fell against the bulwark amidships. Jennifer started back for her. In an instant Hodges knelt at her side.

He helped her up. She leaned against him. Jennifer suddenly knew her insight had been correct. Well, she had waited a long time for her mentor-colleague to . . .

"Slippery even for an old salt," Hodges said.

"Right," Jennifer said.

"I'm all right," Susan said.

Right, Jennifer thought, knowing what the problem truly was. The group made its way to the steps leading to the module. Only Hodges had seen Delores engage the ship's intercom mike and heard her command before he had dashed out after the two scientists.

"Engine Room. Reduce all one-half.

"All one-half aye." The voice came back loud and clear.

"Steady as she goes."

"Steady as she goes, aye."

"Wells."

"Aye Commander. Course coordinates plotted."

"Very good, Wells. Those should be, wait, I think a bit of an adjustment here; try that. Good. There we are. That should be right."

In the Ex-Gee, the three occupants engaged a small switchgear and a buss. Reading orally, repeating, and following the numbered directives in their operations manual, they quickly pressed a series of buttons in their appropriate sequences. The generator snapped into a low, comfortable hum. The ship shivered for a moment, accompanied by a high pitch complaint. Then she calmed to a velvet purr.

"She's anxious to go," Jennifer said. She knew Susan disliked her awarding inanimate objects anthropomorphic identities and characteristics. Still, Jennifer had a mystical edge to her. She had a favorite writer who always had one of his characters state that everything, God made or human made, once it has shape and form and is complete has sentience.

"Where should I--" Hodges began.

"There," Susan said. "In the lower chair. We need someone to work the aft view."

"Checklist three: Ship Release checklist," Jennifer said.

"Proceed," Susan said."

"Fuse Buss 1-2 connected to 2-3. Switch to on. Push-button indicator will show green."

"Fuse Buss 1-2 connected."

Seamless, she sailed like silk in the depths of the sea beneath the waves. In the depths of the sea, as though, long lost, she had come home, she glided. Later, Jennifer would compare her maiden voyage to a lost petal of a flower washing ever so slowly down a clear sparkling creek bed. She glided this way and that, almost like a manta ray. Indeed, in a dreamy moment, it appeared those strange bat wings undulated like a ray's, gently displacing the water all around them. Jennifer had the sense once that they were comfortable free and floating in a new amniotic sac, gaping in wonder down a yet darkened channel. Only in reverse, she realized, for the light dimmed as deeper they fell away.

For a short time, the storm so violent it churned the waters several meters below the surface, the doughty little vessel shuddered, as an aircraft entering turbulence. Then they were well below it and entered the great silence of the deep sea.

Getting off was not as bad as they had predicted. All instruments had sprung to light as they proceeded through their launching and operations checklists. They had to wait a few moments for the angle of the Starr to be right, then Hodges set the sequence in. They waited a tense twenty-eight seconds for batteries activated sequence charge and the command signal to the devices to be generated.

Jennifer remembered those windmills at old miniature golf courses; one had to plan ahead some seconds to ensure the sufficient opening for her ball to roll through and not be blocked.

Jennifer liked miniature golf. She had not played in a long time. The new courses did not seem to have the windmills any mor . . .

Then, the flashes of red and yellow sparks illuminated their window panes against the lightening strikes now close but still beyond.

They felt the ship shudder. Suddenly, they found themselves roiling beneath the high waves of the ocean. In haste, to prevent her being buffeted about, they adjusted their ballast as any crew would adjust that of any submarine. Considerably smaller they, they sank beneath the waves much sooner.

Soon enough, they entered the deep calm joy of drifting silence.

"We'll go slow," Susan said. "We need to make sure everything operates OK. This storm may be a blessing in disguise. We can use this as a dry run check. Pardon the pun."

Trapped fathoms beneath the sea, Jennifer had to tolerate not only the old cliché, but that damn girlish, nerd-scientist giggle. She glanced at Hodges. Incredibly, he seemed almost besotted. Music to his ears. In silent retaliation, she made up her own bad pun, keeping it to herself. Water on the brain.

"Monitor all warning lights and gauges," Susan said.

They gazed at the various panels and consoles. The indicator lights lit in their appropriate sequences as they had trained to regard them, as Barnstone's engineers (or the Navy's engineers) had designed them, following the concept of Susan's and Jennifer's overall design schematics.

"Operations array."

"Navigational array."

"Guidance system aligned."

"All systems normal," Hodges said. The women noticed he had paused prior to acknowledging the weapons systems control panel. "We're a go."

"All normal here," Jennifer said. There was a pause. Susan continued. Before she completed her sentence, Jennifer interrupted her mentor.

"Well, as the Commander said, 'Steady as she goes.' We'll follow the high S curve, to check our pressure at each level on the sine co-efficie--."

"Oh my God."

"Jennifer, what is it?"

"Ms. Littleton?"

"We're, we're not far, 20 kilometers and 26,000 fathoms from the site."

It took a moment for her meaning to sink in. Susan double checked the navigation data base that had been entered from the satellite data and the data from the scientists' initial discovery.

"She's right. You're right. We can--"

"Wait," Hodges said. "You're talking five miles deep. What kind of valley rift is that? No one has ever . . . (here he sighed; then he continued) besides, we need to propel this vessel in the opposite direction. I have to link up with the commander at Standhope. And we need to conserve energy."

"Just a minute," Susan said. She calculated distances and reactor output ratios. Jennifer knew she already verified what she had figured in her head.

"At this distance, and with the storm not abated we can run a fly-by, and have plenty of energy to reach Standhope, perhaps even a few minutes before the Starr."

The two women looked at the military man. He peered through his aft window now, turned away from them. They turned to look at him. Four female eyes gazing at him. What chance did he have? The whales sounded about 500 yards away. Still they headed down. They were already at 5,000 fathoms, a mile or so below the surface. Soon the humans would have to close off visual for pressure. He checked his instruments. There was a slight pressure variation in one of the gauges. Nothing major. Besides, they could always turn about.

"It's for security, Hodges," Jennifer said.

"What's that?"

"We won't be surprised next time out. Down. We'll know what to expect."

"Are you certain your numbers?"

"Yes. Positive. That's aff-affirmative. Plus or minus two per cent. Parameters negligible and acceptable."

"All right. But just a quick look-see from a safe distance. Long distance eyeball and out. Set new coordinates. I have a feeling we simply need to follow our whale buddies."

"Wow," Jennifer said, seeing the pod still sounding, still heading down. Then they closed the pressure windows to rely on instrumentation, for now they approached well over a mile in depth.

"Steady as she goes." Jennifer smiled. Susan was finding she liked the military and nautical expressions.

They entered the deep depths of the sea, where, only decades ago, no one knew what to expect.

"Switching on outside lights and cams," Jennifer said.

They gazed, captivated at the screens. At once bizarre eel-like and bloated spine fish creatures passed before their view. Down they spiraled, following the line of descent as a signal along an optic fiber. The lights of the ship sent out in the deep green-black water, thick like an oil cube about them now; an eerie long glow, as a headlamp in thickest fog.

"It's so silent," Jennifer said. "So all encompassing. It's like I've been here before, somehow."

"It's the contrast with the storm," Hodges said.

"Yes, and something more," Susan said.

The Ex-Gee defined its arc with its descent, as a creature in a realm yet undiscovered.

"Commander."

"Go, Mr. Wells."

"All clear and steady as she goes."

One of the other crewmen took issue. She noticed something odd. She asked Delores to gaze at the screens herself. Then, suddenly, it was gone. Delores thought the anomaly might be a ghost reflection. It happened in storms sometimes, even when there were calm seas and heavy cloud cover.

"The storm?" Delores asked.

"I thought so. But it seemed to be closing. One thousand meters off the port bow. Wait. Look. There it is again."

"Wells?"

"I don't, aye, affirmative. Nine hundred meters to port."

"Damn. Attention all hands. Battle stations. I say again, battle stations." Delores then muttered under her breath, covering the speaker-mike with her hand, hoping few or none of the crew heard her. "Battle stations, with a skeleton crew, and a fourth of them untrained scientists, and my best man under the ocean somewhere. Well, probably a trawler blown off course in the storm. Strange to be coming at us though. Too close for comfort in calm seas."

"Commander?"

Though she spoke to a woman, Delores, as did most in the navy, continued to use the standard military honorific. What was the seaman's first name, Naomi? The girl had a sharp eye. "Proceed with your report, Mr. Jerrolds."

"It's the profile, Commander. I've seen it in radar school. I'm sure of it. A Russian cruiser, Pushkin class. Seven hundred fifty meters and closing."

"What the hell. All hands. Battle Stations. Prepare for ramming. Get out weapons. Man the 5 inch. Come on, people. Move! Move!"

Another of the newer crew assigned, Joel Harris, was the first to see it. He had made it to the 5 inch. He locked, loaded, sighted to port. "Visual contact, twenty degrees port bow, 600 meters. Closing. Incoming. She's opening fire. Permission to return. I say again. Incoming."

Like the wraith Mephistopheles materializes from the blackness of hell, the Russian made cruiser's lightening bolt whistled across the Starr's bow. In the storm, they were not aware if another whitecap lifted them or if they had been hit.

"Green light. Fire at will. Return fire. Fire at will. All hands. We are under attack. I say again, we have been fired upon by unknown vessel at this time. This is not a drill. Damage report."

"None indicated, Commander."

"The storm's become our friend. They can't judge or figure with accuracy range or azimuth."

"They're firing again."

This time spray from the ocean rained upon the deck, well over the bulwarks. It was not the same as before, when merely from the severity of the storm.

"Off the starboard bow. No damage, but close."

"She's closing in. Wells. Hard aport."

"Command--"

"Hard aport, man. Now!"

"Hard aport, aye. What is our--"

"Forty degrees and don't spare the inches. Jerrolds."

"Commander."

I think you've manned a 20 mm cannon before."

"Aye-aye, skipper."

"Can you make it to the gun?"

"On my way."

"Harris. Come in."

"Commander."

"They won't be expecting us to come along side. Wait till we're flank amidships. Then fire at will."

"Roger that."

"Norwich. Christensen. Magruder. Get those M-16's. Step out on the starboard platform. The old Civil War firing lines, top line, stoop line (first and second, technically, but no time for old time training), just think, people; obviously ladies and gentlemen, no need to wait for the re-load. At will as we pass."

"They're firing again," Wells said. "Clear miss again."

"They didn't expect our turn. Steady, Mr. Wells. Maybe we can make them believe it. But do keep in mind we really do not want to ram her." At the last moment, Delores grabbed the main wheel. "Watch, now, bridge crew, everyone watch now she makes forty degrees, not 36 or 38."

Down, down, down the Ex-Gee floated, seemingly in a suspension of Jell-O, seemingly in an ocean of black pit crude oil. The whales were in front now. They clearly were attacking something.

"Hodges. Jennifer. Look here. We're witnessing something no one has ever seen before. A pod of whales attacking Archetuthis."

"What?"

"A giant squid?" Jennifer said. "No one's ever seen one being attacked by--oh my!"

"Cameras? Recording?"

"Just a, yes, now, fully operational. Our first marine zoological submission article. 'Observation of Gray Whale Pod Feeding Upon Archetuthis at 22,000 fathoms.' We'll be the first to . . ."

"What's that?"

"Where?  What the hell?"

"It's another sub.  But how."

"He was in the pod. Back dropped," Hodges said. "I thought I caught his signal earlier. Now he's--Jesus! Torpedo away. Susan!  Evasive maneuver Beta-Charlie. Remember, I showed you. Damn it, don't think, just do it! Go, girl. Launching decoys. Decoys away! That's it, ladies. Now you've got it. Amazing how the training kicks in, isn't it?"

Oddly, in such a moment, Jennifer realized it was the first time he had called them by their given names.

"Where the . . . Damn. There."

"Don't say 'there.' Say, 'Decoys launched aye. On screen. Fish averted.' Susan, Jennifer, let me have the con."

"No," Susan said. "She's my ship. I've got her now. Hang on boys and girls. Jennifer. We're going to see what she can do. Aft rockets on my command. Now! Fire rockets!"

"Aft rockets engaged.  Whoa!"

"Hang on."

"Damn. It's not a ship. It's a bullet in the sea. We're riding a damn bullet in the bottom of the ocean."

Jennifer would always remember Hodge's simile. The vessel rocketed in the darkness of the deepest deep. A little sub trailed behind, somewhat similar in design, but unable to make the speed of the Ex-Gee. The torpedo chased the decoys and exploded.

The mystery ship followed the water trail and the ever dimmer lights of the Ex-Gee.

Hodges worried. He worked a simple equation. Impossible! No torpedo at this depth could keep its integrity. The thing would at once implode from the enormous pressure. How did that, that fish continue even for while? Then, as a thought unable to be processed suddenly streaks through one's brain, he knew. He had heard about a concept so unique as to be thought beyond capability. Clearly someone had conquered the problem, a problem that had dogged U-Boat and Submarine designers since the inception of torpedo development. But who . . . ?

"Jerrolds, at the 20mm Gatling. Now, damn it! All hands, on my command. Fire at will. Open fire! Fire! Fire! Rake those bastards. Wells, give coordinates to gunners, damn it!

"Roger that. Connecting."

A blaze of withering hail of bullets came from the defense line Delores arranged. The Starr was an Arleigh Burke class destroyer, an older version. Nonetheless, under ordinary circumstances, she would provide a formidable weapons phalanx of an 8 inch and 5 inch, and 2 75 mm guns, 2 20mm Gatling cannon, up to 20 torpedoes, Aegis and Tow missile systems, heat and sonar seeking depth charges, and, with modifications, 10 to 15 Tomahawk cruise missiles. Other guns and weapons array, including anti-missile and anti-torpedo systems could be included. Now, however, she was stripped down for scientific research, she hadn't been as well maintained as a regular ship of the line; nonetheless, her commander knew her 30 knots capacity in open seas, and extraordinary maneuverability with her 2 large screws. She was capable of turning even in rough seas her 415 feet, 750 ton displacement on a quarter, if not a dime. Delores had used all of her skill and the ship's response, and what military personnel she had to fullest advantage.

Harris assisted Jerrolds. The Seaman fired the Gatling. The line of men and one woman the commander of the vessel under attack arranged fired their rifles as uniform as musketeers of the early and mid-19th century. Hot lead projectiles zipped through the cold rain from starboard of the Starr to port of the mystery aggressor. Its personnel, amazed at the daring maneuver, turned to getting away as fast as it could, with alleviation of as much damage as possible.

"Damn, we're close. Too close!"

"Whites of their eyes!"

"If we had hooks and chains, we could board her."

"We won't go back quite that far in time, Mr. Wells," Delores said. "Firing lines are enough sentimental journeys for one day. But I am satisfied to perceive you are aware of your naval history."

"Aye, Commander. New heading. She's on the right oblique. Her port thirty degrees."

"Come about. We'll chase her a short while. Only somewhat with--cancel that order."

"Commander."

"A wounded bear is more dangerous. I don't want her getting a lucky hit at this point. Storm's letting up a bit. We'll stand down for now. Regroup in strategy later. Let's get our heading back to Standhope."

"New, that is, I say again, old, heading set, Commander."

"Steady as she goes, Navigator. All ahead one-half. As storm abates, come to three-fourths."

"One-half, aye."

"Damage report."

"None of significance. We're in good shape."

"Steady as she goes, aye."

"Track all echoes and ghost images, this time, Mr. Wells. Mr. Foxworth."

"Aye, Commander," Jessica Foxworth said. The 'Mr.' honorific was still employed by many in the Navy, irrespective of the seaman's actual gender. Harris and Jerrolds returned to the bridge. They breathed hard. So did they all.

"Good shooting, Seamen."

"I think I got 3 or 4."

"I counted 3 in the drink."

"OK, don't break out the champagne yet," Delores said. "That was her initial contact. She'll be back. You're entitled to a briefing. Some of you came in after . . . Mr. Wells. Schedule a full briefing at Standhope. Captain's table."

"Aye Commander."

"First firefight?"

"Aye."

"Aye, Commander."

"Don't worry. It will not be your last. You did well. Just don't rest on laurels. The second time you can get careless if you do."

The Starr found its heading again and plowed through the storm. It began to abate, as the captain had noticed. The waves waned down, crests under eight feet. The rain still poured in sheets, but more straight than at a severe angle. Delores sat at the command control, peering out the window. She didn't express it, but she couldn't help wondering how the hell did the son of a bitch know how to find us? Been something very strange about this operation from the get-go. There's more to come. You don't have to be a John Paul Jones to have that feeling. These were her thoughts for the moment. Then she considered her charge.

"Any signal on sonar with the Ex-Gee profile?"

"Negative, Commander. I'm picking up what may be a, stand by one, is a pod of whales. It's fading, though. They must be sounding over 20,000 fathoms. I didn't think they could go down that far."

A seaman brought her a hot cup of coffee. Not much of the original armament, but it would be good to have trained personnel. Fresh scrubs. They acquitted themselves well. Still, after they arrived at Standhope, she would request from CINCPAC a contingent of SEALs, she thought. Damn. Where the hell did that fucking sub go?

"Keep on it, Mr. Foxworth. Any signal. Even if, well, any signal."

"Copy that, Commander."

Babysitting nerdy scientists on their damn fool's errand. Eisenhower was right about the military industrial complex. And this coffee's cold besides. Well, it was a good fight, anyway. That's something. God, I love adrenal highs.

Sometimes in deepest darkest night, when driving one's car down deserted county roads or rural highways, shadows move within shadows. Yet a few hours yearn until the first grey-rose of dawn peeks in the east and only those astute realize the grackle bounding of stag, does, and fawns, have rippled the curtain of blackness by the side of the highway.

That was how things appeared now to Jennifer as the intrepid little ship sped on in the close impenetrable blackness of the fathomed sea. Its flood lamps and CCTV monitors showed less now, as even deeper she reached.

"I think he's still following us."

"Is he gaining?"

"Negative. If anything, the opposite. Signal's getting weak and intermittent."

"Maybe we can do a flyby and get out of here before . . . "

"What is it Susan?"

"No. Nothing. Shouldn't we . . . Hodges."

"Go ahead."

"Could we launch a torpedo at him?"

The military professional was taken aback at the scientist's suggestion. More and more he was becoming convinced this was a special woman. But surely, she, an educated woman, would not consider a pre-emptive strike when not called for. At least so far. And he suddenly knew that he had to be careful, he thought. Twenty thousand leagues under the sea, so to speak, was no place to lose one's wits for any reason. At once his experienced military and naval operations computer brain went into its analytic mode. He regarded his instruments and indicators. He came up to look at the front console banks blinking blue, white, red before the two women, illuminating their faces in primary light.

"Not at this distance. They'd detect it far in advance. At this depth the casement would implode. They'd engage evasive maneuvers or send decoys to detonate. It would be an exercise in futility. In point of fact, it would make them happy, for it would disclose further to them our speed, range, azimuth, and location."

"Still it might slow them down."

"Too many uncertainties for the percentages, Sus--Dr. Arthknott."

"Very well, Hodg--I mean, copy that."

Jennifer caught at once the little interplay. Hodges was becoming less formal; Susan was beginning to employ military terminology. And had she been mistaken when checking their pressure and depth gauges, did she not see reflected in the glass, for a moment, when Hodges came up to look over their gauges, his hand linger a bit on Susan's? Inside the sub it was close, humid. She recalled now that just before they slipped their surly bonds, compelling the ship into the ocean, Susan had fallen a bit and Hodges had caught her. Now she recalled they hadn't broken their accidental embrace so soon. Jennifer looked over at her friend. The scientist's hair, the once taut bun, was askew, frizzing all about, and hanging down. Her eyes were glistening like she had never observed. Well, had there ever been a stranger or less expected spot for romance than the darkest most encapsulated place on earth and only inches and technology separating them from tons of pressure in all its dimensions and implications?

Suddenly she was aware Susan saw something.

"There. Ahead. No. Yes. There."

Jennifer turned to look forward. Hodges came up. "That reddish glow?"

"You see it?"

"We all see it," Jennifer said. "Yes! That's it. It's still there. How much time?"

"Four minutes, possibly three. Fifty-five minutes of fuel left in the verniers; we need to conserve them for the main event."

"We can conserve now. No need to fire. We'll be there in two minutes," Susan said. God. Look at her! My God. Look at that."

"Holy St. Maria!"

"Hodges?"

"Looks like we're coming out of the Utah mountains with Las Vegas on the horizon."

Soon enough the Ex-Gee fairly stopped about 100 yards out from the vent. Reddish-yellow bubbles, flecked and streaked at the top of the columnar stream in a deep green, hissed out of a hole in the earth about two and a half times the size of the ship.

"She's a bit smaller than we saw on the robot video," Jennifer said.

"But she's large enough," Susan said. "We can fit. I'll circumnavigate her. Cameras."

"Activated."

Susan propelled the vessel all about the vent, a deep sea volcano spewing forth steam of a chemical soup the same consistency as the day the earth was born, so old and so ancient that even time had lost contextual meaning.

"What is that? Over there, four degrees starboard. What are those?"

"Mr. Hodges, you're seeing animal life few have ever witnessed. Less people than have been in space, possibly less than have walked on the moon. And then only by robot video. We are the first to arrive here. To see it as it unfolds. We should name it after ourselves.

"The Arthknott-Littleton-Hodges Explosive Event Life Vent. We'll publish it that way.

Hodges smiled. He thought he smiled to himself. Who'd had ever thought an old salt-SEAL seaman soldier would have a scientific phenomenon named after him? His father had not matriculated past tenth grade. One day he left the family. He did not return home to his wife and children. There was a rumor of another woman in another town.

He, Hodges, had to go to work to support his brothers and sisters. Their mother worked, and once the children were older, and on track to jobs or education of their own, he joined the marines. The military had been his escape, where he found the fathers he had been missing. Now he glanced about. Jennifer, Ms. Littleton, smiled back, He must have smiled outwardly as well and she had seen him. She had a knowing smile, he realized. Susan continued, somewhat reducing to her lecture voice.

"Sulfur, silicon, manganese based creatures attached to the vent rocks. We don't know how they generate. Look, see, they're not there, then they're there. Those white blankets all around them are infinitesimally huge colonies of bacteria. Remember I discussed them earlier. If we're lucky, we can see-- yes, there!"

"Where?"

"I see it. Down there, Hodges. Coming out from the third crack. Worm-like tubule creatures. See how the bacteria go in and out, like corpuscles in osmosis. But it's not osmosis. We don't fully understand."

"Seems like I hear a lot of that."

Susan laughed, nay, giggled. Jennifer looked at her again. A girlish giggle at over 30,000 fathoms in the midst of a violent volcano spewing forth substances yet beyond our ken. Well, maybe it wasn't so inappropriate after all. In a way, what better place than an immense amniotic sac containing and nurturing the emergence of new life? Still, it was something Jennifer would remember all her life, the image of a renowned scientist acting like a sophomore high school girl in the throes of her first true love (second, I guess, if you count that jerk who was still pursing her in a malevolent manner) whilst traversing so deep underwater the waters themselves may be the primal waters from the distant age when water formed upon the planet.

"Oh just typical scientist talk, silly."

Silly, Jennifer thought. Silly. Good Lord, they'd start hitting each other next. Then, Jennifer started to worry. They were down by themselves. The ship performed well, sure, better than she had hoped or dreamed. True, the hull pressure gauge was a bit high, but it was within parameters. Her real worry now, if Susan's palsy started . . . albeit she had to admit it seemed to improve the deeper they had dived. Suddenly she saw it.

"Susan."

"Yes. I'm coming around. Say no more."

"Can you go around to the other side and hide behind that outcropping back there?"

"Hodges?"

"Our friend's found his way. I don't think he can pick us up with this turbulence between us. Now we'll just activate the sonar shielding we need at least for a while. I'm sure he's scanning already. Long as we're on this side, I can see him coming on our over the top bounce technology, and I think we can keep him confused until we can sort it out. Good thing Barnstone agreed to it."

"He was concerned about weight distribution, sacrifice of some scientific hardware," Susan said. "At this point, let me guess, the Pentagon convinced him that both elements could be on board with little or no loss of mobility in the sea or in the hostile environment."

"See? And everybody's happy," Hodges said. "Let's see, I make it he's about two miles out. ETA ten minutes."

"What do you have in mind?"

"I know what you were thinking: You want to find the best place and go in now."

"We, it--"

"It's no good," Hodges said. "We need our full compliment of crew. We need to link up with the Starr at Standhope. But you're afraid he'll go in first."

"You're going to stop him?"

"Like you said, slow him down. Jennifer, you're on torpedo launch. Right here. Remember? This, then, remove the safety covers, wait for my command, then, turn key and push. Remember, we've all cross-trained. If our fish hold for even five seconds before imploding, it will be a good screen."

"I know what to do."

"Good woman. Sorry. Copy that. But only on my command. He'll see us and may turn and fire himself. He knows now he can't outmaneuver us. OK. Good. Here. Right here. Settle behind this huge red rock.

"Oh my!"

"What is it Susan?"

"Look at it undulating. It's not a rock. It's creatures gathering as they extrude. They pile on, pile up over the opening they emerge from." Susan said. "This has never been observed before. Perhaps they continue to receive nutrient exchange from underneath. We need to get a closer look, take some measurements, readings."

"That's a negative. Cancel that. It is too late to change our guarded position. It is amazing at that. Truly aston--But our strategy calls for us to stay. There will be at least one more time, remember," Hodges said. "But it will have to do for our defense for now. Four minutes Jennifer. Can you up the sensor scope three degrees? I need a range of sight lock-in. Good. Hold it. There. Positions calculated. Target locked. He's there. Slowly edge around now. Careful. Not too close. We don't want to hit the rocks. Jennifer, remember. Do not fire in the direction of the vent unless it's absolutely necessary to save us."

"Got it. Understood. Roger that. Copy that."

"You're doing fine, Jennifer. Damn, those bubbles are huge. And they're yellow. Yellow-red bubbles, from sulfur and manganese, right? Maybe we can use them for a few more seconds of camouflage. Now, remember, the angle has to take the torpedo away from the vent. I can't risk an explosion caving in the phenomenon."

"Got it. I mean, copy that. All nav coordinates locked in. What a view! It's OK. I'm ready."

She believed her, trusted her once more. Jennifer noted her mentor had transmuted; she was sharp, businesslike again. Susan's first love and hope would always be the vents, Jennifer thought. She could separate her attraction to the man and perform her duties; and she had to ignore the science of the vent to survive this excursion.

Well, and hadn't she changed? Look at her, a soldier in an undersea battle. She shook a little, a palsy, then she got control. She felt fear, she knew. Somehow, though, closest as she had been for some years to death, she never felt more alive. Even the cells of her flesh seemed electric, she saw so clearly, heard so acutely, like that time she escaped from under the raft, nearly drowned, then lived. Lived! This magnificent gift of life truly was everything. It began here!

Hodges barked his orders. It seemed he was ahead of them all somehow. He seemed to be able to draw an immediate synthesis between his military strategy and the scientific approach.

"No problem. OK, ladies. Here we go. It's rock and roll time. Come around in. That's it."

"He's turning. He's seen us."

"Steady, steady now."

"Hodges!"

Like a groaning older woman rising against her will to go out for the morning job, the Starr turned and found her new heading. In the distance, but in their visual field they could see it, the sun cut a swath of bright yellow-white rays across a friendlier sea, dazzling off the waves with a glorious glistening. The rain fell to earth light now, almost a drizzle. Joanne Foxworth looked back out the port side window. A dark wall of cloud still appeared on the horizon, but not as ominous as before. Indeed, already, like a saving grace description from the Biblical text, a sliver of sun seemed to sever the cloud and rays of magic radiated from the once angry heavens upon the earth, upon the firmament of the waters.

She was special forces. A specialist in radar at the SEAL training base on Coronado Island. They had taught her sonar. She had become proficient. She didn't know how she made it through Bcd/s camp. After all, most of the men had dropped out. Five times at least she thought she drowned, and four of them wished she had. Maybe that was how she made it through with her calluses split in half, walking (swimming) pneumonia, and endless tours hauling in portage her boat bark. But, albeit in a purgatory daze, she found and re-found her comrades and they somehow got their boats through and graduated.

She volunteered for the mission. They all did, of course. She wasn't sure yet about Delores. She hadn't been from the beginning.

She never liked women commanders, knowing it was an old prejudice based on little objective reality. Since the daring maneuver of the Starr in battle and her quick strategic thinking and victory at the engagement, somewhat like her boat, she was starting to come around. Delores's cunning was no longer a secret. She'd remember that, keep the matter in mind. For she had one too. After all she had gone through, she had not been given combat command. She still had doubts, of course. It would always be the same story. Damn. Those idiots running the enemy boat.

Then something of beauty so magnificent it affects every person on earth and has since persons have been on the earth, caught her eye. She was the first to see it, the first to be in awe, for somewhere out there, pastel colors of blue-red-yellow-green coursed across the vault of the heavens.

"Look everyone. It's a rainbow. A full one."

They turned, these battle hardened and well trained troops and gazed at the optical phenomenon. Solid bands of primary pastel colors graced and bridged across the firmament of the heavens. It was large, extended to the horizon, and well formed.

"The storm's over, my friends."

"Now that is something. That is beautiful."

"And never again will I come . . ."

"Foxworth? You're a religious woman?"

"My father was a minister. We studied bible at night, before going to bed."

"'When I bring clouds over the earth, and the bow appears in the clouds, I will remember My covenant between Me and you and every living creature among all flesh, so that the waters shall never again become a flood to destroy all flesh. When the bow is in the clouds, I will see it and remember the everlasting covenant between God and all living creatures, all flesh that is on earth.'"

"Commander."

"Well, Mr. Foxworth. There is God, country, and then my Father."

"Yes, sir."

Joanne Foxworth's doubts of resolve about her secret matter started to fade, as, soon enough, God's hue laden sign of the covenant of life began to fade, one cascade-path at a time, as if lights in different rooms of a building were extinguishing. By the time it was gone, she felt she had returned to herself. It was, after all, a great deal of money.

"Mr. Wells."

"Aye Captain. New heading. ETA forty-two minutes at this speed. She's calmer commander. We could increase--"

"Negative. Mr. Foxworth. Any--"

"Nothing on scope, Commander."

"Damn. Where is she? Steady as she goes. I don't want to leave her behind, if she should start looking for us, needed our help. Mr. Wells. In ten minutes, reduce to one-third."

"One-third in ten, aye."

Once again, the durable ship appeared to skim the reflective waters where the waves of sea and the canopy of sky met. The Starr looked as at home in calm seas as she had appeared in turbulent ocean.

The Ex-Gee was getting some pressure gauge readings into the yellow warning lines. They agreed they needed to take her up at a slightly accelerated angle. To get to the higher reaches with little pressure sooner.

"Hodges."

"She blew up just off her port engine. Some damage there, possibly extensive. Weapons on that side possibly compromised. She won't follow us."

"Hodges, I--"

"She won't go into the vent. Not unless they're completely insane. She needs to limp back to her surface ship to regroup and effect repairs. She might be out a good while, but I suspect we'll see her again. I'm sure they have competent repair specialists on the mother ship."

"The Ex-Gee handled well, Jennifer."

"This pressure aberration concerns me a bit. There. Starting to fall now. A little."

"We were a little close to the explosion. That may be a factor. Good seamanship, however, Susan. Going over the torpedo and the enemy like that just out of range of the worst of it. Most would go around and receive collateral force to midships. Your maneuver allowed the enemy sub to block most of the explosive force. How did you learn that?"

"I've been reading some of Delores's ops manuals."

Jennifer recalled now the ops and tech manuals Susan read on the plane and later at sea. She had wondered . . .

"Memory calibration reading; this is the locus for new heading. Vector on screen."

"Roger that. New heading 18° by 48."

"Eighteen degrees by 48, aye," Jennifer said. Continually now, she realized she was picking things up and liking it. She, soldier! I sailor! It had a ring to it.

"Let's get to our hotel for the night, people."

Jennifer entered some data on her console board. Upon the return, the navigational data base would simply follow by memory their line of ascent.

Circling and finding circle-linear co-efficients in a sine curve matrix, the Ex-Gee slowly made her way far up to surface.

"Commander. I've got her. Two miles off our starboard. Five thousand fathoms. Signal weak but growing. Just in range."

Everyone ran and looked over Joanne Foxworth's sonar scope. She held her earpieces.

"Stay with her, Mr. Foxworth."

"Copy that, Commander." Another seaman indicated profile looks good. She may be coming up a bit too fast but she appears to be within safety sine parameters. Angle looks good. Level spiral curve in tolerance.

"Damn. All right. Lower communications array. Can she pick up our signal? We can't pick her up. She'll just follow us straight in."

"Copy that. All systems go." There was another tense pause. Then: "She's got us."

"Mr. Wells."

"Aye, Captain."

"All ahead one-half. Communications."

"Aye Commander."

"Notify CINCPAC we need those caves cleared."

"Already on it Commander. Fleet departing for sixteen hours on my mark."

"Proceed."

"ETA twenty-five minutes."

"I could use a cup of hot tea."

"Hot tea, aye."

Like a pup or a juvenile following the lead of a wizened dog, the mentor not glancing at the protégé yet knowing the responsibility upon her shoulders, the Starr cut through the calming waters, followed beneath the ocean but at an ever shallower depth by its charge. Soon the two ships traveled near the same speed. After about fifteen minutes, Joanne Foxworth called out.

"Surfacing. The Ex-Gee is surfacing. One-half mile off starboard astern"

A few seamen dashed out to the railing to see her. It seemed to some she was like a swimmer who had been down a bit too long and was gloriously gasping in air. Delores came out with her binoculars.

"Doesn't appear any the worse for wear. Wells. Send coded message. Established VC. Inform our destination station Sally Hombre 1 in 12."

"Copy that Commander. Received. They say they're ready for some fresh water above the surface. A hot shower and some hot tea."

The Starr's bow poked out a bit from the ad cave. The Ex-Gee fit in the deuce cave with room to spare. In each cave, a series of ropes bound the ships anchored to a rocky port wall and dock. The designers had used the original natural outcroppings as much as possible. They had blown or expanded a passageway between the two natural caverns. At the far end of the deuce cave, a natural cut limestone culvert gaped above the water level. Again, the engineers had expanded what was already a natural phenomenon.

Deep within the cave, then, in this cavern, different rooms for command and control, galley, sleeping births and conference area had been carved and divided. Electronic gear monitored the Pacific submarine fleet which roamed and prowled the northern ocean, their nuclear missiles ready to launch in retaliation a nation's sudden or planned attack upon the US.

In this conference area, now, the crews of the two ships bent to compare notes. Jennifer and Susan noted the experienced seamen and soldiers were not surprised to learn of parallel attacks upon their respective vessels. They had come a long way since their innocent and naive days of believing this would be mere scientific exploration, Jennifer thought.

All were pleased to learn the vent's aperture could provide entrance and egress. The navigational memory lock allowed them to calibrate time of descent from their location. They also knew that their enemy would be back, perhaps waiting for them. Jennifer knew what was on Susan's mind and the mind of the military personnel. How did they know where to find us? It was a heck of a thing Jennifer thought, no longer quite so amazed she now thought as a sailor, as a soldier, to go into battle with a betrayer in your midst.

Deep into the night, deep in a dark, secret cavern, in the midst of the world's greatest ocean, they palavered. They discussed a two pronged strategy. By early morning Delores called for a full weapons and systems check at 1100 hours. Watch was in shifts again. Susan and Jennifer and Hodges collapsed into deep sleep.

She was a little girl. The monster lay in wait outside her room. It began to enter the room, the big hairy undefined or, perhaps, as adult, she could now describe it as Sasquatch appearing. It started in. That was OK. She remembered how to defeat it. She simply had to close her eyes. But she couldn't close them. Something was wrong. They were already closed. She knew then she was asleep. That was it. The monster kept coming. She had to find some way. Reverse.

If awake, close eyes; therefore, if asleep . . . she opened her eyes. She sat bolt upright in bed. At once she was full awake.

Water lapped all about her bed, a bed of rock and stone. Her head rested on a red rock outcropping. She was alone, on an island. The water rose with rapidity, and the monster was still there, swimming toward her. Where was she? Then she saw herself. She wore a white shift. It had red on it. She reached her hand down. It was blood. But it wasn't hers. A deep horn she had heard before was sounding underneath the water and blaring forth a whirlpool of bubbles.

She woke up. Truly this time. Wide awake this time.

It was the klaxon, a sound similar to the one she heard at their secret seaside resort. People ran around outside their room. She ran in to the control room. Video sirens showed blips. Personnel monitoring were talking.

Delores stood at the center of things.

"Delores."

"Not now, Ms. Littleton. We seem to have intruders all over the perimeter. I've got gunners at various locations. I'd say we're in our second battl--whoa, here we go." Delores picked up a two-way microphone-radio. "Fire at will. Green light. Mark intruders as: 12° off rock face 1; 14° off rock face 2. Sectors Beta-Zebra and Gamma-Zebra. Green light, all hands. I say again, green light."

Jennifer heard the reports of small and large arms now. It was staccato. Later she realized it was advanced automatic weapons fire.

"Commander. Torpedoes approaching cave entrance. ETA forty-seven seconds."

"Launch decoys front range 8:00, 10:00, 1:00."

"Aye Commander. Copy that. Launching. 33 seconds. Torpedoes following decoys. Twelve seconds."

Jennifer prepared herself. The explosion shook the walls, but not much else appeared.

"Foxworth. Command to gunners on six inch. Open fire with range, azimuth calculated. Damn it woman, now. Here, this one."

"Aye, Commander. Calibrated. We have a lock."

"Open fire. I say again. Lock in. Fire. Fire. Fire."

Above her Jennifer heard the roar of large canon. There was a pause. A strange eerie silence.

"They're retreating. Dingy mission retreating. Enemy vessel retreating."

"Monitor a while, then stand from battle station status. Maintain high alert status."

"Aye Commander."

"That includes double watch tonight. Full night vision gear and automatic weapons locked and loaded."

"Copy that."

"Well, Ms. Littleton, it appears we have surprised them again, once again being better prepared than they thought."

"But who--"

She stopped because they all knew who it was.

"Communications."

"Aye Captain."

"Send signal, code alpha Bravo to CINCPAC. Request Dallas or Nebraska class ship to accompany Ex-Gee to DC safe fathom. Report second attack encountered and repelled. Request additional SEAL team and ANS ASAP."

"Copy that. Encoding. Crypto ESI complete. Transmission complete. Received. Awaiting reply."

"I'll be in my quarters."

Jennifer realized she didn't know where Susan was. She needed to tell her she would now have a US Navy submarine watch over her on the way down. She began to look for her. She was not in their room. Not in the galley. She turned a corner off the bunk rooms. There, at the end, she saw her. She stood waiting, as if in anticipation. Hodges appeared, in battle array, his weapon cradled in his arms.

The man and the woman saw each other. She stood his weapon against the wall. He was hot, flush with victory in yet another battle, as men since before the time of history had returned to their woman with the blood of killing upon them, and the blood of the joy of victory coursing through their veins. As the woman had always done in this dance of death and sex, two human experiences that were somehow oddly connected, she was suddenly in his huge arms, this slight, perhaps frail woman. Their lips met, hard and deep and sweet. Jennifer couldn't help herself; she felt enthralled. She stared, as one who is offended by his or her own voyeuristic behavior, but, compelled, cannot turn away. They kissed a long time. The scientist allowed the soldier to let her hair down, wavy below her shoulders. They kissed again, perhaps even more passionate than before. Then Hodges pulled her into a small day room off the bunk row, and closed the door. Jennifer turned away. She returned to the control center.

# 5

---

## UNDERTIDE

This the day! It came! The Ex-Gee had been gone over thoroughly. Jennifer and Susan, along with some engineers from the Nebraska thought they had resolved the pressure differential problem. The odd design of the outer wing surface and the inner hull of tiles and spent uranium could establish the difference in pressure within the heat of the vents, but in the depths of the sea, the pounds per square inch made uneven distribution on one frame or the other. Some adjustments in distance might bring it more within tolerance it was thought. Jennifer worried. She would not be aboard the ship. The last several hours, she was like a mother hen, giving redundant suggestions to her crew, who grew impatient, then intolerant.

For a while Susan's nervousness was obvious to all. She wanted to get going. Every day's, even every hour's, delay meant the possibility of the vent's aperture narrowing, or perhaps in one traumatic gasp of energy, closing altogether. Lately she had the anxiety-arousing thought that their faceless enemy might torpedo it; wait, what did Hodges say? No torpedo at that depth can possibly . . .? Sill, some device could be brought to bear to close it to scientific investigation.

The old battle between scientist and military officer reared its ugly head. But Delores had a platoon behind her now, and it was clear they would await the arrival of the fleet's submarine. Jennifer and Susan realized, this time with resignation, the thing clearly was out of their hands. The government was spending considerable resources, and must consider this even more valuable than they thought.

The Nebraska arrived. She slipped deep at night. One moment the sea was calm, the next a rippling smooth splitting of water, and a giant grey shadow loomed over them. Jennifer thought of Moses holding his staff out over the Sea of Reeds and the waters dwindling. Jennifer didn't realize how huge submarines were. The slipped water cascaded down the concave side of the gargantuan tableau as if a waterfall in the mountain had suddenly appeared. Jennifer had the strange thought it looked like one of Susan's bizarre creatures. Perhaps our collective anachronistic subconscious heralded back in time further than ever we thought. The coning tower reached above the cave entrances by half. They must stay partially submerged in the caves, she thought. Later, toward dawn, she took a quick tour, then stayed on board when the ship submerged for most of the daylight hours.

Another day's wait. Susan was getting even more nervous. The military strategists wanted to cover as many possibilities or probabilities as possible during the operation. The Captain of the Nebraska was informed of the underwater, surface, and port battles. Charts, graphs, data bases, undersea plots, surface and depth charge attributes, satellite imaging, ultra-sound undersea mapping imagery, weapons check, and procedures review--all were laid out for any eventuality.

Jennifer noted that, in the afternoons, when briefings were at a minimum, Susan and Hodges were not to be found.

Then, on the third night following the Nebraska's arrival, Delores and Captain Coralis, Commander of the huge submarine, called them in.

"Dr. Arthknott. Ms. Littleton. We believe we're ready. We're going vent exploring in T-six hours. Prepare your vessel."

# 6

## VENTIDE

She drifted out of the cool wet chamber, the new one. She drifted into the fire chamber, the red hissing chamber, the old one. Millennia beyond eras, eras beyond eons, past a time lost in time's memory had she drifted in her fashion. Through channels she had known which erupted at the beginning of time, and through channels she had not known as new channels exploded open. Known meant nothing or meant little. Little anatomical or physiological pre-primitive conglomeration of cells to produce cognition, an awareness existed; it was only a growing near-awareness and even that had taken her endless eons to develop.

Still, whatever it was, however its primitive sentience was there now and to whatever extent she knew or almost knew, sensed or almost sensed, the new near-feelings grew stronger. There was almost an awareness that something occurred beyond. There had been a rush through a chamber, rendering it the cool chamber, the new wet one, a stream, then, suddenly a flow stronger than before.

She drifted. She flowed. She undulated. She floated on fire. She was. She is. She will be. Time, as always, passed not for it meant nothing. Its spectrums existed only as non-existent. She waited. She waited as she had waited through the meaninglessness of the absence of time for so long time was lost and beyond itself.

# 7

## SUBTIDE

The Nebraska is top of the line above D-class, modification Delta Prime. Commissioned and launched between 1993 and 1995, she holds dimension of 560 feet, stem to stern, and bloats a hull diameter of 42 feet. Although the exact dimension concerning bridge height is classified, it is known from observation that the coning tower rises about 36 feet above the outer deck.

She boasts armament in sufficient quantity that, by herself, she could effectively demolish and eliminate more than three aggressor nation states, including Russia, China, and, say, Iraq or Iran: Twenty-four Trident MRV undersea launched ICBMs, each of the MIRV warheads capable of 1 to 5 megaton destruction; how many RVs rest upon each missile is classified; it is estimated to be between 3 and 5. She can launch underwater projectiles with ultra-sound computer lock-link guidance from 4 torpedo tubes, 2 to port, 2 to starboard. Albeit classified, each tube typically can store and fire at will 10-12 torpedoes. It is rumored some of these carry small nuclear warheads. It is rumored that there are oblique port and starboard, and multiple rear, launching tubes as well; however, this is denied by the Navy and the shipbuilder. There is no question, however, that she can launch, from stem or stern, decoy projectiles and aluminum sensing foils, chaff material, to fool enemy projectiles headed toward her in a hostile ballistic. She also has surface weaponry including a six inch laser guided cannon, and a computer lock-in 50mm Gatling gun, capable of 300 rounds a minute.

She contains Top Secret quiet machinery with stealth design for low detection profile above or beneath the water, and the most advance long range sonar to detect friendly or hostile forces. There is a Top Secret ESI (Extra Sensitive Information) space as yet unknown in its capacity or equipment.

In terms of survivability, one thought about the unknown space is an escape pod sub within the sub with about nearly half weapons systems capability, and undersea communications low frequency sufficient to command and direct the compliment of missiles and other weapons remaining on the damaged and abandoned mother ship.

There is another thought concerning the mysterious space. It is a concept growing in favor from professional and amateur military sleuths; the Navy has not denied it, as it has other suppositions. To appreciate the proposition, it is necessary to understand that since the beginning of World War II, the extended safe depth of all submersibles, excepting special deep-water designs such as the EX-GEE, is somewhere around 2,000 feet. This is especially true of a warhead projectile, that is, underwater torpedoes. Typically, they are designed to operate in shallow waters, so that more weight may be advanced upon the propulsion, guidance, and explosive systems. In this fashion, the Navy's Mark 46-50 series has operated in design and function quite successfully since the Vietnam War. The Mark 55,if this supposition is correct, revealed here for the first time, is a Deep Sea Encapsulated Launch Self Propelled Guided Projectile From Deep Sea ASRoc (Anti-Sub Launched Rocket), that is, from a deep submerged weighted free-floating sensor platform that releases the projectile (in essence, a deep-bell encapsulated pressurized chamber with a computer brain, searching through its comparative data bases of hostile audio vibrations, when hostile audio contact is detected, establishing a comparison, and, when a not gate fail command is offered to it, assured of recognition of aggression, thereby initiating a launch sequence command). Fully declassified since the end of World War II, yet not significantly known by the public is the alternating code sequence designed by Hedy Lamarr, actress and brilliant mathematician.

Now, to reduce it simply, in essence: A deeply submerged highly technologically advanced robot, with an unknown compliment of projectiles; if an enemy submersible is detected within its range, it compares the vibrations of the water displacement with its data base; it identifies it as friendly or hostile; if hostile, it reviews a set of parameters, as speed, direction, course, permutations and combination probability analogs of intent under prescribed and proscribed circumstances; it prepares to launch one or more projectiles; a signal from a friendly submerged or surface vessel may and commonly would offer a not-launch command, effectively shutting down its launch sequence. Of course, there must be further fail-safe measures, but no supposition by the authorities concerning them as yet exists. Presumably, there is some sort of additional recognized hostile intent by the data bases, but this is mere speculation in this romance.

If this is true in whole or in part, as in all things, for the advantages gained, there are losses: Surely, the range, speed, and explosive level of the warhead must all be less than a standard "surface" torpedo.

Therefore, again as an extrapolated guess, thus, since the MARK 46-50 series torpedoes typically average lengths of 22 feet, the DS55 (Deep-Sea) may be as short as 5 to 7 feet; MARK 46-50 series typically weigh in at about 3,600 pounds, the DS55 may be reduced to 600 pounds (400 pounds for its own self-contained encapsulation protection at depths below 3,000 feet; 100 pounds for guidance and improved MARK series pump-jet rocket propulsion system; 100 pounds for the warhead). The MARK series warhead explodes at standard depth at least 650 pounds of explosive; the DS55 probably less than 300. An average speed for the MARK series is 32 mph, with a range of 5 to 8 miles; here, the lighter weight of the DS55 would compensate for the deep-sea expressed difficulties to some extent, allowing it to remain close in speed; nonetheless, at the huge pressures exerted upon the object at extreme depth, speed and range would be reduced, perhaps to 20 mph or less for one-quarter mile to one-half mile at the outside before depth pressure implosion, despite all encapsulation design. Standard diameter of the MARK series is 21 inches; suggested diameter for the DS55 is about half that. Again all not much more than mere speculation and extrapolation guesswork.

No dimensions for the launching platform brain are suggested. It is probably safe to suggest the size of the ALVIN class deep-sea submersibles, including living space and air pressure for temporary visits by human technicians. A connecting portal to allow their own deep-sea submersible "tunnel" exchange access would be a necessary design modality.

Return now to the mother ship: The Nebraska boasts an officer crew of 16, and enlisted crew of 157. There are 2 crews, gold and blue. Depending on the ship's mission, they will each tour out to sea 3 to 6 months at a time.

She is so far advanced in design survivability, maintainability, and reliability, she knows no peer in any ocean submerging weapons system. She was once rumored to have been seen by unidentified fishermen in the Black Sea, home of the major fleet of Russia. It has been rumored she discovered (or created) an undersea passage channel between the Persian Gulf and the Red Sea. These accounts, of course, seem the stuff of legend; however, it is known she broke all records passing under the ice caps of the North Pole.

She is, along with the fleets' aircraft carriers, the strongest and mightiest arm of American military might and political will in oceans off the eastern shore. Now, in a mission classified TS-ESI, she found herself in the less familiar western sea.

Even so, it was not the first time. Several times on secret missions she had slipped in at night to Standhope; recharged and refitted, undetected by any enemy's spy satellite, she slipped out again at night, traveling by surface for good fresh air, then diving before dawn. Her crew's compliment were well trained and competent. They respected Captain Corales. He respected them. The men and women who serve for short tours of duty or for careers in the U.S. Armed Forces truly guard and keep the freedoms all Americans and much of the free world. Heroes and heroines all, they deserve much more than this brief moment of entitled salute. But we take this moment to salute them, and to thank them, every one.

Night fell upon the western regions of the planet. Like a stone placed upon a lily pad on a pond deep in the woods, the tubule shaped dark craft slipped her surly mooring bonds. Purring with less sound than any submarine or ship before her, slowly, imperceptibly, she united with the waters; she became one with the ocean beneath the waves. Her advance sonar revealed the target at once. Another submersible, much smaller, about 40 feet in length with an odd signature. This one, too, had slipped out of the cave of Standhope about a half hour earlier, to go the place she had been designed to go, where no other ship could go, although there were now some doubts about that. The screens also revealed another vessel, one above the surface.

Corales ordered up scope. The refit hydraulic gears lifted the optical array, much more sensitive and complex, with digital computer imaging enhancement and distance reckoning, than even four years ago, above the surface of the waters. The lights of the Starr were quite visible. An enemy sub could bring her down easy, with one shot.

"Sonar, any other vessel signature?"

"Negative, Captain. Only our large friend above and small friend below."

"X0. Full sweep, wide range throughout."

"Full sweep, wide range throughout."

"Full sweep wide range, aye."

"X0. Stay with the EX-Gee 500 feet till she goes extreme deep."

"Five hundred feet, aye."

Like a mother whale letting her child try some independence the Ex-Gee cut through the deep mystery of the sea followed above and behind by the huge underwater ship.

On the Starr, Jennifer monitored her instruments on the central berth on ship's bridge. With Delores below in the Ex-Gee, Wells guided the old destroyer and occasionally barked orders. It was night, deep night, and that helped. Jennifer always felt better at night. Her mother had always told her she was nocturnal. "At night, darling, you seem one with the universe," her mother once said.

Deep at night, as she slept or if she were out on city streets or at sea, the anxiety of life, so harsh by light of day, disappeared into the deep reaches of heavens, the twinkles of stars, the vastness of space, and night witchery. Gazing from the vast sea to the even more vast firmament of the heavenly spheres, she could feel that she might not be noticed only for her beauty or, later, her intellect. But for just being, for the profound gift of being a creature aware of being a creature, for having a sense that there was meaning and purpose though it would always remain a mystery and even knowing that it was a mystery, an enigma within a riddle with no solution and always just beyond our ken, a conundrum really, aye, even that made it worthwhile.

"Approaching the coordinates, Ms. Littleton," Wells said.

Was there an edginess in his voice; did she still, after all this, seem distrustful? Was it something else, something she could not penetrate, but seemed to bother her as just out of reach, like a fly buzzing inside one's house, deep in the month of July, the insect nearly spent, but still avoiding the final blow, still bringing annoyance. Increasingly, he seemed aloof. More than once now, she found him in hushed conversation, hunched over with that Foxworth woman at her console. Was it her imagination, or did they fiddle with something quickly when she approached? She had a fleeting thought that they--but Foxworth was a trained SEAL, and Wells had been with Delores from the get-go, hadn't he? From the get-go. She had a thought dancing about her mind. She couldn't quite capture it. Then, she almost had it . . .

"Ms. Littleton. The coordinates in one."

"Copy that." She was fully accustomed to the military formal communications line now. She appreciated it. It made things clear. Precise.

"They'll be heading deep soon. Umbilical's will detach at 1,500 fathoms. They'll be on their own then. Except as far as our large friend can follow and determine.

"Stella Alpha to Ex-Gee Bravo. Do you copy? Over."

At first there was static. Then Susan's scientist-teacher's voice came through 4 X 5. And yet not exactly. A different voice for her somehow. More, no, less arrogant, yet more precise somehow. "Stella Alpha. This is Ex-Gee Bravo. Copy. We are away procedures for deep descent Over."

"Copy that. Procedures for deep descent commencing. Firebrands ahead. Good luck and Godspeed."

"Copy that. See you on the surface in an hour or two."

"Copy that." Now static.

Jennifer watched the blip on her screen fall away, until the ocean's tides were so deep, even the blip shimmered, grew steady for one last spark, dissipated, shimmered-sparked again, then disappeared.

Susan sat to the left, looking at the monitors which showed the front facsimile pictures. They were X-ray and thermal videos; the visual cameras would not be unsealed until within the channels. Magruder sat to the right. Delores sat between them, monitoring a redundancy of each of their console, video, and computer screen displays. Hodges sat below, from the rear gazing at the wide scan near display. He also had a redundancy of the front display, for he also was in charge of all weapons systems.

They had learned three on bridge deck could handle much of what needed to be accomplished. After some reconfiguration at Standhope, including considerable heated disputation into wee hours, they determined the crew of four could be quite sufficient with some quick cross-training and on the spot ops modification. It would lighten the weight of the vessel and might re-calibrate its speed and maneuverability fourteen per cent faster response. Certainly it would conserve fuel, and, with the unscheduled first trip behind them, a commodity most valuable. Unsaid was it was one less person to risk.

The four monitored their consoles. Delores and Susan had developed a truce of sorts. Delores would be in charge for the submersion to target; once in, Susan would direct the ship. It was thought they had a better chance if each person's knowledge and training were used to best effect.

Susan for now ran diagnostic checks. Her thermal readings, spectral analysis, and X-ray readings would be more important as they entered the undersea and under-the-sea bottom world, as she had begun to call it. Delores and Magruder monitored current pressure, hydraulics, guidance, and memory for each of these, especially, now, the arc of the curve sine descent.

"Pressure gauge edging toward yellow, Commander."

"Steady as she goes. Arc line of descent?"

Hodges monitored this from his console. He watched his blue line and green line. To a casual observer they appeared synchronous. To a seasoned eye like Hodges's, there could be the beginning of a problem. "Point Oh-five three per cent co-sine left of projection and memory. Within parameters."

"Copy that. Within parameters. Continue descent, Mr. Magruder."

"Aye-aye, Captain."

"Capt--Mr. Wells."

"Proceed, Mr. Foxworth."

"Losing signal. Descent may be off point five degrees. Pressure gauge ris--damn. Lost her. She's on her own."

Jennifer felt her right foot begin to shake in that damn uncontrollable busy leg syndrome, which usually afflicted older persons, but which she had endured for as long as she could remember. And if it were so bad now, what would happen to her when she was old? The sick irony of it. She was not the one with the palsied disease, but she was the one who the whole world could watch her big foot quiver.

That damn pressure problem. Maybe they should abort. How could she communicate that now? Besides she knew Susan, Delores, Hodges. They'd carry it through at this point even if it were getting too close for comfort. She wondered if the Nebraska still had them. And she could still pick up the Nebraska. For an instant she thought she caught another image on her screen; then, as quickly, it disappeared. "Mr. Wells."

"Aye, Ms. Littleton?"

"I, I, never mind. I thought I--never mind."

"All hands. Carry on," the XO said.

"Bridge."

"Bridge aye."

"Sonar."

"Report."

"She appears to have a five point five per cent drift to leeward. Still within parameters, however.

"Say again sonar."

"Copy that X0. She is one deep down ship."

"Copy that."

"Sonar, bridge. Understood. Maintain constant surveil. Report changes."

"Changes, aye."

Corvales ordered down scope. "Proceed to maximum depth. X0. I want to keep as close to her as possible."

"Max depth, aye. Proceed to max depth, all hands. Max depth approaching in seven minutes, my mark. Mark."

"ETA drop zone at this time."

"She should be at the entrance to the vent in twenty-two minutes on my mark. XO mark."

"Roger that. All hands. We are descending to maximum depth. Monitor all equipment, quarters, bulkheads. Maintain stations. Report anomalies. Captain out."

The two submersibles in different planes of existence, cut unseen through the deep hidden world of water at the heart of the planet's living system.

The Ex-Gee plumbed the depths of the planet's deepest valley, 9 miles down from sea level, deeper than the 28,000 feet Mt. Everest rose above the land. Already fantastic albeit familiar creatures appeared on their thermal view screen. Susan voiced astonishment at seeing a large sea anemone swirling, shaking, rocking back and forth, its outer frills swishing in an ancient swirling depth-rite. How could it be so far out from the shelf, so deep? Did they come this far, this deep to escape their predators? Surely this was an aberration, or a new species undiscovered until now. Then she saw others and then the reason. Susan had never seen a starfish swim before. Usually they maneuvered the suckers of their feet across the continental shelf floor or inland bays. But here, somewhere in front of them, about 75 feet she would say, were giant versions of these common yet unfamiliar and bizarre creatures in a depth of sea dance of victim and predator. She checked her instruments. Yes, good. The auto recorder had come on. She would have yet another paper. She began yet another lecture in new discoveries in marine biology at deep ocean environment. After a while, she was interrupted by Magruder, answered by Delores. This time, she didn't mind.

"Captain, navigator."

"I see it, Mr. Magruder. Weapons."

"Weapons, aye. I have it," Hodges said.

"Thermal readings appear to have signature," Susan said. "Run calibration against memory to verify."

"No question, Susan," Delores said. It was one of the few times she called her by her given name. It's the ridge. Those thermal and X-ray readings are in the red line and we're still twelve miles out. It's the vent and it's still huge. Navigator."

"Navigator, aye."

"ETA."

"ETA, aye. Seventeen minutes thirty seconds.

"My God. Look at the size of it."

"And it's smaller than last year," Susan said. "Here, compare with this overlay. Video and readings from the Alvin and deep ROL."

"Weapons. Navigator. Calculate feasibility of mission intent."

"Calculated Captain. Within parameters. She'll fit in with a little room to spare.

"Susan."

"Delores."

"We're on our way. Into the very bowel-pits of the earth.

God help us. If She can find us in hell."

"X0. Sonar."

"Sonar aye."

"X0. Sonar. Picking up a second signature at . . . delay that. Disappeared."

"Sonar, this is the Captain. What's happening?"

"Captain. Chief of the Boat."

"Chief of the Boat, aye."

"Maximum depth. I say again: Max depth attained at this time."

"Copy that. Max depth. All hands, this is the Captain. We have attained maximum designed spec depth. Steady all hands. We're going to be here awhile. Air may get a little stale. All hands monitor bulkheads for pressure variations. Sonar. Captain.

"Captain. Sonar aye. I believe I have the signature of the vent."

"Bring it up to the bridge, sonar."

"Sonar to bridge aye. Printing out now." Joshua Tree, Sonar, from Nashville, Tennessee: he wondered if he should return to the harmonic pattern where he saw or thought he saw the other ship. The captain should see that too. But he wanted this right away. He'd run it again when he returned to station. It bothered him; but it was only later he realized something out there was throwing a harmonic divergence pattern. He had a program for countering the divergence pattern. But he had to realize that that was what it was. It would almost be too late before it occurred to him.

The Ex-Gee continued to the lowest depth any human occupied submersible had been. Even the Alvin and the ship on its previous adventure had not come so deep for so long and so close to where the interior of the earth belched its magnum generated substances into its higher realms. Now the waters were fully black, blacker than black, for no sun's rays could penetrate this distance. Only the burning, churning, bubbling brimstone cloud gave heat and thus some illumination, as though flashlights and torches diffused through a cold dark night of wet and fog.

"Commander. Pressure gauge in high end of yellow scale. Point one off red. It's too deep, Commander."

"Specs and ops systems check. We've come too far down, Dr. Arthknott. It's time to consider an abort."

"She'll alleviate, Commander Delores."

"Do you hear the bulkheads moaning, groaning? The bolts will start flying off soon. Now say again, Dr. Arthknott."

Susan noticed the two women were on formal terms again. "I say again she'll alleviate once we're in. That's the concept."

"Concept. I'm responsible for three other lives."

"As am I. We've come too far." Later, as the story was told Jennifer realized she was the only one who understood the gallows play on words. Too far to abort, not to abort. She aborts, she aborts not, she abor--only there were no flower petals down there. A fathom too far, this way, that way.

"Systems check complete. Within parameters."

"Pressure," Delores said.

"Climbing, Magruder said."

Susan looked at her instruments, at the electronic and thermal imaging. She was still adamant. "We can't turn back now. Look at those visual readings. It's exploding with manganese, silicon, and sulfuric life. Sending out robots at this time."

"Wait. I'll, dammit, Arthknott."

"Robots away," Magruder said. "Entering vents. Telemetry and visuals coming in. My God. Look at that."

"It's alive! It's alive! It teems with life," Delores said.

"It is so beautiful," Susan said.

"That's it. Camera's gone," Hodges said. "They lasted fourteen seconds."

"So beautiful."

"X0. Sonar."

"Sonar, aye. These readings are amazing. The thing must be 110 yards long and 60 wide."

"Like a football field."

"Bridge, Sonar."

"Sonar, X0, aye."

"X0. New signatures, two smaller signatures entering the target.

"The robots. Understood, Sonar. Any others, wide range scan?"

"Aye sir. Tuned on multi-phase oblique bounce sequence return."

"Report, Sonar."

"There's a submersible behind the highest rock formation on grid, mark eighteen degrees left, elevation at vent level, twenty meters. Sonar to X0."

"Copy that. Weapons. Dispatch missile capsule array, laser sight, at Sonar's coordinates. At will. We can't fire; not with the Ex-Gee close and going in. But we can rattle their cage."

"Weapons. Missile capsule array Sonar's coordinates aye. Coming up, X0. Capsule array away, I say again, capsule array away."

"ETA."

"On self-propelled. Memory guidance lock in effect. ETA on my mark, eleven minutes."

"Damn. It'll be too late."

" Depth encapsulated Torpedo?"

"Negative. We blow the Ex-Gee out. Or in, destroy the whole works." Corvales paused. He pondered the moment. All hands were silent. On the bridge they looked at him. The air was heavy within as the sea without. "Weapons."

"Weapons aye."

"Send out torpedo decoys."

"Captain."

"I think they'll have some good sonar. We only picked them up from our harmonic bounce. They know what they're doing, whoever they are. But I'm gambling they can't yet distinguish between the fake fish and the real thing. I'm hoping they'll think six torpedoes are heading their way. It may give the Ex-Gee the time she needs."

"X0. Weapons."

"Weapons, X0. Set coordinates to follow the capsule array. Launch six decoys. At will."

"Weapons aye. Coordinates programmed in memory lock. Guidance affirm. Decoys away."

"Copy that. Maintain all stations. All hands. Steady as she goes."

Down into the open pit of the lower realms, their arcs defining the helix-shape they sought, descended the man-made object. Far beyond time, in this flaming arena materials and marvels that developed helix shaped proteins yearned for air and water, prepared to utilize these elementals even prior to encountering them in the space of the swirling primeval soup covering the rocks and channels that was the womb-birth of their creations. Countless eons later they had combined within the watery swamps' realms and the most powerful force in the universe was unleashed. Spreading like the wildfire from whence they had their genesis, it combined and grew and became hundreds, thousands, millions, teeming minions, until so great its power some of its progeny grew sentience and awareness. Endlessness passed yet again. So far removed from their fire origins, they could no longer withstand heat and magma, expanding their metabolic process into anabolic and non-confining physiologies, great rocks from beyond the planet hurled into the seas and mantles, destroying their delicate margin of life. Again and again, when time itself was ripped out from its fabric-semblance of form, the life of carbon and oxygen entities waxed and waned. Now great numbers of species of extraordinary diversity engorged into existence and disappeared into oblivion. Still sentience increased.

For the first time since that so far long ago time of molecular burst of birth, the fragile descendants, as removed from the birthing place as time itself floated in their encapsulated object of their own creation poised to return at last. The pre-diluvian fire-cracks in creation itself had, as it must, produced life as it attracted life. Now, life's offspring, earth's children, the inheritors of dominion of the planet and its diversified forms, faced death straight in the eye, preparing to spit in its inflamed retina. Besides this journey now into the unwelcome, hostile warmth of the pre-womb, the only place left for this inheritor of the world to go, this last great species that seemed to grow smarter but not wiser with each century and decade it measured of its own accord, visited or would visit soon the distant black cold oceans of space from which the hurtling rocks of death and destruction and rebirth had come and were probably still coming. Some day.

Co-sine angles and polar coordinate curves had been measured. Now Magruder guided the small ship into the breech, as a bullet following a laser sight. Susan let him know if the angles were too severe. They calculated in haste. They adapted. Their machines calculated and adapted. Delores fairly screamed when the pressure entered the red zone. She wanted to abort. Magruder mentioned that were he to abort the angle margins, the stress could disintegrate the ship. Then, of a sudden, while the argument hinged on whether to pull out at the next valley of the curve, Hodges saw it.

"Commander, weapons. Rear recon measure. We've got a bogey visitor. Signature--Stand by. Coming in. Memory compare—Damn! It's our old friend. Damn! He's closing. ETA two minutes. How? Calibrating ascent-descent ratios. Damn! He must have hidden behind the high rocks on the leeward side.

"Carstairs. Fucking bastard."

"Susan. Focus. Can we target rear torpedoes?"

"Bastard."

"Dr. Arthknott. Damn it! Hodges, damn it!"

"Copy rear targeting torpedoes. It's affirm. Locking now. Battery activated. Guidance activated. Come on. Come on. Locked! Fuck! We're lit. He's locked on to us. Wait. He stood down."

"Angle of intent we passed the last curve value. He'd blow us into the hole and destroy it. That's not what he wants," Magruder said.

Susan had a brief flash of thought. But she never finished her sentence, and the thought died too. "How did you know what he wa--"

"He's coming around. Calibrating. I think he means to paint us, off and on and follow our descent angle."

"We're entering the threshold. There's no turning back now. My God. Look at those readings. Watch out. She's banking."

"Stabilize. Compensate. Draw wings in ten degrees."

"Copy that. It's too violent. We'll crash into the threshold rocks."

"Fire verniers alternative side. Damn, what is--port. Fire port verniers. Three seconds. Auto pilot design alpha huron. Now dammit!" Susan screamed to Magruder.

"She's turned in. Turned in."

"Aggressor ship aborted. She turned about. But that's impossible!"

"Steady now. Steady as she goes. What is it Hodges?"

They could barely hear themselves speak, the violence of the turbulence was so huge. And something else. A great knocking in all patterns of the hulls, as if fire itself was attempting to bang its way into the capsule.

"Heat index rising. 90°; 105°; 109°."

"You don't say."

"Torpedoes coming at them. That's why she turned," Hodges said."

"Impossible," Magruder said.

"Unless," Hodges said. "Unless the Nebraska launched—"

Then, all images disappeared from Hodges's screen. He turned. All he could see were his three shipmates ensconced and illuminated upon their skins a great glowing red-yellow, as if they were embers in the midst of roaring flames. He was reminded of Mather's sermons, in which he always called himself an ember plucked from the flames, for indeed he had been rescued as a child from a burning house. But the analogy, he realized at once, was false. We four, he suddenly knew, were dry fuel cast into the fires of hell itself.

Hodges wondered, as he had from the beginning, if there really was any way out.

It was as if the mystical essence of the spirit of the living flames incarnate glowed and glimmered upon what they imagined still to be their flesh.

They yelled. They screamed. They screamed over the screeching roar of a horror they had each attempted to envision but had not possibly imagined. They could barely hold their bodies in one place, and even less assuredly the ship. Somehow they discerned that the vernier on the port side could compensate and grant them passage through the threshold. The ion pulse had silently, efficiently flowed into effect, seemingly unconcerned about the fire-heat. Later they would realize time and again it was this device that had saved them.

They knew they headed down; or down and up were suddenly the same. They felt they were rising. Alternatively as they slipped the bonds of ocean's amniotic sac, they felt they rose up; they felt they descended. Then, suddenly, as a spelunker snakes through the initial opening up, down, and around rock, then fairly falls into an open cavern, they knew they were through. The bubbling reduced. The screech-floom of flame metamorphosed into a low muffled roar.

The ship's navigation still somehow worked.

"Susan. Commander."

"Weapons."

"Negative. At 115° and rising. 116. 118 . . ." He knew they knew it. Who could not feel sick and dying with such heat?

"Increase compressor."

"She's in the red zone now."

"Delores. Damn it. Just do what I say this once. For the love of God, if God be down here, burn the fucking thing out. We'll flame up inside ourselves."

"My God. Look at our pictures. The lateral aux back-up cameras are still working. That extra shielding . . . "

They gazed at their main screens. Red-yellow hues all about them danced, a pattern of fire and bubbles of flame never witnessed by eyes capable of comprehending.

"It's the world as she was, the planet at the time of its creation. We're in the middle of the beginning of the universe," Susan said.

The ship shook. The ship quivered. Minions of white floating snow-like objects passed before them. Minions of red tubules against the yellow and blue fire red line flashed-swirled about them. Bubbles of steam within fire, a pillar of fire cloud carried them up, or to the side or down, for they were no longer certain.

Susan continued. "Life forms all. Manganese. Sulfur. Compounds of living rock rising out to the waters to live and change. See. See! Observe! They form bonds. They, they, wait a minute, wait, yes, look, helter-skelter, they hook, they link. There! See how that part cuts in, how it cleaves the weak bond, then bounds up both loose ends. My God! The top section cuts loose, slides along the binding edge, and inserts further down. Transposon activity at the very heart of creation! Real-time evolution even before there's anything to evolve. Don't you see? Don't you see it? It's so obvious now. It was part of the original design!"

Delores and Magruder looked at her. Her eyes were aflame, impossibly brighter than the brightest flame without. Their lungs breathed in searing heat. All panted like dogs on an August Mississippi farm.

"One hundred twenty-one degrees. Sweet Jesus's Mary. One hundred twenty-four. My God. My God. I can't breathe. Can't feel my flesh."

"My skin is no longer skin. It's fluid, a running river of flesh, I . . ."

"We're losing all our water weight. We'll start dying from dehydration in another minute or two. Drink. Drink. Drink. We're got to get out or . . ."

"Verniers ion left 137°, my mark. Now dammit!"

"Susan. We've got to back out on our memory arc line trajectory."

"There's no time for that. Do you want a chance at life? Mark! Mark! Mark! Now! Now!"

Somehow Hodges turned. Sweat poured over, drenched his eyes and ears like huge steady sheets of an all-day rain. Before he passed out, he managed to program in the coordinates and the rocket flowed. His last thought: He hoped the outer hull at the rocket propulsion chamber exit hadn't melted fully. He prayed. He passed out.

He thought he might be able to open his eyes. He tried. His lids stuck together, as though glue had been poured between them. He rested. Perhaps he should try again. At last his lids parted, with a strange squeak. Once more he saw.

Susan bent over him. She hooked up his IV for hydration. He did not feel the vein prick. He wondered why. Soon he would figure out they were no longer on earth. That was why he did not feel the vein prick.

The ship floated in a lolling, rocking motion. Calm. Peaceful. At one and at peace with the world. He felt cooler. Susan's hair frizzled down, matted and somehow loose at the same time. She had removed her clothes but for her sleeveless T-shirt and skivies. When she leaned over him, her breasts swayed in a similar motion as the ship. She was charming.

God, he was lost in the body and mind of a mad scientist. He looked down.

She had removed his clothes as well.

Diffused white lights formed red-yellow halos defining gem-shine circlets about her mated, frizzed, and hanging loose hair all about her head. She looked so beautiful. If only he could move. He found he could not.

He thought: This must be heaven. All the talk about coming back or meeting with loved ones, it was all so much talk, nonsense. Obviously he now knew one was stuck with the people one was last with. That was it. Of course, he hadn't been in heaven long. Perhaps people could visit one another in their assigned capsules or pods. Well, it didn't matter. After all it would not be so bad to be with Susan for eternity. Even eternity and time and infinity itself had to have transference to nothingness. He was suddenly pleased with himself. Being with Susan had made the books he read and had been confused about make sense. She had a way of explaining things to him that clarified it all somehow. Was there any other couple in the world whose languid pillow talk concerned the truth and projections of science? But if he was in heaven, why did he need an IV? He understood. In heaven, they needed to start out a person with something a man or woman was familiar with. Then they eased you into it. That was it.

"You're my angel, I guess."

"Sorry to disappoint you. And pardon my French, but our asses ain't quite cooked yet. Look out the window."

"Window? How in --" Hodges sat up, a tiny incline. A thick, black-gray dead weight, like lead, pressed deep into his mind. He fell back in his chair.

"I can't."

"Give it a minute. Let some more of this drip filter into your veins, arteries, capillaries, to bathe the cells." That's it. You're doing fine. Tough guy."

She removed her shirt. Her perfectly formed breasts that no one else knew about glistened and seemed to regenerate a life of their own. The ugly duckling transformed into the beautiful swan, he thought. His swan. His intelligent, beautiful swan. But it was useless, hopeless. All they could do as lovers now was die together. When it came down to it, maybe that wouldn't be so bad after all. Maybe it was time. The truth was, he had already enjoyed his share of narrow escapes. Yet one more seemed unlikely. Still, one thing he had learned; there was always a chance, and a man or a woman had to take it or surely die.

She wiped his brow. He thought of his mother wiping his brow in a memory so long ago distant and until now lost, he had not thought of it again until this moment. Susan, like his mother so long ago squeezing the cloth, the drops dripping back into the bucket, squeezed her shirt. Wetter than before she somehow managed to put it back on. She now left nothing to anyone's imagination. How could no one else have seen how beautiful the woman was, hiding it all these years?

"Susan. There's some things I need to say. We--"

"Shh." She put her fingers on his lips. "There'll be time. Up there. On the surface. Here. Try again. Let me help."

The first woman to realize he wasn't just a dumb hulk. Maybe he was feeling better after all; for he allowed his thoughts to tell himself a silly little joke. The woman was intelligent in more than one way. The private self-joke elicited a slight smile. Yes, he improved. Already he could feel some of his strength, his power, as he had referred to it for a while, return.

"Well, a little smile. I think you can make it up now."

He sat up. He turned. He found he could fight off most of the blackness in his mind. He looked up. Susan had opened the Plexiglas sheath. Cool ocean water swirled about them, bubbling gently. Beyond, it stretched toward a horizon, channeling and churning into steam. He turned to the pressure and temperature gauges. Pressure gauge in yellow, closer back to green; temperature gauge read ninety-one. Still hot, but now tolerable, yes, very much better. She wiped his brow again.

There was at last a hint of coolness in the cloth, an essence of heart-felt coolness and comfort only women's hands can provide. It was an odd thought: He knew he was about to die, he felt about the worst he had ever felt, and he was suddenly happier than ever had he been in his life, so full of joy he thought his heart would burst, and not from the hostile environment.

"We made it back? No. I've never seen anything like that."

"No. No one has. Until now. The horizon edge, the event horizon of water and fire. We're still down in it. Got a long way to go. And only twenty-six minutes to figure something out."

Hodges glanced over at the oxygen tank readings. Twenty-eight minutes. Susan was allowing a two minute differential margin.

"Where are we?"

I didn't see it at first. It was the day I gave the lecture. You remember. We played the video. Then I saw it. Maybe I looked away and looked back. Something. But there it was. I thought the camera or disc had an anomaly in it.

Later, that night, Jennifer and I went back and reviewed our thermal scans. There was no question."

"I don't understand."

"The vents exude, belch black smoke. Black Smokers they are sometimes called. Great degrees of heat rush through the ocean floor. This, of course, we all know, and we in this ship know all too well. But something else, and I should have intuited it. I knew I missed something. I couldn't figure what it was."

"Susan?"

"Nature abhors a vacuum. One of the most basic principals of science. This is what I missed and should have known: From this great pressure of fire, winds of fire, soil of fire, and, at last, water, vacuums are created. And into these breeches, these . . . "

"The ocean water pours in."

"Most of these pools are miniscule, burned to steam in instants. But our vent is so huge, the flow is continuous. As long as we stay in this part (I estimate it is about the size of a small lake, roughly a quarter mile average on all tangent sides), close to its entrance, away from the event horizon, we'll be safe. At least for twenty-four minutes. Unless we can grow gills, live off the fish that come in, and live out our days in this stream-pool." She giggled her girlish-woman scientist giggle Jennifer found irritating, and Hodges had come to love. Well, almost.

"Can we slip out through the water stream?" He was fully alert now. Amazing what enough water in the body and mind will do. We are water creatures, as far removed from the fire-life as death itself. Earth's creatures long ago time left their birthing place behind, so far behind it was now fully hostile and what was once out there was now what sustained all the descendants of being. Really, it was a mystery.

"Susan?"

"Hmm? Oh. No. Negative. It's too narrow. Just some cracks in the rocks. There's only one way out. How we came in. Hopefully our computer will remember and the auto pilot can get us back."

"Your thesis?"

"There's a great deal of telemetry. We can review it later if we make it."

She wouldn't admit it. He sensed the disappointment in her voice. The source of life had no doubt been found; but its empirical evidence was as elusive as on the surface laboratories: Like water in a boiling pot when it turns to steam, rises, and vanishes into the ether.

He gazed out again. He was reminded of those psychedelic posters and paintings of the 60's and 70's, a shattering of reds, golds, yellows, greens, a rainbow phantasmagoria of a phantasmagoria. Gregor Samsa flailing his useless stick-legs in psychedelic pattern: They had metamorphosed into the Beetles in their yellow submarine.

He realized there was no up nor down and they would need the auto pilot memory chip to guide them their way out. Silicon logic to rescue them from silicon hell. How had they arrived here? Had Susan been the only one to survive?

"Delores? Magruder?"

"They are starting to come around. Magruder's the worst for it. I think he bumped his head. I barely got my own IV in before I passed out. I prayed the vector I gave was the right one. I woke up when we were heading along the stream into the horizon-fire. I turned her and somehow got her here. Set her on a circular path. Then I tended to the three of you. Hooked up IV's, took off clothing to allow for surface skin cooling. I did as much as I could.  I, I'm a bit--"

She fell into his arms. They perspired. They sweated. Not as much as before. The man's IV tubes intertwined with the woman's IV tubes, as though two tubule creatures lightly danced and shimmered in a rudimentary mating ritual. The man kissed the woman. The scientist kissed the soldier. For a short while at least, they knew they were still alive. "Come on tough guy. We've got much important work to do. And only twenty-two minutes to do it in. Oh my. Oh, that's not, that's, I just want to go back to sleep. Sleep forever in this amniotic sac and never venture again into the heat of the world outside."

"Susan."

"It's OK. I know. Come on now. We'll either make it or we won't. If death awaits us, death awaits us. But we will die trying."

Jennifer scanned her instruments. The day waxed. The day waned. It had been over two hours since the two submarines slipped the surface and prowled the great oceanic depth beneath them. Once she thought she caught blip-lights of the larger vessel. But it was the small one she sought somehow returning in safety and that was the one that eluded her. She knew time was running out . . . or ran out.

Not back yet meant not back at all. Not ever. Never. Tolkien had been in error. Never was worse than too late, much worse. Unless Susan had somehow found . . . they had gone over the directional coordinates many times; but the unknown factor, X, the chaos element, the blessing and the bane of science, even a one degree shift in their calculations from a lava flow, or a steam stream or a sudden cauldron could cause her to miss the water pool. Still she hoped, clung to it as a half-drowned woman at sea who had just seen the gentle cold waters close over her lover now clawed her way upon her half-sunken raft loaded with frozen dead men and blew her whistle in a desperate breath-reach for the life-boat that had moments before passed her by.

She observed an unmistakable feature on horizon sight. Closing fast. Her heart sank, for she knew what it was. At the same instant, she heard them behind her. She had that feeling in her stomach. Like just before the starter's gun at her swim meets. She also knew what she would find when she looked out at the soldiers on deck.

"Mr. Wells. Mr. Foxworth. You slipped something in their drinking water this morning."

"We're not cruel, Ms. Littleton." Joanne Foxworth didn't sound so eager and innocent any more. "It's just for forty-five minutes or so. We'll be gone by then. Or is it an hour and a half?

Oh well, they'll be fine. Or dead if they wake up. Interesting situation for them, don't you think?"

Jennifer turned. She stared down the 9mm Glock and the M16. The old "16 Tons" song came back to her at that moment. Strange how the mind works that way. "If the right one don't get ya, then the left one will." Or was that "John Henry, A Steel Driving Man?"

"So, Wells. It was you. All along. Susan was right. Carstairs had people in who knew the codes."

"The three of you. Arthknott especially almost had it. The three witches. I barely made it back up the stairs and behind the doors when Delores came down. I thought with your great imagination, her logic deduction, and Delores's powers of observation, I would be found out. But the two of them were at odds ends. Huh. Interesting oxymoron that. Almost. Odds ends. Don't you think? Well, anyway, it gave me, us, the time we needed to regroup."

"It won't work. One of the most powerful weapons systems in the world circles beneath us. You can't outrun her; you can't out fight her."

"We won't have to. Our own vessel, the Marduk, has cloaking sonar. It'll disperse the signal and she'll just think there's one ship here. Stealth technology, you know. ESSS digital beaming. By the time she finishes her futile efforts, trying to protect the Ex-Gee, we'll be long gone."

"With what? The answer to all this is down there."

"Is it? Is it underneath the underneath?" Foxworth said, coyly looking at Jennifer as a lover. Good God. Is the woman coming on to me?

"Then what. At the entrance . . . oh my God. The steam smoke at the entrance. The differential in pressure . . . ?"

"Keep going. You're doing fine."

"Wait. Wait a minute. That's it. That's the connection I needed to make, what bothered me the whole time. I couldn't figure-- the damn energy co-efficients never matched. Always we had that damn gap."

In spite of herself, in spite of her predicament, Jennifer in an instant turned to her computer. Quickly she brought up the simulation program which she had handled many months ago before the project had even officially begun. She began adding embedded functions in the interface state transition matrix, this time carrying the residual energy differences to the output vector.

"None of us thought, here, I'll output the energy differential curve. With the heat co-efficients and chemical compounding controlled for and subtracted out, you have, wait, there, wait, there! A phenomenal, vast net energy . . ."

Then, like it occurs to all scientists and artists, she had the total discovery in one flash in her highly intelligent brain. The Eureka phenomenon. She thought the Word, and all its implications. Then she said the Word, the Word that the Lord God surely uttered to create the Universe, for even before the beginning of time, there was only the Word; and this is the Word that S/Hhe said:

"Fusion!

"Controlled fusion through a chemical-interface that siphoned off and yielded up a net energy differential from the unique transposition of matter across the vent's membrane boundary. Replicated underwater to capture a natural cooling exchange, you could generate unbelievable power with essentially no consumption of natural resources."

With the rapture of the moment and the depth of insight, every bit as gratifying as any of her most deeply felt orgasms, she let the realization cascade down through her body as she had with her lovers. Each one special; yet Allen . . . Allen: For a moment, Jennifer almost forgot where she was, that an iron-formed tubule containing the potential of plasma controlled burst-energy expunging a projectile of death was pointed at her heart. She continued to the synthesis of her conclusion.

"The end of pollution, the reduction and salvation of expensive and depletion based energy resources, the restoration and return of ecosystems, medical cures, space travel to the stars." Her eyes glistened like they had seen the eyes of her teacher, Susan, glisten when her hypotheses, premises, analyses, evidences, and conclusions involved her utterly. Jennifer indeed forgot the danger she was in. For the moment, she dreamt the eternal dream. Her dreams and thoughts continued without regard to where she was, until one of her thoughts slammed into her brain. This heavy thought returned her to her ship-borne reality.

"Why, with endless energy available we could design . . ."

Her voice trailed off,

"Go on. Why stop there?"

"A weapon of such magnitude all the good could be destroyed in an instant."

"Or the threat of its use. Or of a low yield use. It's all in the permutations and combinations. We think we have it; we know Carstairs does."

"Then your submersible never needed to go in, into, to enter--"

"By George I think she's got it. Now, then. Why you didn't drink any water today is most unusual. But if you'll please come over here, we'll be glad to tie you--What the hell?"

Jennifer knew at once it was the whales returning to surface. By chance they came up close (later she would ponder if it was indeed mere random occurrence), very close; it was most unusual, as if they knew to help her, as if they heard her in her mind singing whale song, singing the secret siren song of the sea. Up they broke surface, on the port side, in an uncommon maneuver, the entire pod at the same time. The ship rocked just enough to tip her captors off balance.

Jennifer, seated, held on. Always take your chance when it comes, and early on, Allen had taught her. Never go to the second phase. You may die trying, but you will certainly die at the second scene of the scenario. She bolted out the door of the pilot house on the starboard side. Onto the outer deck of the bridge she dashed. She needed to get to her quarters. She ran on wet slippery surfaces. She raced without slipping or falling. Her huge feet gobbled up decks as fast, sure, and true as they had gobbled up pool-lane water at a more innocent time of her life when she triumphed over her competition. She had long ago lost or misplaced her trophies.

She made it halfway before the bullets struck along side her or she heard them whizz past her ear into the ocean beyond.

She had another odd thought, hoping at that moment with her own life in dire jeopardy that the 20mm and .45 caliber superheated projectiles miss the whales sounding now on this side also.

A desperate woman in desperate circumstances, she dashed down the companionway toward the poop deck. Just inside the small room, she stopped. She saw it leaning against the wall. It shouldn't be there. Then she recalled, Hodges had secured it. "You never know," she remembered him stating. Allen and Hodges. Perhaps two men had saved her life without their knowing. She grabbed it. She headed back up onto the main deck. She saw they were halfway to her now. It was twenty feet to the ocean, a little rough today, and surely cold.

She didn't hesitate. She leapt, as from a high dive, remembering her form to dispel the impact of her arrival. Bullets zoomed, whistled all about her leaping body, which, seemingly suspended, hung in a profile icon familiar even to those not in regular attendance at poolside. In an instant, suspended between heaven and earth, air and water, she sensed a warm sensation as she felt her left side whammed by a hammer.

She tried to maintain the gracile profile of the dive. But the hammer blow was consuming, mighty, powerful. She felt herself spin out of control. She slammed into a high wave of the sea, as if Poseidon had sent the whitecap to break her fall.

Like the submersibles before her, she slowly sank beneath the surface, her body spinning slowly, a small stream of crimson for an instant about the blue-white circlet of her entrance incarnadine.

Then the waves of blue and white covered her and the red dissipated, then vanished, as though the lives of the cells had returned from whence they had come.

The flukes of the whales raised above the ocean surface, on both sides of the ship now, allowing a knowledgeable person who had chosen to follow this pod the unique identification of each individual through the striations and cuts of that fluke. They had received sufficient air. The bullets had whizzed by them. Wisely, they dove again beneath the surface, carrying with them, as they had for eternity, the mystery of the firmament of the sea.

Captain Mitch Corvales walked the length of his bridge. He walked back to command. Something wasn't right. He was concerned. If that small submersible had been able to elude his sonar, even on a temporary basis, then it was conceivable it had been more than mere rock that had thrown their operation for a while. He knew, as commanders of every submarine and task force in the fleet knew, that, prior to its breakup, the Soviets had been well along in developing cloaking sonar, an anti-sonar series rapidly shifting harmonics sent in sound wave omni- directional currents with pulse interludes on piggy-back carrier bands. The result, highly complex and sophisticated, but, in essence, was to jam return signals without the operator realizing interference or jamming occurred. He or she would merely perceive the device as having found nothing to reflect and come back. An empty screen, in effect; nothing out there when something in fact out there lurked.

What was that ditty in Tolkien's The Hobbit? By the twitching of my thumbs, something evil this way comes. And we, with all this sophisticated software cannot discern it. He felt a sick kick in his stomach.

The Russians, they knew, had continued their work, perhaps to expand their best economic output, military measures and counter-measures to rogue nations, or bankrolled terrorist groups. Josh Egerton, his Sonar man, was the best or one of the best in the fleet. For what he'd about to ask the boy would need all his training, all his skill, and considerable intuition. He would take his chance. He believed in him. He believed in them all.

"X0. Go to red. Silent running. Underwater visual on scope."

"Aye Captain. All hands. Switching to red and infra-red on my mark. Three seconds. Mark."

Like a photographer's dark room, the lights on the vessel deep beneath some unknown latitude of the Pacific Ocean transformed red. There could be no glare now. There would be less chance of eye fatigue. There was at this point, Corvales knew, no margin for error. This was what they had trained for.

Corvales was reminded of the search for the Atomic Bomb. The entire matter had begun as a mere intellectual exercise in quantum mechanics and theoretical physics. Only the impetus of World War II and the fear that Nazi Germany developed the device along with ballistic delivery rockets compelled a massive development project orchestrated in the main by escaped Eastern European Jewish scientists throughout the late 1930's and early 1940's.

Now, here he defended what had started as a mere scientific curiosity of biological significance but had quickly caught the attention of military professionals. The more he pondered the matter, the truer the analogy of the two events seemed. The enormous significance of it all was not lost on Corvales nor his superiors in Washington nor at Stratcom in Omaha. For there was something else being pursued that only a few persons in Washington or Langley or Omaha knew about. If it were true, it were amazing and profound.

Classified still at this writing is the particular design capability that gives the Nebraska its silent non-signature to any Sonar while allowing the ship over eighty per cent efficiency to which noise and vibration ordinarily would be a factor. The major theory concerns a counter fan turbine run in a calibrated opposing interval, processor matched to the actual outer screws that propel the vessel through surface and deep waters, along a cognate counter water flow produced along the wake.

"Engineering. Silent running. Counter turbines activated. On my mark. Three seconds. Mark."

Classified still at this writing is the Nebraska's underwater visual scope with both full pressure lens and laser guided miniature (nearly microscopic) camera on the needle of her prow. A separate imaging system allows the viewer gazing through the little window at the top of the periscope shaft an actual and T.V. generated forward split screen underwater view.

"Underwater view scope. Activate on my mark. Mark."

Corvales peered through the small window with special glasses. "Sharks."

"Captain."

"A wall of sharks. Hundreds. X0."

"Aye Captain. School of sharks sighted."

"Have Egerton report to the bridge."

"Sonar."

"Sonar aye."

"Report to bridge. ASAP Mr."

"Copy that X0. ETA twenty seconds."

"Sharks," Corvales said. "A wall of sharks."

"Sonar reporting as ordered, sir."

Corvales removed his glasses. "Never saw so many sharks. I think they sense something."

"Sir?"

"Or they're running from something." Corvales paused.

His men worked their screens and stations. They wiped sweat from their brows. They had been at deep depth for over two hours. "Did you see the sharks, Mr. Egerton?"

"Sharks. Aye, Captain. Begging the Captain's pardon, sir, I didn't think they would--"

"No. No, no. It's quite all right, son. I was merely curious. Status of the hostile."

"Your strategy worked, sir. At least for a while. She turned. The Ex-Gee spiraled in. It was something. I never thought they'd be able to maneuver--"

"Current status, Mr. Egerton. Of the hostile."

"Sir. Just hanging out, so to speak at the vent entrance. Occasionally turns toward us. I, it sounds crazy I know."

"Go on."

"I think eventually she plans to fire a torpedo at us."

There was silence. "I mean, she does seem to be working with some probes she sends out to the edges. But I think she also . . ."

Egerton looked up at his captain. He was sure he would see easy and impatient dismissal on the man's face, this man he respected as much as anyone he knew and would die in battle for. He had spoken as a first day student at submariner's school. He had not spoken like a knowledgeable, trained professional his commander and crewmates depended upon, as he depended upon them. It was absurd, anti-physics, and counter-intuitive. It was one thing for an Alvin class submersible to explore the deep beneath the deep, quite another for an underwater rocket. The pressure would cause its implosion in instants. Yes, we had some encapsulated top secret weapons, launched from undersea housings; but the girth demanded would all but eliminate such an object from a relatively small, deep sea vessel. But his commander's face was serious, that rock-etched line face of a man always thinking twenty fathoms deeper and twenty miles ahead of everyone else."

"Roger that Mr. Keep a good eye on that. Mr. Egerton."

"Aye Captain."

"You've had counter anti-pulse variance harmonic training, haven't you?"

"Aye, Captain."

Again the long pause. Chatter of duty stations filtered about the bridge. Corvales continued. By chance, it appeared everyone ceased their chatter at once. For a moment the silence of the ship seemed deafening. Corvales gave the command he had been pondering.

"Institute full to half pulse harmonics. Random and chaotic variances. At once. Continuous. Three hundred sixty degrees. Long range. Don't worry about the energy excess, Mr. Egerton. That will be the XO's concern."

"Copy that, Captain. To surface als, all range. Aye sir."

"Dismissed."

The Sonar operator returned to his duty station. He reached about his neck. He brought out a key on a ring. He unlocked a red box to the left of his console. A rheostat resistance switch lay inside. He turned the dial to a label written, "MultiPort Seek Rand Sor." He pressed it down. A low hum, like a Tibetan Monk chant, filtered throughout the ship. Lights blinked. Somewhere on board a compressor ceased its work. Then, of a sudden, all returned. The hum lowered. The hum disappeared.

Egerton gazed at his screens, and listened to his headsets. He adjusted the rheostat switch.

Corvales worried now about the probes at the threshold of the event sent out by the hostile ship.

Susan Arthknott fought the queasiness and fuzziness in her stomach, in her head. She knew it took well over a day, in some cases, a week for a normally healthy person to recover from severe dehydration. And the people in this redoubtable ship nearly had been boiled alive. They had only about twenty minutes of oxygen left, maybe twenty-five since any tank monitor always had more than what showed. If they made it somehow they could be taken to a good navy hospital on the west coast to recover for a week. That would be all right; in fact, she looked forward to it, especially as long as Hodges were in the next bed.

Who'da thunk it? Who could have thought it could happen like this, at her age? And a non-scientist. A soldier. Younger. But he was such a masculine specimen.

For a moment she realized she had been dreaming of something but could not remember what it was. A hospital. Well, as doctor or patient, she knew that when a person desires to surrender as patient in hospital, she recognizes beyond question she must truly be ill.

One thing she knew. By any standard her ship's design was a success. Improvements were required, of course. The uranium should be the first line of defense, not within the outer layer. The tiles could be doubled spread at angular quality lines . . . yes, that should work. She would have to figure the calibrations and angles, but it should work.

They had simply spent too much time in, that's all. Susan surmised that the computer model had been in error. Pockets of cauldron spots flamed and sparked far hotter even than they had projected. She'd have to let Jennifer know. Jennifer! She'd only been away from her friend and protégé nearly three hours. It somehow seemed like three decades or three millennia ago.

That was it then. Our lives are eras, unique from any other era on earth or in space or in the fiery middle of the planet. Defined by different periods of time eternal.

First there was the infant, mewling and puking in her parents' crib, then the schoolgirl on her way to school, ignoring the vicissitudes of prepubescence, then unable to ignore them, then the young woman, turning to molecular biology, then the doctor-scienti--

"Susan! For the love of God. Snap out of it. If I read it right, we have only about twenty minutes of air left."

Dehydration. The IV drip was only half empty. She needed more.

"Water."

"Here. Drink it all. We've got to drink all our rations. At least it didn't get to 100 Celsius. The water's still here."

They drank. Delores started to come around. Hodges explained their situation to her. Magruder moaned. He thrashed about. Then, at once, he fell asleep or into a coma. They drank.

"Damn," Delores said.

"Glad to have you back, Commander," Hodges said.

"Damn. OK," Susan said.

Susan explained she was setting in the return coordinates. Or, rather, letting the computer and auto-pilot know they needed to back out by memory as the same approach by which they came in. Delores wanted a systems check. Susan explained that was two to four minutes they didn't have.

"Besides, what difference does it make? We can die here or die out there."

"Are we, what's our position relative to the surface?"

"Only God and our autopilot memory know. And I'm betting on Alfred."

"You call the computer Alfred?"

"Alfred served Batman well. I'm hoping. OK. Alfred says he's ready. Ready now. Get set boys and girls. This is it!"

Sweat dripped off their brows. It coursed down their backs. It collected, nearly pooled, under their arms, even before they left the cool water chamber. They knew not their orientation in relation to surface or depth of sea. The craft once again was about to venture into the most hostile of environments, where no person had ever ventured, the heart of the inferno of the earth. Soon enough, red, yellow, white danced about them. So far, the tiles did not melt. So far the spent uranium reflecting the most radioactive of metals did not begin to break down.

"It. It's not as bad for some reason. 105°. 108. 109. Not rising as fast," Hodges proclaimed.

"We're in a channel of steam from the water chamber. It's giving us a window of some coolant. If this path will coincide with our pathway out, we may be--"

"Commander, weapons."

"Commander, aye."

Delores shook her head. The usually strong, stalwart military officer attempted to fight off the blackness in her mind. The disorientation was almost too much. She had been on ships at sea in storms so huge and horrendous, it seemed her boat had been cast to the virtual bottom of the ocean with walls of sea about her, and she was not certain if earth and sky were above or below. But this, this water and fire all about them, it was, oh the hell with it. She would be sick or weak later. This her moment of greatness! Her time of glory!

"I say again, Commander, aye."

She wiped the sweat from her eyes. An exercise in futility. Still it entered under her lids. Damn. It stung.

"I've got two blips. Strange. They're converging our position. One's huge. What the heck. It's above us. I, no. It's all around us. How is . . . What the hell--104°; 102; 99; 97; 96; 98; 95. Holding steady at 95-97. Blip's disappeared."

"Hodges, Susan. What's our oxygen?"

"Nineteen minutes. Temperature's steady but we're going in a different direction. What the hell is going on?"

"Can we afford to effect visual?"

"Aye Commander. With all due respect, I don't think we can afford not to."

"Susan."

"Copy that Delores. Here we go."

The panels spread again. They gazed at what lay beyond them.

"Mother of God," the scientist proclaimed. And in spite of herself, she continued to express her awe in a place only of awe. She recognized at last how truly full of awe was this place and she had not known it.

"Dearest Mother of God. It is so beautiful. It is. Is!"

The others looked at her, then without again. Susan sat staring in what Delores would later describe a gaze enraptured, as if one who had seen clearly an angel or a demon, a consummate revelation of epiphany.

Then she looked out. She saw.

"Oh my dear Holy God!" the military officer said.

She slipped off her shoes underneath the hull of the ship. She swam. Again she swam in a race. She needed her kick as she had known it.

Once, years ago, when she knew she took to the water, she swam under a lake's anchored raft. She was twelve years old. The world of immortality stretched before her, a mighty unending and unyielding ocean stretching beyond boundaries, beyond the horizon. Then, for the scariest of moments, she thought she wouldn't make it. She knew she drowned. What astonished her was she wasn't frightened. She simply surmised she would either make it or she wouldn't, she would either die or live and, oddly, at the moment, for some reason, it didn't seem to matter. She meant to keep simply swimming. Underwater, she kept her strokes, promising herself she would move her arms and legs until her lungs burst. At last, probably just in time, she felt herself break water beyond the edge of the raft, as a whale bursting past the surface of the water. She inhaled. She exhaled. She breathed deep breaths, gasping, her chest and her mind and her soul swelling with the precious breath of life.

At birth, our first breath in; at death, our final breath out. All else between is this magnificence of life.

The breath is the life. Air is the all. Water, fire, food, drink, soil, but air-breath is the spirit of life. Man and woman, a little lower than the angels, needed the spirit-breath of life and grace.

Where was she? For some reason she had thought of a childhood memory. Her side hurt.

She swam. The hull of the destroyer seemed to go on forever.

She felt the waves of the water. It was cold, freezing, but her side was warm. Suddenly she realized she had swum under the hull of the Starr. It had not been easy. The ship was huge. But it shouldn't have been that difficult. Then she remembered. Something in her side was wrong. Something kept her from her normal strokes and rhythms. It didn't hurt exactly. Or maybe it did. She could not determine.

She held something in her hand. It couldn't be important. But for some reason she wouldn't let go. What was the reason? What was the object? All she knew: She must hold on. What was the matter with her? She was cold. Very cold. Slipping now. She remembered. She had to find the ladder. Climb up. There were bad people there. Susan depended on her. Susan! Where was Susan? She was underneath the water. But she was in a volcano. How could Susan be in fire and water at the same time? And if she were under the water, why didn't she see her when she swam under the raft; or was her swim under something else?

She saw the ladder. She had to climb up it somehow. The answer was at the top of the ladder, wasn't it? Wasn't there always a ladder between heaven and earth? But she was in the sea somewhere, wasn't she? Then how could heaven's ladder be right above her?

But the ocean was so cold and the waves cast so much water in her lungs. It would be peaceful now, simply to let the ocean curl about her, encompass her like a womb of watery amniotic fluid.

To return to the water's womb like she was meant to return so many years ago when she had cheated the lake spirits. To return down to the depths of the sea. That was it! That was what she was meant to do. She would go meet Susan. They would be absorbed by the cold comforting waters together. Or would sharks sense her blood and--well, either way. It was that old familiar feeling of not really caring.

She tried one more stretch to the ladder's first rung. No use. Too far, too wet, too weak. She slipped beneath the surface. She looked down. It was so peaceful. And there was Susan, looking so beautiful like she always knew she would, coming up to her, stretching her arms to embrace her, to comfort her, to welcome her, to take her home. Yes, it was the answer. She felt at peace. Or, well, no matter; let the peacefulness prevail; for thence she felt herself twirling deliberately, spinning slowly, sinking, sinking down beneath the white capped surface of the blue ocean's mysteries and secrets.

Egerton listened carefully. He adjusted his dials. He hearkened to the sounds true and sounds phantom, to the sounds of the sea and to sounds that were not sounds of the sea but of its invader, man.

He never wished to be in a submarine. Who in their right mind did? But when he sat down with his first sonar set-up, he was hooked. It was almost worth the long tours at sea. The stale air, the food long past fresh. Four heads for practically 200 men.

Now, he listened most carefully. Something strange sounded. Then, at once like that fellow who discovered water displacement and yelled, "Eureka," he had it! He charted his graphs. And he had it! He knew!

"XO. Sonar. You'd better come down here."

"Roger that. On my way."

It took him a while to figure it out and now he had to explain it. But they were good, well trained officers. They'd get it. And quick.

"All right, Mr. What do you have?"

"I couldn't grasp it at first. The pulses always came back negative. Then I realized it wasn't a chaotic harmonic she generated. It was a simple random distribution, the Fibonacci sequence."

"Fibonacci. Adding the last number to the prior one in a sequence of numbers to extend the sequence."

"That's it. One, then 1. One plus 1 = 2. Thus, 1-2. One + 2 = 3. Thus, 1-2-3. Two + 3 = 5. One-2-3-5. Three + 5 = 8. Thus, 1-2-3-5-8-13-21. So on. It's a natural sequence, occurring in many places in nature. Tulip or rose petals, hair or fur, brachiation of trees or leaves. But usually not--"

"Not usually in artificial intelligence, not in man made sequences. The perfect cover. Devilishly cleaver. A Russian chess master play. Almost perfect."

"I sent it back in counter sequences, until I found its highest cardinal number. Turns out it's 34. It just sent counter pulses one number lower each in the sequence. Half of it was guess work, really, but--"

"You found her."

"Big one. And approaching our good friend upstairs at flank speed. See. Here. And then here. Here's the full projected plot."

"Damn. Twelve minutes I make it."

"Twelve minutes 37 seconds. Give or take 10-12 seconds."

"It's no good. We're a good 20 minutes from the surface. And another 10 to the coordinates."

"Eighteen and 11, actually." Egerton cleared his throat. "Sir."

"And our guy down here?"

"No change. But when we turn, I suspect he'll come along for the ride or try something."

"Above and below. Well, we have a problem. Two of them. Three, with that cockamamie vessel we're waiting for on that damn fool's errand. Never mind that. Good work, Egerton. Stay on it. I'll alert the Captain."

Thomas Olgelby, Executive Officer: He liked the title. His short stature had always been a problem for him; but being XO assigned to the fleet class submarine of the line and thus in the world made him feel as tall as the coning tower. He had had some advantages, it was true. His Brahman Olgelby family upbringing in Boston. His father had wanted him to go into politics. Even when disappointed at his application and acceptance at Annapolis, the old man had already seen his military career leading ultimately to a senate seat and even to the top office. "Then you could be Commander-In-Chief of the entire army. Maybe it was a good choice after all."

All he wanted now was this ship. He hated beneath the surface of the sea for so long time. They all did, he knew. But somehow, over the months and years, he had come to love this vessel. And he knew every rivet, every bolt. They had given the command to a, well, to a--the man wasn't from an old established family on the east coast, after all. But Mitch Corvales had proven himself to this midshipman. Corvales had a top appointment in the fleet. He was up for Admiral next year. Then this XO would become this ship's Commander. He was sure of it. And he didn't need his father's or mother's help.

Corvales respected his opinions and submissions. He had a whale of a problem for him now. But his mind had always worked quick. By the time he returned to the bridge, he knew what they needed to do.

He took his time. They didn't have much. He knew Corvales liked it that way to get it at one briefing. Neither he nor the Captain liked to repeat matters, if they could help it. Besides, Corvales's mind worked as fast as his. They were from two separate worlds and different in many ways, but there was this ship and her might, her astonishing might that brought them together. Working together, they might soon have to bring her to bear it.

"Recommendations?"

"I think we ought to head to surface. Catch these bastards at whatever stage they are at. We'll catch them off guard. A surreptitious afternoon surprise attack. Come upon them from the west. Sun in their eyes. Our SEAL contingent sent out on the Zodiacs to board the friendly and the hostile. We'll come in close behind, low in the water, decks awash, but our surface gunners ready. They're too close to our friendly now. If we fire torpedoes on her we could take the Starr with her. Sneak in beyond. Get a good visual for the SEALs and for our gunners. Egerton thinks he can fool the foolers. Con the con men. So to speak, sir."

"Our friendly down here?"

Olgelby breathed deep. This was the question he knew was coming. The one uncertain factor. Factor X in his equation. Corvales sometimes waited too long. If the man had a weakness, this was one an enemy could possibly exploit.

"With all due respect, sir, it's been over 90 minutes. Skipper, 45 was our, that is, their, max. I don't think they made it. At least, we have to play the odds. Three lives probably gone compared to a whole group topside, our documents aboard the Starr, our mission."

"Our main mission was down here. A hostile at the vent--"

"Skipper, as we already know, we can take care of the one behind and the one above."

He needed to repeat himself after all. As they palavered, he was certain his captain and he knew what they left unsaid. Mitch Corvales wanted to protect the scientist, to rescue her and the others. They had become his responsibility. He wanted to bring his people back alive.

Olgelby took a deep breath mightier than before. He looked away for a minute. He thought he saw a fly buzz out of the bridge down toward the upper head. The same one as when they left port. Maybe he was mistaken. He kept calm. He stayed professional. He fingered his insignia, a habit many officers enacted when nervous. He took on his Brahmin air of a Renaissance courtier's panache of nonchalance. He knew there was no other way; and he knew his captain knew it. He glanced back to look at the man straight on. And straight on he gave it to Corvales, the only way for a captain of one of the most powerful fleet ships of the line, a captain facing a major decision to get it.

From before recorded time, captains out on their watch at sea have had to reckon such decisions concerning their vessels and their actions without benefit of consultation from superiors. From the age of the Revolution, American naval commanders have brought great credit upon themselves, their crews, the navy, and the United States.

"We have no way to go in after them. We can send the robots for a quick look on video undersea telemetry VH-LF. But that will only be a few seconds and--"

"And this, this thing hovering there will probably destroy the opening anyway."

That was the opening Olgelby hoped for. He wasn't all the way there yet, he knew; but he had his opening. He should soon be able to close the sale. He took a deep breath. He went to his next step.

"We have ways. We could get one through. If she fires on us . . . " Members of the scope crew looked up. Clearly command knew something about the impossibility of torpedo launch effectiveness under deep depth turning possible. Or was there some new weapon? They knew of our own Top Secret deep sea launch platforms, but even the new projectiles launched from them couldn't sustain those enormous pressures more than two or three hundred yards at best.

Ogelby continued. "We'll dispatch decoys and fire from platform Zeta Alpha. Even the pressure-encapsulated torpedoes will never make the distance of course. They'll implode. But the shock wave should give them a start. Then, close to surface, as I think she will follow, we can eliminate her."

"The same shock wave could reverberate along the opening crack, shut down the vent. Then it would be we who eliminate any chance--"

"I think, skipper, that they--"

"You think they've used up all their chances already."

"Yes, sir, I do."

There was another of those long Corvales pauses. One good thing about them. When the decision was made, it was made. Olgelby noted now it was his captain who took a long breath, acquired that at once far away and near look in his blue-gray eyes, then looked back. When he did, the man looked tall again, and once more appeared to peer down at him.

"I presume you have coordinates in."

"Aye, Captain.

"Sonar, bridge."

"Sonar aye."

"Keep your harmonics in pulsed time, Mr. Egerton. We don't want the hostile to perceive we're on to her. Can you do it? It's a ways up there, Mr."

"I think so, Captain. I've just got to stay an algorithms sequence ahead of her."

"X0."

"XO aye."

"Do it!"

His signature on the invoice. Olgelby picked up the ship's communications microphone.

"XO to all hands. We are preparing to surface. Begin procedures. Stay alert. We expect hostile action below and above. Maintain battle stations. Maintain beta red.

"Surface!"

"Surface, aye."

The gargantuan metal tube carrying 200 men turned. Her nose poked up, up toward the surface and the sky. Turbines creaked. Turbines turned. Bilge water exploded from her dive tanks. Slowly she began her upward journey. The special tanks filled with air, the excess waters rushing out the sides.

For a moment, fully expected, even men on their tenth tour felt disorientation. Soon enough, however, she reached her angle of ascent. She climbed through the murky depths of the sea. Up. Up. Up.

"Captain, X0. Sonar."

"Bridge aye."

"She's firing, Captain. Two fish. One on course. My God. Deep depth and still coming. Captain, how--Jesus. One imploded. Prepare for shock wave. Second on course. My God. Still coming; but it's imposs--"

"Helm. Bring about 1.2° on my mark. Steady. Evasive maneuver Alpha-Charlie. Fire decoys. Weapons. Do we have a lock?"

"Helm, 1.2° AC aye."

"Weapons. Lock in 5 to 7 seconds. Come on. Come on."

"Locked!"

"Rear torpedo. Fire 5. Fire 6."

"Five away. Six away."

"Decoys heading true. Second hostile fish following decoy. Our fish on targ--Good God Miss Mary."

"Say again."

"Bridge, sonar. She imploded from pressure. But, but--"

"Go on. As you were, Mister."

"At implosion, something of her or the shock wave, or the enemy fish still going . . . she's gone into the vent. She tried to evade. She tried to evade. She's disappeared into the vent."

"Understood."

"Captain."

"Report."

"Captain. I'm no longer reading any significant opening at the vent line."

There was a long, sick silence, the silence surrounding the soul when the body dies and before it realizes it is due to quit its vessel and the earthly realm.

"Captain?"

"Acknowledged, sonar. Vent closed down. Mark the minute."

"Mark the minute, aye."

One thing he gave Corvales credit for. When there was nothing else to do, he went on to what could be done.

"Sir, what shall I--"

"Impact."

"Impact?"

"Impact, at this time."

"Aye, captain.

"Alert the SEAL commander. Briefing in eight minutes. They need to gear up."

"Sonar?"

"Aye, Captain. I make it sixteen seconds. Eight. Five, 3, 1."

They felt as much as heard the explosion. The ship was quiet for a long time. Then Thomas Olgelby spoke to his skipper.

"Mitch. They were gone nearly an hour ago. It's just as well. No one else can ever, we've seen that hell. Mitch. Captain."

"Steady as she goes, X0. You run the SEAL briefing. I don't want anything to go wrong with our rescue mission topside."

"Copy that, Captain."

The submarine climbed. The whales, sounding again, passed her like cars on a divided highway. Down they prowled, in search of sharks and squid. The man-made cetacean climbed through the sea, hunting more dangerous game.

She didn't feel the hand pull her out of the comforting womb of the ocean's depth, out of range of Poseidon's sirens singing their songs under the sea, to her, calling her to come to them. Somehow she had part of a mind left to know something happened.

She saw the city beneath the sea. She had gazed upon its jewels gleaming from the sun-fed water's reflection's glory, as a woman's diamond floating to the bottom of a pool. Sapphires, rubies, emeralds, diamonds, beryls, agates, and mermaids and mermen, beautiful women, handsome men swimming up to her with their arms open. How welcoming. How comforting.

Suddenly it disappeared in the shimmering sparkle of the water's edge above her.

She coughed. She wheezed. Pain washed over and through her. "Why? Why?" Wheezed she. Coughed she. "It was so beautiful." Coughed. Wheezed. "So beautiful."

"Come on, Jennifer. Come back. That's it. Keep coughing. Breathe. Jesus. You're hit. We've got to get this suit off. It's only going to keep you cold. Here. Oh hell, I'll cut it off. Damn. I've got to get you a blanket."

Who had done this to her? Who had taken her away from her journey in the sea to find Susan and live in that beautiful diamond city forever? The voice was . . . she had been with him once. A long time ago. She heard him return. Hear. Smell. Taste. And pain. In spite of it all, in spite of herself, she came around.

Damn, it hurt. Pain. From the depths of her pain she knew. She thought. She was.

Alive! She was alive! Still alive!

"I'm alive."

"Yeah, that's OK. Here. Couldn't find a blanket. Piece of an old canvas behind that tool box. It'll do for now."

"I'm aliv--Oh God, that hurts."

She turned on the side that didn't hurt. She vomited. Water effluent that no land creature should ever take inside her body projected out, blasted through every orifice-passageway of her pharynx--mouth, nose, ears, yea, even her eyes. Out again and again in waves matching the waves of the ocean's rhythms.

"Jesus. Come on baby. You need to do this, but we need to get below. They haven't come back to the stern but they will soon."

Gasping, vomiting, wheezing, her side splitting. God why didn't he let me die? "Oh God. It hurts. Throw me back."

"Easy baby. Easy. Get it out. But do it soon. Or take a break. We got to get below."

"Who? Allen? Allen, it's you. Oh God. Allen, you bastard. Why didn't you let me die? It was so beautiful. Oh God."

She started to hit him. Instead she fell into his arms. She stank a smell of stink he had not smelled on another human being. It was offensive. But to him she smelled sweet as the pure waters that would wash away her dirt. His brown arms encompassed her white body, and he held her, her matted hair, her nostril-stink, and his heart swelled, so great was his love for this woman. Her eyes poured water again, but this time from the depths of her soul and not out of the ocean deep.

"Come on. Let's get below. They'll see us here sooner or later. They're all over the bridge and prow."

"Where?"

"The poop deck. There's a false entry to the engines. Delores thought it would be a good place to store excess items. The good part is, they won't know about it, won't go there for a while. Come on. You can vomit your guts out down there all you want. You're in a temporary rest phase now. You've got a few more heaves in you. I've got to take care of that wound. Here, let go of it. I have it. That's it. Man, carried that sucker all this time, even when--come on, baby. Hold on. I'll carry you. Don't worry. We've been lucky so far. Just a little while longer. That's all we need. Easy, now. Easy."

"Allen . . . "

"I know baby. I know. Easy now . . ."

Delores figured it out before she asked Susan the question.

The membrane gossamer but thick, tough wall reflected a red hue against red yellow background. It was like that Van Gogh panting where all yellow swirls fill against a night. Only the swirls were lines and swirls of rectangles and curls changing red and yellow and red again. Great waves of white snow, triangle and tubule shapes floated in and out of the keening membrane, for it vibrated with a harmonic tone none had before heard, a far roiling thunder off the distant high mountain peaks, but closer. These creatures great, small, tiny, huge bounced off yet somehow penetrated the solid wall. Tubules of rust-red creatures found and squeezed through the wall as some fictional vibrating time-traveler from the future. Fecund waves of twisting and turning filigreed-topped tubules redder yet than others appeared before their eyes and seemed, as by osmosis, to enter the deeper wider fire halls and hot searing bubbling caldrons.

These and more, an astonishing teeming sulfur, manganese, phosphorus, selenium, and silicon fire of locomoting entities that were not there, then were there, then were not there again.

"We're inside, aren't we? We've somehow been taken inside it."

"Somehow it maintains inside itself a temperature conducive to allowing its progeny or womb-kept life-forms to be fit for both environments; its outer, thick membrane has some kind of anatomic and physiologic and chemical make-up to allow it to exist in both environments. It is a daughter, or rather, mother, of fire, birthing sons and daughters of fire, water, air, and magma. Then, there is a way the creatures work through the membrane with some difficulty, apparently, and, in some cases, with ease.

It is not osmosis, not exactly. It's some other process. I need to observe more, conduct some experiments. It's so awfully gorgeous."

"This is it, isn't it? This is where life is created. All mother's womb."

"Another great womb. The great womb of life on earth. Look, Delores, Hodges. These walls, these teeming tubules, the other hordes of--they're not there really. Suddenly they are. Then, somehow, they dance within her, and extrude out, somehow. Into the cauldron-fire to become ore-living creatures but alive with DNA, like any creature we know, like the first of all creatures ever, this process for, for ten billion years, more maybe, has been the same. Until we arrived. It's where it all began. And now we have returned. And then to bubble out. It's so awful gorgeous."

Hodges gazed at the chronometer. "Susan. Delores. It's a fine gorgeous and true living laboratory. But in twelve minutes we're going to be fodder for it if we don't figure out how to get out of here, and return to our part of the world above the sea." Hodges realized at once the double entendre. They had to get out.

"Delores. Hodges. I'm not sure we can. No. Listen. There is something. This creature is huge. Larger than the Nebraska. It must have taken her centuries, eons, of, well, living down here. But how does she survive? Do you see what I'm getting at? When she gives, God it's not birth, it's something else, generating of generations, a genesis they then supply somehow her nutritive needs."

"You mean, we're her prey? She's going to eat, that is, absorb us?"

"Jonah inside the whale."

"Yes. That's it. Unless we can . . . there's one more thing. She came to us. She, what word. Sensed. She knew.

In some way we may, will, never know, she sensed. She knew."

Though it was the hottest place in the near cosmos other than the sun, chills ran up and down the backs of the people in the puny vessel inside the maw of the great mother-reaper creature from before time itself.

"Come and see. The answer is simple. We must get the whale to vomit up Jonah," Susan said.

"Commander."

"Commander, aye."

"I've got another blip.

"What?" Delores said. She was astonished. They were amazed. None knew what to say. Hodges continued. "Sonar still working by damn."

"A rescue effort?"

"By what? Wait. Computer memory signature matched. Damn. It's our old enemy. Knocking at our door. And following the currents this way. Holy God!"

"What was that?" The women asked almost as a chorus, so close for a moment Susan glanced over, expecting to see Jennifer. But it was Delores; for the first time since she had known her, she appeared as just another frightened woman in a tough spot. How quickly the rough-edges military officer reduces to the quivering schoolgirl, Susan thought. For there had been such a vibration vibrating somewhere even their captor, even in this super-heated environment of continuous explosions, shook in a manner uncommon.

Delores turned. She saw Susan looking at her. At once, she tried the hard veneer, to return the bearing of the military professional.

But Susan saw the woman was shaken with the realization. For she knew the reaction of explosive force.

"I think they blew her up. Blew the entrance. Blew the fucking vent off: My God they blew it up! We, we have no egress. We have no way to back out."

They looked at each other, then, as dead women and men. For now they knew their pathway back had been sealed off, the enemy was closing in, they were inside the belly of the beast, and their element more precious than fine jewels, their element of air, exhausted in ten minutes.

A skeleton, hand-picked crew, an old Navy vessel stripped down to make way for scientific equipment and science personnel: The old warship would be no match for anything with respectable complement of armament. Once there had been five inch guns, harpoon ship to ship missiles, Tow missiles launched from her helicopters, Tomahawks with ranges and satellite guided targeting in excess of 1,500 miles, helicopters with 30mm cannon and Arrow anti-missile missiles. They weren't here now).

Now there was largely only grey peeling paint. She was becoming a rust bucket. More was the pity.

He had gone below. He wasn't sure he had seen the ship out there, or had sensed something was wrong. But he had gone below for some reason. Maybe he was still mad at her. He wasn't even sure what he looked for. He had run engines before. Maybe he wanted to talk things over with the wrenches down below. But the experienced sailor and intel officer in him took over. He began taking inventory of the military equipment below. He found the armory had some weapons left. An AK-47, 2 M16's, an M-60, all short on ammo.

He returned to the poop deck. It took him only a second to see what happened. He saw her leap over. Even in her chosen desperate act of escape, she looked beautiful in her dive. He had his own 9mm. The M16 he lifted from the near deserted armory had only one clip. He was no match against the group of terrorists, and she was already enfolded deep into the waves of the sea.

Desperate, it seemed an eternity before they returned to the bridge and prow. He skulked up the side. There were only two. But another ship was heaving to along side. They were busy with the ropes ship to ship. It was what gave him his opportunity. That same damn vessel they fought before, no doubt. Soon more armed men and women would scurry about on their ship. They were about to be boarded.

He had received his briefing at Langley. He knew what they wanted. The sea spray sprinkled over the bulwark and washed his head and neck, but he sweated none the same. He sneaked back to the stern, away from bow and bridge. They would be busy for a while with the tie-up, and boson's chair transfers, but sooner or later they'd come this way.

He gazed over the bulwark where she had dived twenty feet to the ocean. Only the waves of the sea gazed back at him, sparkling and foaming in the sun. Then it dawned on him. Maybe, somehow, like a soldier running low across the field against an enemy machine gun nest, she made it to the other side without being seen. He ran, low against the wind over the rear deck. Taking a chance, he glanced down.

And she was there!

Her blonde tresses floated on the surface spreading out, like tendrils of a gossamer jellyfish, opening and closing, seeking any living form by chance. She was close enough to the rear ladder. Praying none of them looked back this way, he scampered down. He thought not of the risk. He leapt into the foam. Her left hand reached up just above the surface, as though she waved good-bye to the world. He stretched out his hand. He grasped her fingers, her hand, her wrist, her forearm, he had her!

He pulled her to the ship. Somehow he grasped the last rung with his right hand. He pulled her up to him with his left. He prayed he wouldn't dislocate her shoulder. He prayed he would not tear his own rotator cuff of his shoulder. She was no starved skin and bone super model. She was tall, muscular, with considerable avoirdupois. Somehow, he managed, rung by rung to get up to the rear, lower deck.

A moment to make sure they hadn't come back yet. Good God, she was almost dead weight. It was a herculean task. But he finally got her high enough on the rungs to get under her legs with some leverage, and, at last, over they went, plopping and flopping on the deck. In time, he removed her wet clothes, for she vomited and shivered and bled. In spite of the effluent of the ocean and her guts and blood, he was still in awe of her beauty. Then he saw the wound. He had to stop the bleeding. She started to heave again. In horror, he saw the wound froth when she heaved. He did not tell her of the frothing of her bodily fluids. There was a first aid kit across from the armory, a room he figured had been the dispensary. He had to get them down there.

Somehow he carried her. Then she began half to walk, moaning and weeping and looking half dead. She was his woman now. He would never desert her. Never again in his life would he abandon her.

He was astonished she never lost her grip on the thing she had carried when she executed her swan dive, her leap of life into the sea.

Mitch Corvales had a room he entered. It wasn't on any ship, or land station. It was his room he visited when all else failed and there was nothing more to do but go on. He knew he would soon have to go to his special room. He had been leery of this mission from the get-go. That was the fucking damn problem. There was no clear-cut military mission. A virtual set-up for a SNAFU, another Custer fuck.

He despised supporting scientific, civilian missions. And an unfamiliar ocean besides. The currents, the caverns of the Atlantic he knew as well as the route from his house to his office. But this stuff. Of course he had been informed of the military potential. Even with everything to it, the parameters of the mission were so ill-defined. If there is a biological weapon to be found, then so much the better.

But my God, fusion! That search, of course, made the mission worthwhile. Nonetheless, it was so vague, as if not even theory but mere hypothetical guesswork.

Ah, the first Persian Gulf War: There was a mission! There were clear-cut pathways and waterways for glory. There was victory in sight and in achievement. There was a clear cut mission.

In the end, though, even that mission had been compromised. That idiot former CIA director calling the whole thing off just when we had the son of bitch in our sights. Then the man's half-wit son his commander-in-chief out of a stolen election. And this Commander-in-Chief has the balls to order the Seal team to get

Bin Laden, then wimps out when they were all ready to bring an end to that toady's chemical arsenal.

When he retired he planned to voice all these concerns. Maybe sooner than later. Now he could help defeat ISIS, for they needed to be defeated, utterly; but here on a damn fool's errand instead.

He never dreamed that roach out there would head into the vent to escape his fish. What the hell! Any sane person would have engaged a deep underwater escape maneuver with as much empty sea around, fired decoys and headed into the oblique. Corvales wanted to scare him the hell away and his torpedoes couldn't last longer than a few seconds anyway. No doubt they thought we also had the miniaturized depth-pressure defiant rockets. By the time they realized their own miscalculation, they were trapped within the vortex. The rest was inevitable. Now it was over.

Now he needed to repair to his special room. For he had literally sealed the fate of the Ex-Gee's crew. Still, he knew eventually the XO was right. Forty-five minutes down there it was over anyway. It had been over ninety minutes at the impact time. Well he'd visit his room later. Now, he could still protect the people above.

"Commander, XO."

"Go."

"Approaching surface, sir. In, mark, 100 seconds."

"Notify SEAL Commander.

"Sonar, bridge."

"Sonar, aye."

"Any indication they've spotted our signature?"

"Bridge, Sonar. Negative. As far as I can tell. All looks copasetic. I say again. Negative to hostile sight."

"Copy that. Note coordinates. Navigation."

"Navigation, aye."

"I want an over the horizon surface. We've kept ourselves off their screens so far. I don't want them to make a visual. We'll launch all attack boats in four minutes. On your mark, XO."

"Roger that, Captain. All hands prepare to surface. I say again, prepare to surface. SEAL Team: Equipment check. Prepare launch all attack vessels four minutes on my mark. Mark. Steady as she goes. Surface in 48 seconds. Switch out of red. I say again. White light gradual illume."

"Switching out of red; white light gradient illume at this time, aye."

They had nine minutes of oxygen, less than ten minutes of sweet life and Dr. Susan Arthknott decided to deliver to them another of her classroom lectures. He was captivated by her, thought he loved her, but he considered at that moment cutting her life expectancy short by 7 or 8 minutes.

He had always been a big man, not so popular with the girls. Because of his appearance they hadn't thought him intelligent. But he got things faster than most and knew he was smart. He loved the military. It was the one place he had known they thought him equal and capable and treated him well. He always considered it would be an honor to die for his comrades, for his mission, for his country. He always knew it might come to this. It appeared at last he was about to get his chance.

He never dreamed a woman like that could go for him. Thin, slight, brainy as hell. He knew others could not see her beauty. But he knew how that must feel. He saw it. He saw it from the beginning. He thought her partner, that classic blonde beauty, must know it too. He liked Jennifer, as all men and some women probably did; but he was fully captivated, besotted by Susan. The way she moved, the way she talked, the way she looked at him over her glasses, but mostly when they fell off her nose upon her chest, then gave that especial, enchanting giggle, a girl-woman after all.

When she came to him he had been proved right. She was scared and confident at once, like a scientist careful with her experiment at first, then relaxing and giving herself to it, to him, totally. He understood that also.

She had a large freckle on her right shoulder just under where her hair came down. When her hair came down, he lost all thought of the freckle as she came on top of him. What the hell, let her prattle on. There would be worse ways to go out than hearing the harmony and the melody of Susan Arthknott's voice.

"Look here. Do you see? Those strands there." Susan hit the main console screen playback. The console streamed the visuals again, as dazzling and vivid as the first transmissions from the two lateral cameras, the split image playing in glory and glory on the console once more.

"Those single strands of DNA. Usually they're microscopic, coiled completely to fit in the nucleus of a cell. These are fully uncoiled. Amazing! They are macroscopic, more than a meter long. Look at their shapes. That alpha-helix there, the one that looks like a grappling hook, or that, very possibly a primitive myoglobin involving oxygen transport. Maybe it reminds you of a Swiss Army Knife with all the blades open and the handle missing. And, and, there, look, I, I can't describe them all. But these they are!

"The birth of life!

"Somehow they, how? How? Ah! Of course! They break. They recombine. Then repeat. Then again and again reinsert.

"See how huge that one is. You see, the genome of the salamander contains more than 10 times the quantity of DNA of the human; but we have only 25 times more genes than the lowly E. coli bacteria. So the non-coding parts explain this apparent contradiction, that is, lots of junk, but very few good combinations. Somehow the structure of the useful segments becomes coding sequences for proteins, repeating and repeating, inserting, into the machinery of life. All the variations, combining, forming, and then bubbling out, exploding out, coiling, diffusing. They swim. They maneuver. They transcend. They evolve, practically at once or over millennia, to creatures finding their way all over the world, sea world, land world, ice, desert, soil, sky.

"This is it! We have it! With this life-directed soup, we can format cures to every metabolic process gone awry. We can cure every disease. We can save the whole world, the whole God blessed and cursed world! I, I've got to get samples. Our samples in the lab will grow. Yes, that's it. They'll grow and they'll provide the basic cure for practically any dis--for any illn--"

Her eyes flashed those flames he had come to see, to know, to expect. He had seen them at the heaviest moment of their love making. She was wild then. Nothing else existed. She was mad now. He knew it. They all were.

"What's the matter with you people? Don't you see it? The beginning, primitive molecules forming the coding regions for the most fundamental proteins, protein combinations before any flaws, mutations. This soup is the key. The key is the code unaltered. The code unaltered is the life. Hearken to this herald:

"This is the original blueprint, blown forth upon the firmament from the breath-spirit of God Almighty!"

"Susan," Delores said.

"You must see it. You, you mus--" But the scientist's eyes began to flicker down, to appear a bit more normal. The flares in her irises ebbed to embers. Her nostrils seemed to retreat from flaring. But only for a moment. Following Delores's next admonition, the scientist who held in her hand the key to the end of suffering and misery re-generated her fervent gaze and attitude, nearly as profound redux as it had been before.

"It's practically the temperature of the sun. You can't collect samples. We have eight minutes of air."

They did not think they could be shocked the more. The scientist shocked them yet again, for she said her next sentence with full calmness, with nonchalance, in a matter-of-fact tone. She could have said, "Well, then, let us brush our teeth each morning, floss, mind our manners, and always look left and right before crossing the street."

"Well then, let us get out. Launch robot sample trays port side."

"Susan."

"Delores, listen to me. We've only got about four minutes to get out of this thing and to these coordinates. Look. Wait now. Wait. Come on. Come on. There! Do you have them?"

"Hodges."

"Got it. But . . . OK, got it."

"Now the sample tray may soon explode or may capture some elements on the spent uranium wall as we go forth. The tiles are all but gone. It's going to get damn hot in here in a few seconds, and I don't have time for arguing."

"OK. I'll trust you. Sample tray robot arm launched. It's holding in here of course. Got one."

"It'll hold. Or the thing will stay with us. It is what it does. It be that it be."

Hodges had never seen a look on a woman's face or anyone's face as the look Dr. Susan Arthknott had on her face in that creature's cooling womb in the star-heat of the interior of the earth. Her eyes were dark, deep set, aflame with fire at the same time. Her hair frizzed everywhere. They had stripped to their underwear and he would always swear he observed his favorite shoulder freckle quiver.

"Hodges."

"Weapons aye. Nav aye."

"That hostile vessel."

"Approaching. What's left of it."

"I think we need to get her in here with us before she burns up. If we can give our womb-monster-creature here a good jolt, I think that will create enough electromagnetic wave force to give nature, as it is here, a hand. Is our bulkhead electro-shock array operative?"

"Affirmative. Operative, at least some of it. Enough for her to know there's something else inside her. But how will that help?"

"For God's sake and all the love in the world. Everyone. I haven't time. Please just trust me. For the dearest love of God, trust me. Charge now."

"Charge on. Whoa. She felt something she's never felt before."

"Come on baby. Be a good mama. Take it in." Delores and Hodges looked at each other, then at Susan. They knew it was over. Dr. Susan Arthknott was mad as a hatter, as a March hare.

"What are you--"

"It took me a while," Susan said. "I should have seen it all along. You see the answer is so simple, really. So terribly simple. It is not osmosis at the interface event line. Or rather it is, in a fashion, but it isn't. Nature abhors a vacuum. What is here and isn't there must be there. Don't you see? You see it all now, don't you? It is symmetrical energy harmonic reversal. One of a similar or equal weight comes in . . ."

Susan's voice trailed off. She stopped speaking. But her mind moved in a time and space that existed only for her, only for the sentient vibrations not yet present in this moment, or perhaps full of awe always and she did not know it. Until now. "But if . . ." her mind continued to itself, in that deep place not yet here and not yet there.

". . . the exchange is between substantially different molecular densities there would be a net energy differential, an energy gradient gained strictly from the energy differential of the two."

Dr. Susan Arthknott's mind swelled with the emotion of the thought. There was a whole new Universe being born in her mind, displacing at least for this split second, which may have been a millennia or a million millennia in the Universe's birthing so long ago, her mind holding the rhythm of the womb they were in. The idea awesome and orgasmic would return later, but not now. For Hodges's mind now, trailing far behind, had caught a glimpse of where Susan had been.

"My God," Hodges said. For he had it all now. "One comes in . . . another goes out. That's why you needed the other ship in here. And the energy charge to equalize the gravity density. But will it work? And if it does, what of us out there? Where? Where can we go now?"

"You know Old Faithful don't you?"

"The geyser," Delores said.

"When we came in, we passed a caldron. OK, many of them. But this one explodes in less of a random chaos sequence than the others. At least that's what Alfred tells us. It entered the algorithms three times, and they always came back within two per cent. Well, discounting the two per cent chance that we could be wrong, she's due to blow in 3 minutes; 3 minutes 27 to 30 seconds, that is. Ninety-eight per cent's not bad, unless our calculations are wrong, and the heat has compromised the integrity of the chronometer chip. But it's a chance. Hell, it's our only chance."

Then she laughed.

They gazed at her again, again wondering if they should trust this crazed woman scientist. Then she told them the joke. "A silicon creature we created entrusted to get us out of a silicon trap, with her allies sulfur and manganese."

Now it was Delores's turn to put it together at once. "The verniers, if they work, we can cut them in the final seconds, hell they won't last anyway, and hopefully be directly over it when it blows, expelling us and everything in its path out of here. You mean for us to ride the wild volcano. We'll probably be torn apart. But you're right. We're going to die anyway. It's worth the risk."

They panted. They sweated. Deep dark-eyed gazes. They were three desperate people and one unconscious in a desperate struggle to the end time of their lives, twixt heaven and hell and earth.

"Lots of if's, Susan."

"Yeah, Hodges. A bunch. Like thee and me." They laughed again, this time carrying the laughter for the first time in a long time. A scared nervous ongoing laugh; and it brought them around just past the edge of the madness and unto the wonder and the joy and the hope of their lives. For, whether for a few moments or for fifty more journeys of the orb about the star, they were alive and they knew it.

"All right, this is it," Susan said. "Hodges."

"She's knocking at our door. She can't seem to make it in. She's disintegrating."

"Damn. Any array energy left?"

"We'll see. Charging. Yes! She's in with us! She wasn't and then she was! Just like you said. Just in time, too, by the looks of her. Off to port, make it fifteen meters."

Magruder, for the first time in long time, moaned. He shifted his position. He moved his head up, then bent it down again.

"Strap him in good. You two as well. Mama's got that sucker now. Those poor bastards are in her womb. To our womb. And we're heading out. Hang on. Here we go."

They waited for him. They always waited. They looked at him. It was his decision. He had made a wrong one earlier. He would not make another. He needed updated information. He requested the latest radar and sonar. Olgelby asked Egerton. No sign of their being spotted. Nothing from below either.

The 3 attack crafts carried 12 person teams each plus the equipment of water, plastique explosive, light charge grenades, ammo, radio, contingency supplies. One of the rafts carried a thirteenth man or woman, a medical corpsman. Thirty-seven rescuers, 25 highly trained and valorous men; 12 highly trained and valorous women. All on their mission to save over 50 brave men and women, a good ship, and her scientific-military holdings and discoveries.

The two-cycle engines on the Zodiacs hummed. They started on the first ignition. The group was ready. Coordinates locked on by navigation.

"Radio. Notify fleet of our situation. Request support vessels Thompson and Llewellyn. Attack helicopters. On my mark: 1340 hours."

"Copy that, Bridge."

"X0."

"Aye Captain."

Corvales looked out off the coning tower into the distance. To Olgelby, it seemed as if his captain could see the enemy at this distance, over the horizon. He knew the skipper was looking into himself equally as deep.

"Launch! Launch! Away all boats!"

"SEAL Commander. Green light. Attack plan alpha Charlie away."

Three two-cycle engines revved. Thirty-seven intense people stormed across the sea. They were five miles away from engagement. They didn't know what they'd find. But they knew it was going to be a blazing white-hot fire-fight above the cool green ocean water.

He uncovered a first aid kit. It was old. The bandages and gauze would do. He pressed the wound to stop the bleeding.He cleaned it. He found rubbing alcohol.

"Baby, I'm sorry. This will hurt. Hell, it's going to hurt like hell. And you can't scream. You can't. I'm sorry, baby."

"Tell me you love me."

"I love you."

"Kiss me."

He kissed her.

"OK. Pour it on. Look in my eyes. Hold my hand. Pour it on. What are you waiting for? I'm a woman. I can take it like a man. Damn it, Allen, pour it on and let's get it over with. Wait! Not yet. Wait a minute. OK. Now. Do it!" He poured it on.

Out of the jar, it poured smooth. This was deception.

The mixture of disinfectant and her blood, lymph, pus hissed and bubbled, as though the microbes could be heard screaming in their death throes. Coursing, oozing out of the wound, rivulets in a sick pink color found their paths down her yet undamaged flesh to the floor of the makeshift dispensary.

The malevolent artist had mixed the hues of her blood with the dilution of the alcohol. Small streams of despair and hope, seemingly almost sentient, the pink waters found their channels on the floor of the deck, or pooled, forming small ponds within which teemed myriads of life forms, given re-birth and death by the mixture within the body of the large woman screaming in silence.

"Jesus," Allen said.

The look on the face of the woman yanked from death, out of the depths of the sea, with sea-stuff and stink about her, in an agony awesome to behold was terrible, a contorted, writhing despair. Anyone else peering in might not have seen her beauty. He knew he would always see it.

Then, she relaxed her face, her lines, her wrinkles. She gave in to the pain, sweet and horrible, horrific for its terror, joyful knowing it was temporary and sweet release would someday come, a day would one could look back and remember being in torment and alive and hoping only for it to pass, when life was reduced to no discipline, no direction, no plans, no back stabbing, no greed, no avarice, no sexual desire, nothing except the person and her hideous pain, with only one desire, to be rid of it.

She opened her mouth to scream. Again she screamed in silence. From somewhere deep in her throat he heard a whispered yell. "Oh God. Oh God. Allen."

"Yeah baby."

"You came for me. You searched for me. You came for me."

"Couldn't let anything happen to a good scientist, right?"

"Oh God that hurts. Allen, it hurts so bad."

"I, I'm sorry, bab--"

"No. It's OK. It's wonderful. Who'd ever think they would welcome pain? I know now why we have pain. We know we're still alive. Oh sweet Jesus, Daddy Joseph, and Mother Mary."

"Here baby. It'll feel better in a couple of minutes. I promise. Just let me get it bandaged up here. It'll feel better soon. You will see. You will feel better. I promise. There. There now. You will see."

"You, you promise?"

He took her in his arms. He cradled her head against his chest. He fought against the stench overwhelming his nostrils. She beautiful. She repulsive. She his. She woman!

She smelled-stink of blood, vomit, sweat, tears, engine oil, salt spray, fish, and something else, something indefinable, something putrid-sweet from the sea, something almost but not quite recognizable and at once fully recognizable, as on the first day we know autumn is in the air, about to turn the corner, but we can't say exactly why. Somehow he knew it was something that had existed on earth, in the ocean slime and scum long before cognizant life appeared. It would exist still even after the next extinction level event.

"Allen. I've, I've got to get to the bridge."

"No! You're going to rest now. They'll come for us soon enough."

"No. Susan. Oh God. Foxworth and Wells. Susan. Susan. Susan, I'm coming for you now. I'll dive off again and I'll come down for you. No. I've got to get to the bridge first."

"Jennifer, calm down. You're delirious. Probably have a fever. Damn. That won't help. Susan is, she's been gone a long time. I'm afraid she's--"

"No. No. She'll find a way. I've got to get to the bridge."

"Listen to me. Listen. You're going to tear your wound. There are about thirty men and women with guns out there. You can't even walk. You'll never make it. Now rest. Rest a bit. Then we'll see."

"Rest. Yes. That's it. Rest. Just for a, for a, a minute."

And the world changed at once. There was no gradual drifting or dozing off. She recognized she was of a sudden, instantaneous, in a deep sleep.

The monster was at her door. That was strange. She had closed her eyes. She was sleeping. How could he have penetrated her defenses after all these years? Had he finally broken through? Why didn't he go away? Why did he keep coming toward her?

Suddenly the other ship was there. Susan would always remember she saw a man's eyes filled with a terror she could never imagine. She almost knew it; but it was so horrific she could never fully imagine it.

They had by chance each opened their window coverings at the same time. Then she closed hers for she realized they were at once through the membrane-like skin of the creature.

They had done nothing. It just was. But no vehicle of any comparable size closed in on the huge creature. The men left inside the hostile submersible were doomed.

However, their cells, their DNA was not doomed. They would escape some day, but not the way they were. They would slowly, in an agonizing fashion be broken down into recombinant DNA and sometime in the future they would be expelled through the vents to enter the life cycle of the upper ocean planet. Who knew? Perhaps someday she would drink them in a glass of water, or inhale them in a deep breath, or consume them in a hearty salad of vegetables.

She hoped they had enough sense to run out of air or turn off their air supply, suffocate in seconds, and not suffer a suffering terrible end beyond description.

"105°. 108. 110. Jesus. We'll be burned to a crisp before we . . . "

"Fire verniers ion propulsion. Damn it, now, before they melt or blow up."

"Firing. They worked. 112. 115. Oh God they're gone. Refrigerator compressor gone. All systems gone. We're on sheer momentum. Hull on fire. 120. 128 . . ."

"Susan. Old faithful dead ahead."

"Dear God blessed be Thy Name, please fire the fucking fire-fucker up now." Weeks later, it would occur to Delores that the scientist had prayed to the Divinity. Well, that is, in her fashion. And she knew that God looked down from heaven and heard the woman in the lower spheres of hell.

The volcano erupted in a huge explosion, spewing forth its magma into the upper reaches of its ecology, a mighty force, mightier, unstoppable even in the midst of mighty forces.

"Hodges, oxygen."

"Two minute warning Susan. I can't even think or talk. Our flesh is aflame. 131°. 139. 1,4ahohh--"

Flames sparked upon the skin of the vessel. Flames sparked upon the skin of the vessel's inhabitants. Searing, bubbling heat and smoke and steam swirled everywhere about them.

Steam, Susan thought.

Steam?

That became her last thought. Then all she knew was not knowing, a sweet, dear, dark oblivion blackness, so void and truly void, a plane of non-existence so deep, so dark, so full in its emptiness, where nothing is, where nothing was, where nothing came into it.

She felt better. He had been right. With the cleaning, the antiseptic, the bandaging, the throbbing, unyielding, hideous pain eased. The bandage held, although blood, red oozing ocher, like ink tapped upon the old elementary school blue-lined yellow tablet paper, spread. And something else, some other bodily fluid, thick clear-green-yellow. Then, suddenly, her obsession with her wound faded, for it didn't matter.

She heard them approaching. He told her to try to hide behind one of the cabinets. He left her to see what it was. She crawled to the door. Reports of gunfire blew about the room. Stray bullets whizzed, all quite close. She chanced to peer around the corner. Allen had shot one man. Desperate, he fought hand to hand with another. He hit the man with the barrel of his gun. He hit the man square with his right elbow. The man crumpled. But another man, another terrorist appeared at the outer door to the first deck. He drew down a bead on Allen. He would soon discharge his weapon, bringing death to her man. If only she could get her own weapon spring loaded in time.

Where had he put—there! Oh, she couldn't move as fast as before her dive to the sea. Now, at last. She fumbled with the mechanism. She remembered the day with the damn videotape in the machine. Damn her side hurt. She had almost for a moment forgotten the pain. Be a soldier. Ignore it. Finally she loaded the device. She heard the report of the rifle again. Two more. A fourth. God she was too late. Allen was dead. She knew it. At least she could take her revenge. Payback, she heard one of the men say once. She struggled to stand. She turned the corner.

"Jennifer, no. It's OK. Don't shoot."

She lowered her weapon. The man she saw at the doorway was the man now lying dead on the floor. Allen stood back in the hallway. Another man, a third man in battle armor, stood in the doorway. He held a layered weapon she did not recognize. He had an earpiece. A thin but firm wire formed a microphone curved around, almost in front of his mouth. This man spoke to them.

"You're Littleton? Johnstone?"

"Yes." Jennifer simply nodded, looking at the three dead men and the two living ones.

"Alpha TL, this Alpha 18. Blondie and Browser secured safe. Blondie requires medical aid ASAP; gunshot left side; appears clean entry, exit. Deck Level 1 secured. Do you copy?"

The commando listened, obviously receiving confirmation. She recalled then the dream with her monster. It seemed that none of her defenses worked anymore, and she was doomed. Then a soldier in battle dress had pierced the darkness of her vision, and slaughtered the mystical entity. She had seen his face twice now; for it was the man standing with them.

For the remainder of her life never again was she threatened awake or asleep by her monster. That day, triumphant, she buried her monster.

She listened. She heard. Rapid fire weapons, men and women yelling, screaming, running. More weapons fire. Explosions. Bright lights, seen even under decks. The soldier told them to stay put. Help was on the way. Then he was gone.

"SEAL team, Jennifer. Spec Ops. From the Nebraska. She'll be along soon enough. She'll hold back a bit. We won't see her at first, I don't think; I mean, she'll come low, with decks awash. I, damn, I am tired. She won't want to risk a torpedo launch or a missile strike from the hostile. And she can't sink her without endangering the Starr."

"I've got to get to the bridge."

"That's a negative. You stay here. You heard what the man said. You can't go anywhere in your condition. You hear me?"

He wanted demure, submissive, contrite. She gave the man what he wanted from his woman.

"Yes, Allen. I hear you. I'll do as you ask."

"All right then," he said, somewhat taken aback, somewhat surprised at the power of his male authority over his woman. At first he skulked. Then he dashed. He disappeared out the door, turning right, following their rescuer to secure the rear decks.

Jennifer Littleton waited. A hint of a smile crossed her filthy, bruised face, her hair flowing up and about, as Medusa's snakes coiled and hissed. She peered out the door. With the blanket around her and the fire-fight going on above her, they might not notice her. It was a clear day. "It's a beautiful day today," she said aloud to herself. "It is a good day to die."

Reports of weaponry, light grenades booming, screams and shouts above and beneath her continued. The ship might be nearly secured, but obviously it wasn't a complete job yet.

She quit her infirmary. Suddenly she found herself in the hallway of the deck. She did not recall the three or four steps it took to get her there. Dazed. I'm dazed, she thought. Still, to press on. Susan must be avenged. She turned right.

Wait! That was wrong. Left, yes, left.

Then her Epiphany: Her vision of light drenched her in light. The light shone down in great rays from the heavens and showed her what occurred off the ship's starboard bow.

It was so bright, and it stayed with her throughout, she saw reality with a crystal clarity she had never before witnessed. After that day, she would never again see things so crystal clear and bright, and she knew few people even had half a day of such a gift. It was the way reality could be perceived by all of us, if we could but let go of the barriers that keep us from seeing.

She saw the movement against the shimmering waves. She gazed out to sea. In spite of her pain, in spite of the blood dripping from her side onto the wood of the floor, in spite of the fire-fight and men and women killing and being killed about her, in spite of her invincible mission, she stared for a moment in awe. The sun seemed fluorescent, radiating, the light scintillating. Ray beams glistened upon, under, and reflected off of the whiteness of the surface of the deep.

Boobies dove into the water, fishing for fish. An orgy of dive after dive. Their wings outstretched until the last second, then pulling them in to their bodies, then diving 5 or 8 feet under water to get the sardines, a huge school, the school desperately but in futility attempting to escape this way and that, trying to head deeper; and if they could, it was in vain for thence attacked by sharks, whales, dolphins rising from the deep, catching the scent of terrified prey, a gathering of predators swarming from miles and fathoms abounding.

As happens to human beings caught up in the middle of oppression and war, despair and death the only choices of the pursued.

An orgy of death and survival, blood now streaked the white-blue of the water, whilst human blood poured over the decks of the ship upon the sea.

Somehow the birds so obsessed with their own prey and the athletic grace and brilliance of their own dives to capture it, they twirled into the waters oblivious to the hunters and hunted upon the man-made floating machine, now transformed to place of valor and death. Death wreaked a wide range across and beneath the splashing froth of the ocean that day.

She saw all this, illuminated with the great light that God must have ordered upon the firmament, above the waters and below the waters. She watched, transfixed, for a long while, and only for a few seconds at the same time.

Stray bullets whizzed past the birds. Jennifer watched, praying the projectiles missed the animals, willing their trajectories to bend in ballistic flight. Then she knew the other reason she had waited here. She had gathered her strength, her will. She was transcended. A wraith with light of justice a halo over her. The light of vengeance radiated from within her.

She could no longer feel the pain. In her large bare feet, she padded up the deck to the companionway, grasping the rail.

"XO, radio com."

"Bridge aye."

"Reports coming in from Alpha Leader. All decks. Starr secured. Holdouts still engaged. Bridge not yet secure."

"Anything on the enemy vessel?"

"Hostile secure all decks. Torpedoes, missile controls and overrides in friendly lands."

"Navigation."

"Nav aye. Course plotted."

"Take her in X0. One-half speed. Remain decks awash."

"One-half speed aye."

"X0, Captain. Sonar. I don't believe this. It, it's impossible."

"Calm down Mr. Egerton." Corvales thought to himself. Now what. At that moment when we were starting to get things under control.

"Sir, I'm showing something one and one-half miles west south west. Now due west. Now sout--it's like it's under no direction or control. Yes! That's it. It's being buffeted about . . ."

"Egerton, X0. Calm down, son. What the hell is it? Report on the QT."

"X0, aye. Copy that. Holy mother of God. It has the signature of the Ex-Gee."

The entire ship heard him. At any given moment, there is constant chatter on board, internal communications back and forth. For the only time he had ever been on any vessel, other than silent running, silence washed over his fleet ship of the Navy. After a moment, Corvales broke it.

"Nav, bridge."

"Nav, aye. Course plotted sir." The man had almost shouted it. Hope reborn in joy had arisen in his voice.

Corvales had it also, Olgelby noted. But he also knew the people aboard were probably dead, as Egerton already knew. Clearly the small submersible was being aimlessly buffeted about in the valleys and crests of the waves.

"X0. Turn about. Flank speed. Notify Alpha Leader he's got to be on his own a while longer. We'll be there as soon as we can. Get the medical team to the bridge. Expedite. Rescue teams equipment check. ETA two minutes."

The huge ship turned about on flank speed. It was a maneuver she didn't often make nor was designed to do well. Soon enough water foamed along side her bow and stern, as she listed 300 degrees to the turn before righting herself in ballast.

She fairly cut the water to the new coordinates.

A pitched battle, she surmised the final one, circulated about the bridge steps. It was grisly, knives flashing, and no sound other than flesh tearing, grunts, groans. They were mean looking men, a motley group, and they did not seem to realize they had already lost at the hands of these professionals.

They did not see her. No one saw her. She realized then she had her mantle of invisibility on. She was a wraith. A demon-harpy. A chameleon-ninja. Lilith in resurrection. Females are the more dangerous, she thought. Poor men. They know nothing.

It was easy then to open the door. In fact, she did not need to open it. She passed through it. She caught a glimpse of herself in the mirror. Fire in her eyes, her hair matted into the spikes of the wraith, snake-tongues flitting in and out from the ends of the spikes, sniffing the putrid air of anxiety and gunpowder and blood.

Then, there they were, the two. The traitors. The ones who had caused her to lose any chance of helping Susan find her way back. Now her comrade, her teacher, her colleague, the woman she admired and loved was gone and this bastard and this bitch still stood, the last holdouts.

When she spoke, it was with a voice rained upon with ice, a voice seemingly to echo with a meaning beyond time and place, beyond air, beyond water, beyond fire. They turned.

"Wells. Foxworth. Meet thy fate. Turn. It is over." They turned. They had been posed to shoot it out to the end. The plan of great wealth and power was over. They were unprepared for rafts from the sea transporting to the fray well trained men and women.

It was as though at first sight they saw her not. Then, they did.

"Well, Littleton," Foxworth said. Sweat beaded upon her face and arms. Her hair matted to her head. Her eyes were mad and wild, as though a part of her were no longer alive. There wasn't much pretty about her now, Jennifer thought to herself, recalling her own image in the glass. And not just from the fighting. Good. It was just as well. There was no beauty in this. Only cold revenge that reached into a place deeper and darker than beauty could ever penetrate.

"We thought you were dead."

"Not hardly. Just decided to go for a swim is all."

"Yeah. Web-footed bitch like you could survive the drink, I guess."

The traitor lifted her weapon. At last the beautiful scientist transmuted into a killing wraith pulled up her weapon. She fired. Jennifer released her harpoon from within her blanket. Unerringly it passed through the woman's throat. Blood spattered all around. Blood and snot and tissue sprayed all about her head. That pink mist surrounded her already dead body suspended in space, then slowly, as in a dance of death, fell to the floor. Foxworth's body levitated in the air, vibrated, and fell back against the opposite door. "The one below, the one still bel . . .," the woman gurgled, in an awful bubbling from where her throat had been. Then she said nothing, heard nothing, saw nothing.

Wells fired at her. He was a sure shot and they were five feet apart. But of course the bullets couldn't hit her.

She knew this. She was a wraith. The projectiles whizzed to the left of her, to the right of her, above her head. She took her time. This time her fingers did not fumble. She felt the spring of the second dart seated in its housing.

She didn't bother to aim. She knew its aim would be true. She released the spring. The harpoon dashed through the air, spinning. The barb pierced the eyelid of his right eye, closed against it, then straight through his pupil into the jell-like substance in the cavity of the orb, through his retina, on into the optic nerve of his brain and out through the brain's membranes and its skull. The Team Leader and three members of the SEAL team ran in, guns at the ready. They surveyed the scene before them.

Wells looked at them with his remaining eye. Blood flowed forth as from a large fountain with a human figure sculpture from all his orifices at once. He fell to the floor, slowly, spinning, floating.

"Med corps, Alpha Leader. AL to all Alpha team. Bridge secured. I say again, bridge secured. Complete final phase. Med corps, we need medical help here ASAP. Ms. Littleton's wounded."

"Copy that. We tried to find her earlier. We're on our way."

She looked down. The blanket had fallen off. She stood naked before them all. Nude, blood, snot, lymph, salts from the sea, filth, sweat ridden.

Again her wound opened. Her blood mixed with the blood of her enemies against her naked body. Like an Amazon in the days of yore, or a woman-warrior in the ancient days of dim historical beginnings, she rubbed the bloods together against her cheeks, her neck, her breasts, her stomach, her thighs. She clenched her hands. She flexed the sinews of her muscles, more powerful and strong than ever she had felt them. She spread her powerful arms wide above her head, fists at the top of the great Y formed. She bellowed a chilling skirr of victory over the corpses of her enemies. So loud the victory yell penetrated the walls of the pilot house and carried over the ocean waves as far as the submarine. The crew there turned from their tasks for the moment, as though they had heard the songs of Odysseus's sirens.

The soldiers peered at her in astonishment. She gazed back at them with a gaze penetrating from before life on earth. Then she closed her eyes, one lid slowly after the other, and she fell, down, slowly, spinning and floating like Wells's body had done, falling into the soldier's arms, finally releasing the harpoon gun she had held onto all this time. It clanged when it hit the floor, bounced, clanged again, bounced, thence, at last, whirled to a spinning rest.

A small pinpoint of light penetrated the sweet nothingness. She had been in a void, in oblivion, unaware. Now they were coming for her, to take her to the light. It wouldn't be as peaceful as the oblivion, but it would be all right. Then the light got larger and mightier. The voices of men, and cool rush of air: It was heaven or life on earth.

But whichever it was she knew she'd never go to hell for she had seen it and been there. Now, men and cool air sought her out. Ocean fluids came for her. The ocean poured into her veins, restoring life to her body. So it was life on earth still. That was OK. For now, she knew it was a taste of heaven. Soon the pain would return. She would welcome it. She was alive.

It took a while. But they were experts. They released the hatch. The two men and two women lay strewn about the cabin, as if someone had picked them up like sticks and dropped them. Arms and legs splayed everywhere, intertwining. Air rushed in. The rescue team rushed in.

"Pulse weak, spotty. BP, 95 over 45." So the reports went, back to the Nebraska's bridge. They were barely alive. But they were alive and might yet survive. Somehow all four of them were alive.

Olgelby saw his commander punch the air, dance a little jig step. His decisions had been good ones after all.

"Bridge, radio."

"Bridge, aye."

"All areas secured by Alpha team. Resistance ended. Twenty down. Thirty wounded. Fourteen prisoners. One casualty AT. One casualty civilian. Code name Blondie. Receiving medical attention at this time."

"Copy that. Notify ATL our situation. Ex-Gee secured. Well, what's left of her. Huh. The only thing left is the cabin with them in it. All hands alive in critical condition. Rendezvous ETA--XO."

"Forty minutes, skipper. We need to secure these people with care, and secure the vessel. As you say, sir, what is left of it. Forty min--forty-five minutes."

"Copy that X0." He received another report on the medical condition of the crew inside what was left of the small submersible. "Better make that ninety minutes."

On the Ex-Gee, the men worked furiously to hook up IV's. The Corpsman instructed full bore wide open drip-piggy back second bag saline solution, prophylactic vaccines and antibiotics.

"Jesus. Carl. Look at their skin, eyebrows. There. I've never seen, my God. It's their second layer of skin. The outer has been excoriated. But how--"

"Burned off I suppose. Damn. Move them gingerly. Here, the burn cot. They've got first and second degree burns everywhere. Going to be a long hard recovery for these folks."

"Keep the IV's pouring in, the oxygen masks and bags going. They've been to hell. Let's give them a fighting chance."

"Copy that."

# 8

COOLTIDE

She drove into the parking lot. She parked the rented car. She opened the door. She turned to exit. A soft swift breeze caught her skirt, billowing it high, exposing her well formed thighs. Two marines happened by. In an ages old interplay of stolen glances and furtive turning at the last timed second, the men walked by.

She didn't mind. She felt flattered. She felt good that after all she went through, there were those who felt she still had her figure. She was beginning to feel it herself, that enviable, confident inner feeling of being a beautiful woman and knowing it.

She opened the back door. She reached in the back seat. She pulled out the plant. Susan liked ferns. They reminded her of sea plants, reaching upwards. Everything in the sea seemed to reach up, to try to reach the surface.

On land we reach, Jennifer thought; whilst into the sea we dive deep. Or try to.

Only three days ago, she had been released from the hospital. Her wound healed well. In a few days she would return to have her stitches removed. Now she came practically every day to see Susan. Hodges came to see her also. He stayed by her bedside as long as he could. He held her hand.

She thought of Alan. He was home most weekends now. That was nice. As for Magruder . . .

Magruder was, well, she couldn't say. He had always acted strange, a little strange man. It wasn't just the close call of sabotage and his also being a patient. Something else. Something she couldn't quite put her finger on. Well, what did it matter, after all?

The thing bothered her as it had bothered her before. She had deduced it. She had tried to tell them, but kept slipping in and out of consciousness. Foxworth mentioned the other one down there. She hadn't been able to understand that at first.

The woman meant there was a third. A third conspirator on board the small submersible, on board. The third traitor had been on the Ex-Gee after all. Only he couldn't do anything since he had been unconscious. Fortunately, his recovery was slower than the others. She had finally been able to tell Barnstone. Magruder was now somewhere else, in a prison hospital. There was sufficient evidence. He would heal. He would make a deal and serve some time. After all, there were still others of the conspiracy, probably world-wide linked, out there.

This was the day Susan might be able to sit up. Perhaps later in the day, she could walk out to the hall.

The doctors were amazed that the crew of the Ex-Gee had survived. Indeed the outer layer of protective skin, the exoderm, had been excoriated. Only the second layer of skin, the endoderm, had saved them. And these were blisters, abrasions, deteriorated conditions. There was no skin to transpose or transplant. They gave them full drip IVs, demoral and morphine in high dosages, heavy Vitamin E and other vitamin injections, and Vitamin E gel rubs gingerly upon them, and frequently they were kept in ice baths or cool water baths.

Mostly however, they were compelled to wait it out.

As the days and now weeks proceeded, they all realized with serendipity that those resultant hideous masks-skin-scar of burn victims would be only subtly apparent. In effect, they would not form the grotesque so often formed in a patchwork quilt of healed and inlaid skin.

The doctors and nurses were amazed.

Susan, Jennifer, and Barnstone thought this curative generation resulted from some unknown exposure that had happened to them in the vent, in the heat of the volcanic chambers, or in the belly of Leviathan, as they now referred to the creature. Or, creatures. They recalled they thought they had caught glimpses of others.

The doctors were uncertain the cause of this beneficent dermatological phenomenon. But Jennifer and Susan believed the answer indeed lay in the fires under the sea. For something else had occurred there.

Susan's palsy had disappeared. Her blood tests showed none of the disease's remarkable presentations.

Was there some sort of electro-chemical energy generated by the myriad, teeming pleomorphic life down there, a sort of Rife Ray blast that cured diseases even without needing to dissect the genetics? Jennifer, seriously wounded, and not tending to it proper at all at first, should have taken longer to recover, and also astonished her physicians. Perhaps someday they could return. The design had to be improved though. There was a way . . . if they could . . .

Her mind turned the design over again, the nips and tucks, the double bat wing of titanium and silicon she considered.

Jennifer Littleton walked up the circular concrete walk. Azaleas bloomed from the center round median of the walkway.

At a distance she heard a sprinkler. Men and women in surgical greens, in military uniforms, in day to day civilian business and casual wear came and went through the circular revolving doors she was about to enter.

She stopped at the entrance. She turned. She looked up. She had thought she heard them. Three gulls glided low over the area. They seemed to gaze down upon her. They turned with a masterful grace. They swooped back out to sea. She continued on her way. She knew the route well by now.

"Susan, you're OK."

She was sitting up in bed for the first time. She smiled. Yes, she was beautiful once and would be beautiful again. "We're going to publish a paper."

"I know."

"'Non Photosynthetic DNA origins Within Sentient Entities in a Large Aperture Thermo-generating Deep-Sea Vent: Silicon and Magnesium Origins of Carbon-Based Systemics.' Something like that. You're better with titles."

"We have time now. We'll put something together."

"It's a momentous discovery, Jennifer. Momentous."

"I know, Susan."

"Look at us. We should be dead. Or appearing like it. We're practically back on our feet. Hell, you have been for a while. What, a day, no two or three."

Jennifer noticed that since she had been back, there was an earthy, non-academic side to her mentor and friend that had not been there before. The vents changed many things, she guessed. Or men did. A man.

Susan. There's something else. Alan, Hodges, the investigators. They're trying to put something else together."

"Carstairs?"

"Yes. And the others. I'm afraid his group, whatever it is, knows what the army is up to."

"Well, military people know the truth of the matter: Military secrets are the most fleeting of all. The misguided genius bastard. Damn him. The son of--

There was a long pause. She was talking too much, expending too much energy. She was becoming agitated. Jennifer knew she needed to rest. She shouldn't have come. She shouldn't have said--"

"Oh. Oh my. I don't feel well. Ring for the nurse."

"Here. Lie down. No, not, wait, let me get this sorted out. OK. There. Lie down. Easy, now."

Jennifer rang for the nurse. She brushed Susan's hair back from her face. Susan somehow managed to brush Jennifer's own long blond hair behind her ears. Then her arm fell back for she was a woman fully exhausted.

"You have such beautiful hair, Jennifer. I've always admired your hair. Like flax. Like waving wheat on a sunny autumn da--what was I . . ."

"Susan. Please. Rest now. The nurse will come. Don't speak. Just rest."

There was a pause, then, as the teacher tried to follow the student's instructions. Jennifer kept speaking, as much to keep her friend from speaking as to indicate what it was she wanted to say. She knew at once she had chosen the wrong subject. Susan suddenly had a little energy, and answered her clearly and cogently.

"Susan, I'm sorry the specimen was lost."

"It's all right. I knew it would be burned up or drowned. I somehow thought we'd be OK when things turned to steam. That meant we were into the water of the sea. If I could have brought it into the lab hold of the ship at that point. But impossible. I was half dead. Cooked into oblivion."

"Susan."

"No Jennifer. It's all right. Really. I saw the sweet blessedness of nothing, and the sweet blessedness of beginning. I've been reborn, you see. Reborn from the sea. Next time though, a slower ascent. The bends really take it out of you."

Despite themselves, they laughed. Jennifer winced.

"Damn, Jennifer, it wasn't that funny, to split your sides." And she suddenly lapsed into sleep. Just like that. One moment she instituted her wry wit; the next instant, her eyes rolled under her lids in deep REM patterns.

Jennifer held her friend's hand. She would tell her the good news later, when she, when they both were much better, and could walk and hug and laugh in joy without concern for the other's welfare.

She gazed out the window. The sun reached toward noon. The palm trees rustled in a slight breeze. A gull landed onto the windowsill for a moment, then headed back out to the ocean. She could almost see it, if she stretched up a bit, a thin blue line a hint of the great mass of the moving firmament waters upon the earth.

Susan stirred a bit. Out of her drugged-sleep state, she managed to barely call out, "Jennif--?"

"It's all right, Susan.

"Funniest thing."

"It's all right," Jennifer said. "I'm here. I'll always be here." Jennifer pressed the call button again.

Together they waited for the nurse to come.

# 9

## EPILOGUETIDE

The waves washed in foam caressed her feet gently. She now loved the more gentle rush, the soft entrance of the predictable waves, the way they felt upon one's feet, one's precious skin where cool water and gentle caresses were gifts, astonishing gifts she had only realized but never fully attained in fullness.

The water is warmer here, she thought, as she remembered thinking it a short time ago, eons ago, millennia past days of her years.

She heard the unmistakable footfalls in the softness and hardness of the sand, the footfalls of her friend behind her. Without turning, she said, "You took a bit longer than I thought you would."

Jennifer Littleton approached her friend, her colleague, her mentor, who was barefoot in the sand-water of the Gulf waters. "I can say you're just about cured. Back to your old self. He was in a conference. He'll see us at seven. Seven after, he said."

"Seven at seven, I know. He has time down to the minute. Next time I think he should go with us. To see time begin, end, and stand still," Susan said.

"I think he wants to actually. For now he expects his full report. I told him that your idea of scraping every millimeter of the Ex-Gee paid off. Some of the DNA of the creature or creatures was found. Enough for some genome investigation. He sounded like he thinks there may be some pharmaceutical breakthroughs. It think he's going to throw us a party of congratulations. A celebration. And he asked that we bring our videos. I think he thinks we're heroines.

"I asked him if Hodges and Allen could come. I know Hodges just received his orders. They're tracking that ISIS terrorist I suspect. But I thought some strings could be pulled. Susan?"

"Yeah. That,that will be fine. I miss him, that's all. I just miss the big lug. But when a woman falls hard for a military man, she has to take the times she can see him. Or if a man should fall for a, well. That will be fine, Jennifer. Satisfactory."

She peered out to sea, as women and men had been doing for centuries and eons. Gazing out into the great wonder and mystery, as they peered out into the oceans of space and upon the stars. There was a connection between the two, but only hints and glimmers of understanding washed briefly of a moment into even the most brilliant minds, and then, like a spring which bubbles up only at random, uncertain times, the clue, the insight, almost gained, was lost again.

"It's still out there. The answer to the mystery. Somewhere. Deep down under. Fire and stardust under the coolest of deepest waters. We came up from there. And we keep trying to go back. Back down there; back out there."

Jennifer put her arm about the shoulders of her friend. Together, the two women stood upon the shore, the foam of the surf dancing about their feet.

A Gulf breeze rose up. It blew their hair.

The sun descended deep into the horizon, far away yet seeming quite close. The bright red-yellow star cast a sparkling glow upon the dancing waves of the waters of the earth.

# Suggested for Further Reading

The following list is only a suggested beginning: Innumerable books, articles, and on-line resources abound for those interested in microbiology, the phenomenon of ore-centered DNA life at the vents, commitment to scientific discovery, or in American military strategy and its ongoing ability to ensure and to conduct the political will of the people of the United States.

**Books:**

Garrett, Laurie. The Coming Plague: Newly Emerging Diseases in a World Out of Balance. New York: Farrar, Straus and Giroux, 1994.

Lynes, Barry. The Cancer Cure That Worked! Fifty Years of Suppression (The Rife Report). Mexico: Marcus Books, 1992.

Rhodes, Richard. The Making of the Atomic Bomb. Touchstone Books, 1995.

**Articles:**

Gold, Thomas. "The Deep, Hot Biosphere." @www.people. cornell. edu. July, 1992.

Jannasch, H.W.; Mottl, M.J. "Geomicrobiology of Deep-Sea Hydrothermal Vents." Science, 229: 1985, pp. 716-725.

"Ships, Naval Surface." Compton's Encyclopedia; Encyclopedia Americana.

Stover, Dawn. "Creatures of the Thermal Vents." Popular, Science, html, "Ocean Planet," 1998.

USS Nebraska (SSBN 739) website. @www.subaseckb.navy.mil

Donald Ray Schwartz has published nearly 200 works, including short stories, essays, articles, reviews and criticisms, a novella, and non-fiction works. Lillian Russell: A Bio Bibliography, in collaboration with Anne Bowbeer is considered the definitive resource on the late 19th, early 20th centuries chanteuse and a significant contribution to that period of American theater in general. Noah's Ark: An Annotated Encyclopedia of All the Animal Species in the Hebrew Bible was the Jewish Book Club Selection of the month in the year it was published, and is still considered the definitive resource for that subject.

His play, Review, won the Sarasota (Florida) Theatre National Playwriting Contest. His epic poem, The Cross Country Run of Jennifer X Dreifus, won the Mellen National Epic Poetry Contest. His sabbatical monograph about Philo Farnsworth's invention of television, published by CCBC, is available online as an ebook, and now in print form from Amazon. His latest publications, two novels, a science-fiction, and one in the form of a memoir, are now available.

Professor Schwartz has directed or produced over 40 main stage productions (including full stage musicals). He has directed television commercials. He has featured cameo roles in two independent major motion pictures. He was a featured performer for Nebraska Public Television's industrial film series.

Donald Ray Schwartz is Associate Professor of Speech, Theatre and Mass Communication (ret'd) at CCBC (Community College of Baltimore County). He resides in Baltimore County with his wife, Ann.

# STEVEN EVANS

A true scientist, Steven served as a rocket scientist in NASA's earliest manned missions. Following research at Carnegie-Mellon, he moved to Omaha to assume the position of Director of Instructional Science for the Schools of Medicine, Nursing, and Pharmacy at Creighton University. At the world conference in Beijing he was designated an Expert in Nursing Informatics. Back at Creighton School of Medicine he was a Senior Research Scientist for the Hereditary Cancer Institute (publishing an eBook, *Cancer Control*). For the past several years, he has provided Protocols of Care as Senior Research Scientist for the Therapeutics Research Institute. He is the Project Leader for an ongoing autism clinical trial to reverse this syndrome. As collaborator, he feels he has integrated well cutting-edge genetics research in this work.

CPSIA information can be obtained
at www.ICGtesting.com
Printed in the USA
LVHW031504071119
636673LV00002B/288/P